Lars and Anna

LARS AND ANNA

A LOVE STORY

ELISABETH MAI JOHNSON

Telemark House Publishing
821 Moraga Road
Lafayette, CA 94549

Book design and editing by Nels and Randi Johnson
Cover photo-Minnesota hay field by Randi Johnson
Back cover photo-St. Nicolai Kyrka by Nels Johnson

ISBN 978-0-6151-6348-2

Printed in the United States of America

This book can be purchased at www.lulu.com

Preface

This novel is based in truth. When I was young I heard stories of how my grandparents came from Sweden, stories of various happenings along the pathway of their lives. Later, my mother and each of her sisters wrote accounts of what they remembered of their childhood - some happy, some funny and others poignantly sad. I have woven these stories upon a warp of ornamental fiction. I have changed some names and added imagined detail. Authentic truth does not lie in meticulous recording of facts, but rather in a revelation of character and personality.

My grandpa Lars died in 1920, at the age of 70, three years before I was born. My Grandma Anna lived until 1938. When I was fourteen years old my cousins and I sang at her funeral in the little white church beside the Leaf River. We sang *Min Fremstigdag*, her favorite hymn. I remember her kindness and sweetness. I remember Grandma Anna as a tiny woman sitting in her rocker, crocheting lace. Most of all, I remember that she loved me. I felt it!

My mother's sister Emma reported the details of their father's conversion to Christianity during the Thomastown 'awakening'. His quotation about Jacob wrestling with God was a literal translation from the Swedish Bible: "I have seen the Lord and my soul is saved." (Genesis 32:30) The Kristofersons (Christophersons) recalled the amazing change his conversion made in all of their lives, even though he had always been a kind father and an honorable man.

The cupboard Grandpa Lars made stands in my home today. The grain on both sides of the cupboard seems to resemble the head of a mystical animal. When I was a child I would imagine it rising mysteriously out of the cupboard in a train of golden mist. My mother said that she and her sisters thought it looked like a horse. That is the source of the *Julahasten* story.

My mother was Betsy Matilda, known as Bessie. I was her only child. All the Kristoferson children are now gone, united with their parents in Heaven. May God bless the precious memory of their lives. I wish to thank my son, Nels Johnson, and his wife, Randi Scalise Johnson, for their hours of work, editing and preparing the manuscript for publication. Without their encouragement and help this would never have become possible.

Elisabeth Johnson-December 2006

Illustration by Jon Rolf Johnson

September 1879

"Lars is gone." Anna's pale lips moved in silent staccato as the wrenching sobs deep within her quieted into patient resignation. "Gone to America. Maybe gone forever. And I love him so much."

With a breaking heart she watched the shining white dot, that was his ship, disappear with suddenness beneath the churning breakers of the sea.

Only the crystal canopy of the sky remained, a symbol of confidence that God's love and faithfulness would endure. The beloved young husband upon whom she had leaned was gone. She felt that he had somehow failed her. But beneath the hot tears and pain, Anna sensed something she could not explain.

"God is with me," she whispered, "I still have his promises."

Comforting arms surrounded Anna and Alma, her baby girl. A soothing voice spoke. *"Kjaredatter,* let us go home now." It was the voice of Kristofer Jepson, Anna's father-in-law, a man of unmistakable authority and great kindness. Home was his modestly affluent white house overlooking Ystad harbor.

It was a short walk. Soon Anna could smell the fresh bread and fragrant coffee her mother-in-law, Kjersti, had prepared for their return.

Kjersti had not wanted to go with them to the harbor to see Lars off today. Early in the morning he had kissed his mother goodbye. After their little talk, Kjersti did not expect to see her tall, rebellious son again. He was her youngest, her baby. Kjersti's pain was piercing and steady. But she was a Swedish woman, a woman of discipline and composure, remembering not to cry or scream, not to beat her fist upon the table, saying words like, "Why, Lars? When you could have a good position with your brother Marten? Why, Lars? Why are you such a proud and disobedient son?"

Of course Kjersti never spoke any of these words aloud. Instead she told Lars she would always cherish the memory of his strong and sensitive face within her heart. She told him she would pray for God's blessing and protection upon him every day as long as she had breath. She told him to be honest and truthful and to do the will of God. She told him that she believed in him, and that she loved him.

After saying these things and watching Lars walk determinedly down the path, she dried her eyes and stoked up the fire for coffee. She had a brave smile for those who returned from the harbor; for her petite daughter-in-law holding Lars' sleeping baby in her arms, and for her husband, Kristofer, whose broad shoulders drooped slightly on this day.

They were three hurting people. But they were Swedes. And so, because it was time for morning coffee, they sat with stoicism and dignity around a red-checked tablecloth upon which were arranged yellow buttercups and tall white candles. They talked of ordinary things, the beauty of this early autumn day and baby Alma showing promise of a first tooth. They wondered how long it would take Lars to get to America.

After the lunch, Baby Alma settled down for a nap in the fine birch cradle Lars had crafted. Kjersti suggested softly, "Now you rest Anna, while I wash the dishes and start the soup. So tired you are, so..." Kjersti stopped herself from adding, "So disappointed." A woman of tact and compassion, she did not wish to intrude upon the private grief of another.

"*Tack sa mycket.*" Anna was glad to go behind a door, where her tears could flow, and her sobs would be heard by God alone.

As Anna lay down on the narrow bed with its feather-filled coverlet, dumb disbelief held her small body rigid. Everything seemed to be right as usual...the cheery afternoon sun, lavender and subdued, sifting gently through Kjersti's spotless windowpane with its white lace curtain...the bright pink azaleas and red geraniums on the sill standing straight and tall...the carved black clock on the wall sending out its steady beat, and the appearance of its cheerful resident, Mr. Coo-coo, gaily proclaiming the hours. How could this be? When nothing was normal at all?

Lars was gone. Anna clawed frantically among the furrows of her memory, trying to ferret out a reason for this eerie turn of events. How did it happen that Lars had left her? It had occurred so suddenly, beginning only three weeks ago.

2

One

"I have something to tell you," Lars had said with disarming simplicity, "But first, nothing must be allowed to spoil this moment, this night. I shall wait until morning."

"Is it good news?"

"Well, it all depends," he had answered mysteriously.

Anna had not pressed him further; there was a happy aura of excitement about Lars that she had not seen for a long time. She settled back to enjoy it, and to let his 'news', whatever it should be, wait until morning.

She puzzled over the splendor of that night...Lars laughing and playing with Alma with unrestrained delight, the fish soup they had eaten with simple relish, the night of love under the down comforter. Lars had tiptoed about as he made the morning coffee. She remembered the kiss with which he had awakened her, the feel of his strong arms caressing her. All this, and then, his 'news'.

Like a bolt of lightning from the heavens, he finally told her his astounding 'news'. He held her close. He told her it was hard to get the words out that somehow they were sticking in his throat like gooseberry brambles. And when he had finished she closed her eyes, feeling only the enormous shock of an unbelievably slow hemorrhage as it crept into every nerve of her tiny body.

Did she hear Lars right? Did he really say, "Anna, today I bought one ticket on a ship going to America" Did he really say, "Today I went to the *prast* to have my name removed from the parish list"

He had searched her face and was afraid of what he thought he read. "My darling," he explained, "There was only enough money for one ticket. But I will get a good job in America and send for you and Alma soon. You will see...the time will fly like the birds of summer. And in the spring you will come to me."

Anna could only shake her head. He could see that she had not comprehended the enormity of his words. Her white face and trembling lips communicated the hurt he had inflicted, the darkness that his words had drawn about the daylight of their togetherness.

"Sweetheart," he began helplessly, I don't understand your silence, the look of horror on your face, your hands trembling."

"Lars, give me time to take it all in."

"But Anna, it's not like we hadn't talked of it before. Remember the moonlit nights in Solvesborg when we sat on 'our' bench in the village square after the dances? Remember when we talked of my dream of going to America? You said that you wanted to go too, even that you longed to go."

She did not respond. So Lars had continued to explain. "I realize I haven't said much about America lately. But the dream has never left my heart."

"It's no longer in mine," her choked whisper revealed. "Not since our wedding. Not since the baby came."

It seemed like only yesterday that Anna had been a child, singing and dancing in the village square, a free spirit. The future was something to be plucked with the gaiety of plucking a flower in the field. It was fun then to plan, to dare, to dream of going to far away places like America. But now, everything was different.

As she rested now in Mother Kjersti's guest chamber, Anna remembered that she had said to Lars, "I was so busy being a wife and mother I didn't think about that old dream anymore. And just to think, all the time it was still in you, festering. Lars, why didn't you talk to me? That's the part that hurts the most!"

When she told him this, he answered, "Oh, Anna, I don't know. I put it off. But only about a month ago I started thinking about that old dream again. For me it had faded too, I wanted the same things as you did, home, family, to be a good husband, and then…"

"Ja, Lars, what happened?"

"My dream came back. My old restlessness began to stir."

"Hmm, a likely story. Lars, what really happened?"

"Ja, well, the truth is, I had an argument with my brother."

"So? What was it about?"

"About my place in the family. Anna, I have no place. Marten explained to me that our family business is just not large enough to support all the sons. And he is the eldest. I don't want to talk about it. Not now. Not ever. I only know that after I talked with him, I had to go away!"

4

"But Lars, you are a craftsman in wood! We could go back to Solvesborg and my brother Jon could help you find work." Anna's voice revealed her desperation.

"Surely you know, Anna, about the hard times now in Sweden. Few new buildings are planned." Anna thought she detected a trace of cruel sarcasm in his voice. She was hurt, and she said no more.

"I must go to a land that is large, where opportunities are endless. Why can't you see that, Anna?" Lars shouted as he slammed the door.

Although Anna was curious about the incident with Marten and had often pondered its meaning, she never mentioned it to anyone. Nor did she speak of the incomprehensible pain she felt because of Lars' sudden decision, the sadness, the suppressed anger at being excluded from his thoughts, the questioning of his love for her, and the terrible fear of being left alone. These were unspoken, indeed unspeakable things. Instead she busied herself with tasks of mending, washing, and sewing; for it was not easy to get Lars' trunk ready on such short notice.

Lars would need so many things: woolen clothing for the winter, warm quilts, dried fruits and meats, knackebrod and skorpa (crackers and dried toast with sugar), and a few pots. How would he ever make out without her to cook and care for him? A man in a strange country? To be sure, he had his skilled craft, and so the precious woodworking tools must go into the very bottom of the trunk.

Lars had been even busier than Anna in the two weeks following his announcement. He was going here and there to attend to many matters about which Anna was left wondering. A coldness grew between them as each drew curtains around their private thoughts. Their laughter departed. And the bright light of their passion had quietly extinguished itself.

Anna had to make preparations to leave their small rented cottage, the only home she had known since the death of her mother, the home she and Lars had shared since their marriage one year ago. She remembered with tenderness every detail of the tiny white cottage. Three rooms, the walls lined with birch, the treasured family pictures in their gilded frames, her mother, father and her brother Jon looking down with solemn dignity upon the carefully embroidered motto: GUD VALSIGNA VART HEM (God bless our home). She remembered the scrubbed pine floors with their carnival of bright rag rugs, the sturdy table with its blue woven cloth, and the chairs Lars had made so meticulously with his own strong hands. He had made the kitchen cupboard too, with painstaking attention to detail.

"Someday," Anna mused, "if I should ever get to America, Lars will make me another one just like this one!" Lars had also made the cradle in which Alma slept at this very moment.

Anna visualized her copper teakettle, a wedding gift from her Uncle Berg, singing grandly in the large corner fireplace. She could almost catch a whiff of coffee, of soup, and of fragrant bread slowly baking in the oven. Only yesterday she had said good-by to the dear little house. And today, she had said good-by to Lars.

Anna awoke to the sudden realization that Alma was fussing, and that the delicious fragrances proceeded, not from her own stove, but from the spotless, cozy kitchen of her mother-in-law. Kjersti's creamy fish and potato soup was done, and the candles were lit. Father Kristofer Jepson called Anna to come downstairs. He smiled, thinking about how cheering and comforting it would be to share their home with her and little Alma.

Two

A nna wished fervently that it were not unthinkable to share her innermost thoughts with Kjersti and Kristofer Jepson. The need was great for her to express her anxiety for Lars' safety, her lingering doubts about his love for her, and the pain of her loneliness. But there was something else. A special and beautiful wonder remained constant in the corner of her heart. In spite of everything, she felt a quiet, reassuring Presence. Right in the midst of her turbulent storm was Jesus! He would suffice. Each morning she read from her Bible and *salmabok* (hymnbook), and the cry of her heart was heard by God alone.

And so perhaps it was even a blessing that Lars' parents were hard to talk to when it came to inner feelings and personal thoughts. Perhaps, Anna thought, these were to be shared only "in the secret place of the most High" (Psalm 9 1:1). Like most Swedes, the Jepsons expressed their kindness with deeds. Words were few and well chosen. One kept one's emotions, whenever possible, hidden within. Anna knew how much they were suffering, especially Mother Kjersti, but life went on with its predictable path of order and tranquility. Seldom did they speak of Lars, but every time a ship came from America into Ystad harbor, Kristofer looked for a letter. Nothing was said when he returned empty handed, his blue eyes vacant and detached, reflecting the disappointment that remained unspoken.

To pass the hours Kjersti taught Anna to tat and crochet fine, delicate lace doilies, and yards of lace for sewing on garments. Previously Anna had only time to knit practical woolen stockings, sweaters, and warm mittens. Crocheting came easy to Anna's deft fingers, leaving her mind free for reflecting upon the events that had led to her present situation.

Anna reflected on how different she and Lars were. Perhaps that was because their lives were not the same. His family was large and prosperous. Her family was small and poor. She and her brother Jon were the only ones left now. Anna shuddered when a furtive memory

7

of her father's death intruded itself upward from the black pit of a buried subconscious. Quickly she pushed it away. What happened to her father, when she was ten, remained a dark mystery. All she knew was that suddenly he was gone and no one ever spoke of him again, at least, not aloud. She recalled hearing grownups whispering. And once she thought she heard them say that her father had taken his own life. Too horrified to ask her mother, the matter had been deeply repressed, leaving a wounded, hurting place in her spirit. It was there even now, as she wept for Lars. From the day that her father was hastily buried, her beloved mother had rarely smiled. Anna realized only that something unspeakably terrible had happened. Although they had lived in a comfortable home in relative prosperity, suddenly there was no more money. Anna had received the impression that her father had done something so awful that he could no longer bear to live. If only someone could have told her the truth. If only she could know that her papa was now in Heaven!

Gustav Lindberg had been a warm and wonderful Papa to Anna. How she had missed his tender words of encouragement, his goodnight kisses, his laughter and charm! The trauma of his abrupt departure had left three people stunned and desolate, her mother, brother, and especially ten year old Anna.

Anna recalled with compassion how hard her mother had worked, spinning and weaving wall hangings and rugs, selling them so that she could set a simple, nourishing table for her children and so that they could keep their home. A cultured, thoughtful woman, her dearest wish was that Jon should attend the University in Upsala, and that Anna should go to a fine school for young ladies.

Fru Lindberg found such a school in Solvesborg, a place where Anna could work part time for her tuition. It was a place where she could obtain a fine education in the arts, in manners, and in appreciating the beauty and purpose of life.

Some of the hurt was gone that morning when Anna, a girl of twelve, left for Madame Yjerst's School. It was as if all the dark memories were left behind as she skipped brightly through an open door.

She recalled that day, a new day which felt like the first morning of creation. The sky was a canopy of ice-blue velvet, reflected in the passionate cascade of a liberated brook. The crocus, together with new grass, bravely edged upward between patches of gray, receding snow. The air, spicy with blended fragrance, when inhaled, seemed to produce a peculiar euphoria. Anna could remember it all so vividly. "I felt like a bubble about to burst!" she whispered.

Then she saw Madame Yjerst, a tiny, wispy, gray-haired lady sitting straight and tall in black lace. Gentle solemnity framed her face. Her intent blue eyes regarded Anna with kindness. Perhaps she perceived in this plain girl in faded homespun a poignant hunger for God and truth.

The years with Madame Yjerst were years of quintessential growth and meaning for Anna. She never forgot them. There were twenty adolescent girls in the school. Classes were held in the teacher's home, the largest and most beautiful house in Solvesborg. She taught them art, needlework, literature, and singing - subjects in which Anna excelled.

Madame's stern-faced husband helped with the school part time. He taught a class in composition and grammar, with strict discipline and total intolerance for schoolgirl silliness. Anna sensed he was a little bit afraid of the girls. He had been a professor at Upsala before he developed an illness, the nature of which was never discussed. An irrepressible girl named Helga, who once put a frog in the professor's desk drawer, was never forgiven. The girls had laughed hard behind their books when he had screamed uncontrollably. "How unkind," Anna thought in retrospect, "Poor sad, sensitive man. I wish I could ask his forgiveness for laughing so hard."

Madame had permission from the local *Prast* to tutor the girls in the catechism lessons he had assigned, for they were in preparation for Confirmation. It was a big day for all Swedes, a day to be celebrated in the Church and in the home with great festivity, a rite of passage into the world of the mature and the responsible.

The *Prast* would have preferred that the professor serve as catechist. However, he refused, assigning this duty to his wife.

"How providential that was!" thought Anna, looking back. For Madame Yjerst, God was someone real, a personal friend with whom she often visited. When they sang the chorale, JESUS, LORD AND PRECIOUS SAVIOR, ALL MY COMFORT AND MY JOY, Anna would see peace and light shining in her teacher's face, and soft gentleness lingering in her smile. This was a startling discovery, a pleasant uncovering for Anna of something she had never dreamed possible. Just to think that one might actually experience the reality of the Savior! To realize God's love personally.

Everyone in Sweden belonged to the State Church, unless he had requested his name to be withdrawn. Most people were religious. They believed in God. Christ was in the second article of the Apostles' Creed. Surely He was on the high altar of the great Cathedral. But for many, He seemed so far away.

Anna had resolved to have a talk with Madame Yjerst about her God. One morning the lesson had been about Jesus feeding the five thousand. It seemed the perfect time.

"Please, Madame, I have a question," Anna began.

"Yes, my child?"

"You have taught us that Jesus is alive. Can you tell me if he still feeds hungry people?"

"Are you hungry, Anna?"

"Not like when my stomach is growling."

"Good," Madame Yjerst smiled, encouraging her to continue.

"But I do have a hunger. I can't really explain it." Hot tears began to trickle down Anna's face.

A soft arm encircled her. "Oh yes, Anna. Jesus still feeds His hungry children. He is called the Bread of Life. He gives himself to us, if only we ask Him."

"Ja, so?"

"Anna, would you like to ask Jesus to satisfy your soul hunger?"

Anna nodded. After the other children had left the room and they were alone together, they prayed. They knelt on the bare floor of the empty classroom. When they arose, Anna felt clean, renewed like the garden after a summer rain. At that moment, a spring came into her step and a new song came into her heart that had never gone away...even in the bad times.

Three

Kjersti's table was beautifully set with blue and white porcelain. "*Var sa god*," she invited briskly. The three came to the table, sat down, and bowed their heads reverently. The prayer was spoken in unison.

> "*I Jesu nam, till bords vi ga,*
> *Valsigne Gud den mat vi fa,*
> *Gud till ara, oss till gagn,*
> *Sa fa vi mat i Jesu namm. Amen.*"
> (We go to the table in Jesus' name.
> May God bless our food.
> To God the glory, to us his gifts.)

"Amen," whispered Anna, remembering that day long ago at Madame Yjerst's when Jesus had given her the Bread of Life.

After the meal Father Kristofer reached up on the shelf for his old Bible and his reading glasses.

Just then, they were interrupted by the clang of the *klokkerstrang* (doorbell). It was Bengta, Lars' eldest sister, who lived next door. Bengta had never married and was a respected schoolteacher in Ystad.

Bengta's accustomed dignity had fallen away like the leaves in autumn. She was disheveled, out of breath from running, and glowing with excitement.

"I've come from the post. A letter from Lars!" Bengta waved the large brown envelope skyward, like a flag.

"Open it!" she commanded her father with uncharacteristic impatience, flinging it upon his empty plate.

"But it is addressed to Anna," he murmured "Anna, here. It is for you."

Anna rose slowly. Trembling she took the letter from Kristofer's hand and withdrew to her bedroom upstairs without a word to Bengta.

"Well," Bengta sighed, a trace of anger burning in her glance toward Anna on the stairway.

"Lars is Anna's husband," observed Kjersti kindly, "It is only right that she should have her privacy."

"But he is my baby brother!" Tears dimmed the blue eyes of this middle aged spinster who would never hold a child of her own, tears of longing for a brother twenty years younger than she, a baby brother who had seemed more like a son to her. She had not been brave enough to go down to the pier on the day his ship had left. She did not trust herself to go.

Upstairs, Anna was shedding tears of joy. "Oh Lars," she cried, "Your words, so tender, so intimate!" She kissed the paper. She wept. She laughed. She exclaimed over and over again, "*Tack, tack min Gud...tack sa mycket!*"

Meanwhile, to the three sitting at the kitchen table, the wait seemed interminable. At last Anna came downstairs, a radiant smile adorning her entire person. She sat down carefully, still clutching the letter. Three pairs of eyes fastened upon her like burrs in a summer field.

"Well?" Bengta almost shouted, "Well?"

Anna paused. "He greets all of you. He sends his love," she began slowly, with just a hint of amused mystery in her voice.

"But how IS he?" Bengta's bottled up resentment and impatience was about to explode. However, as a true Swede of the cultured class, she had carefully held on to her cork.

"He is in good health," Anna continued, "He has a nice place to live near Central Park. He has work in a piano factory. On Sundays he goes swimming at the beach on Long Island. And he has learned to eat raw oysters!"

Suddenly the tension in the room was broken. Cleansing, healing, glorious laughter spilled over the four of them like a rippling waterfall. And the coffee had never tasted so good.

As the months went by, more letters came from New York, all of them addressed to Anna, with only a warm *halsa* for the rest. If his parents resented this, it was never expressed, even by a look or gesture. Only Bengta betrayed her feelings by her silent looks of resentment and frustration. She thought that surely Lars would have written to her, that he would have confided what had happened between himself and Marten. Did Anna know? One day she, Bengta, would just come right out and ask her.

At Christmas Lars sent Anna a gift, a small broach of semi-precious stones set in silver. It was indeed a *gladige Jul*. Alma cut her first tooth on Christmas Eve. In church she smiled and waved to the candles at the beautiful *Julotta* service early Christmas morning. Anna was beginning to feel secure again in Lars' love for her. She was sure this would be her last Christmas in Sweden.

Her hope was a tiny seed, growing imperceptibly each day. Spring came at last; and with it, THE LETTER, containing a steamship ticket to the new land. Lars had at last saved up enough money.

Four

For Anna, breaking free became almost like the travail of childbirth. She had not realized this at first when the ticket came and her anticipation of seeing Lars again was fresh and new. But now, in spite of her deep faith, Anna seemed to carry with her small seeds sown in the trauma of the past. She often dwelt on her father's tragic death. Sad tears for unnamed longings, for home, and for the fear she felt of that unknown world which lay before her cascaded down her cheeks as she packed their simple belongings into a trunk.

Anna packed her treasured linens, a few dishes, warm clothing, and some bright rag rugs and woven wall hangings. And of course, the dear family pictures and the practical copper teakettle Uncle Berg had given for her wedding gift. Then they must travel to Solvesborg for a visit to her brother Jon and his family.

"It will surely be the last time I'll see Jon in this life," Anna sighed deeply. It was a fact of life she must steel herself to accept resolutely, however searing and hard.

Jon was her only close relative. She loved him still, just as she had when he was her rock to lean upon after their mother had passed away. But when she had married Lars Kristoferson, a cold knife of estrangement had somehow thrust itself between them. Jon had never cared much for Lars.

"It may turn out he is not dependable, that he may not always be good to you." Jon had worried, spoiling the joy of Anna's wedding day.

Thus a strange ambiance of ice surrounded the older brother and the sister who had come to say good-by. It enveloped them as they recalled the day when she and Lars had come together to ask for Jon's signed affidavit for *lysing*, the banns without which they could never become husband and wife. They remembered the words they had spoken…words like arrows that had pierced, but had never been extracted from the gaping, bleeding flesh.

"Jon," Lars had announced briskly, "Anna and I need your consent to have our banns declared in church on Sunday."

"Because we love each other," Anna gently added.

Jon disregarded her simple reasoning. "I will have to think about it," he snapped. "Is there some particular reason why you should be in such a hurry?"

Very angry at Jon's implication, Lars had walked back to his rooming house without a word. Anna said nothing more to her brother concerning the banns that evening. He could not know how deeply the implication of his remark had hurt her. He did not apologize. And yet, he had tried to smooth things over by being especially kind to her at the supper table. Lisa, Jon's wife, was her usual cheerful self as they talked of the children, the flowers, and the fine weather. Anna recalled how cozy it had seemed around the table. There was a kind of serene orderliness about Jon, Lisa, and their two children, Agnes, and baby Oscar. Their home was a place of refuge, tranquility, and comforting predictability, a place where Anna had felt totally accepted and loved.

Since their mother's death Jon had been very protective of Anna. It was taken for granted she would always have a home with him and his family. Until Lars appeared on the scene, there had never been even the slightest discord between the three of them. Anna and Jon were quiet, soft-spoken, kindly people. Lisa brought her own special sparkle and cheerfulness to the home. Jon was a capable, respected teacher in Solvesborg. His life had structure and peace. Anna had her sphere in the home helping with the children and housework, while sensitive to the leadership of Jon's efficient, fun-loving wife.

Anna tried to sort it out in her mind. "I suppose he sees Lars as an intruder, someone who will take me away, someone who might be careless of my needs. Jon is wrong, but he is acting out of love for me."

It was true that Lars could be perceived as pleasure loving, adventurous, and unstable. Lars had a kind of burning restlessness that irritated Jon. "He doesn't see Lars as I see him," Anna concluded sadly.

Even with his doubts about Lars Jon had finally given his consent. They could be married in the church.

"Anna," he had assured her, "I admit I have worried, but I only want your happiness."

Lars and Anna were hopelessly, irretrievably in love!

"It would be perfect," Anna sighed, "If only..."

Jon's attitude had indeed cast its dark pall over their wedding plans. Lars, however, did not care at all about Jon's feelings toward him, at least, that is what he maintained.

"Sweetheart," he had whispered as he held her close, "What does it matter if he wants to hang on to his beautiful little sister? We have our whole lives to love each other. So why should we have to prove to him the genuineness of our love?"

"Oh, yes, my beloved," Anna had whispered back in that tender moment, "You are so wise!"

As Anna rummaged through some old trunks in the attic, looking for her mother's wedding crown, she reflected on the unbelievable circumstances that had brought the two of them together. Once more she would retrieve and linger fondly upon these tender memories-and then put them away for a long time. She was going to a new life in a far away country and she must travel light.

Five

Every Saturday night the young and old of Solvesborg would assemble in the Town Square for music and dancing. Since Anna had a strong, clear soprano voice, she was asked to sing while the fiddlers played and the people danced to the lilting old folksongs of Skane. Sometimes when the fiddlers took a break, Anna sang a solo. While the old folks watched wistfully from their benches and tapped their canes, the young would dance and laugh and rejoice until the curfew sounded in the church steeple.

For Anna those were carefree, joyous days and nights to be cherished forever, especially that day in which a stranger came to the square just as she began to sing. He watched her intently, listening to the strength of her melodious voice, and scrutinizing the curves of her tiny five-foot figure.

"Who is he?" Anna queried when the music stopped.

"Oh, he is that young fellow from Ystad," she was told, "He is a woodcraftsman working for Herr Ingvaldson."

"I think he is perfect, even though I haven't met him yet." Anna said with conviction.

As she expressed that thought, the church bell sounded twelve sonorous peals echoing across the fragrant midsummer air. Fireflies skittered about and the nightingale began to sing.

Gathering her bright blue shawl around her, Anna heard a deep voice beside her. Startled, she turned to behold that same tall, blond young man from Ystad.

"My name is Lars Kristoferson. May I walk with you?" he asked, with a hint of fun in his voice.

Walking home with a stranger? Unthinkable! Delightfully adventurous!

"Of course!" Anna laughed. Somehow, ridiculously, Lars did not seem like a stranger. As they walked along, it seemed to Anna they had known each other forever, although few words of consequence had passed between them.

She didn't dare invite him in. That would not be proper, for they had not been introduced.

"*God natt.* May I see you again?" Lars bowed politely, with a happy smile on his lips and a sparkle in his blue eyes.

Anna was about to answer him when she heard footsteps approaching from within the house. "It's my brother!" she whispered, "Go, quick!"

In a moment Lars disappeared down the narrow street. "How stupid of me!" Anna thought, "I may never see him again!"

Just then Jon opened the door. "Anna, I was about to come for you. Who was that man at the door?"

"What man?"

"The man I saw through the window."

"Ohh...that was Lars Kristoferson of Ystad. He walked home with me."

Jon chided Anna for permitting a stranger to walk with her. Then he asked many questions about Lars, none of which Anna could answer.

"Be careful. Don't encourage him. If he comes to the square again I will meet him."

The first move, however, was not Jon's. The very next week Lars went to Jon's school to introduce himself and indicate his interest in Anna. Boldly (too boldly, Jon thought) he asked permission to call on Anna.

Politely, but with cool reserve, Jon had consented to let him come over for one hour on Sunday afternoons, provided this should be agreeable to Anna.

After a month of dances in the square and coffees on Sunday afternoons, Lars proposed marriage. He told Anna he had nothing to offer her but his love. He had no permanent position. In spite of this, and of her orderly, practical brother's reservations about Lars, her answer was an immediate, unqualified "Yes!"

"Yes, Lars...oh, yes! I don't need to think about it. I just know, somehow, we are meant for one another."

"And I too, my dearest Anna. I loved you the moment I heard you singing. And now that I have discovered your beautiful soul I love you even more."

It was at that point they had gone to Jon with their request and he had coldly promised to think about it. Meanwhile, he had been making some inquiries of friends in Ystad who were acquainted with Kristofer

Jepson's family. It was a very good family, he was told. However, this youngest son, Lars, might be a wild one. He had left his master craftsman just before he himself was to become a master. No one knew why. Jon also discovered that, as a youth, Lars had been seen in the village tavern with companions of doubtful reputation. Jon locked all these letters in his desk.

"No," Jon confided to his wife, "I don't think Lars would be a suitable husband for my sister."

"I have a sense about this too," Lisa began, "and it is that you are wrong about Lars. Let Anna follow her heart. Can't you see how they look at each other? How much they are in love? Have you really forgotten how it is?"

"No, but we have had more than feelings. And have I not been a good man for you?"

"Lars is a good man too. I can see it in his eyes."

There was no arguing with Lisa. "Why are women so sure they know about these things?" Jon wondered.

"Of course you must give them your blessing, Jon," Lisa concluded, "Otherwise, instead of being married in the church, he will sweep her away and we will never see them again!"

"You think so?"

"Ja, Lars is just such a one. And have you noticed how she clings to him?"

What then could he do but give them his reluctant blessing?

The day came when Anna donned the pretty, hand-embroidered bridal dress her mother had made before she died, and placed the silver bridal crown upon her thick brown hair. She wore a white lace shawl that Bengta had made for her. They all met at the village church, where a small group of relatives and friends waited. Kristofer and Kjersti Jepson, together with Bengta, had taken the train from Ystad.

It was a simple exchange of vows from the Swedish prayer book, followed by the singing of a hymn followed by the warm wishes of all the assembled relatives and friends. All, including the black-robed prast, were invited to the delicious dinner served in the garden of Jon and Lisa's home. Bright autumn leaves adorned the tables. The sky was ice blue and cloudless, and a hint of pungent crispness lingered on the sun-filled air.

"Oh, Lisa," Anna exclaimed to her sister-in-law, "How can I thank you for this day, for your kindness, and for this dinner! Everything was perfect...except for one thing."

It was hard to hear above the laughter and the chatter, but Lisa understood. She noticed that Jon was the only one there who seemed quiet and unsmiling. It was so unlike him too.

After the wedding, Lars and Anna went to Ystad, where Father Jepson had promised a job for Lars in the family business, and had leased a tiny white cottage for the young couple.

Anna had been so happy, so thankful, in that cottage, so glad that Lars had "settled down", and especially thankful for their precious baby girl. In retrospect, for the first time she could understand how Lars must have felt. His father and brother were doing everything for him, making all the decisions, creating a place for him where he was not really needed. How blind she had been to his feelings! No wonder he had found it hard to confide in her.

She had felt safe and protected when Alma was born the following June. The summer had been filled with love and contentment, with the brightness of the sun and the flowers in her window box. Right up until the day when Lars had come to her with his "news".

Six

For three days there had been a storm at sea. "Why is the cabin so cold when it is June?" questioned Anna in a lucid moment between waves of nausea. She shivered, holding baby Alma close. The stench was gagging her. The ship rolled crazily from side to side as the screeching wind pounded against the porthole.

"Who will empty the slop jar? Who will watch Alma? What will happen if I die?" Anna's frantic cries were directed at God. She knew He was able to get her through this time of fear and agony. Knowing this, however, did not take away her human feelings of weakness and helplessness.

"Oh God, help me," she moaned.

She heard a pounding on the cabin door. A kindly middle-aged woman entered the small room.

"I am Kristin Andersdatter. I never get seasick," she announced matter-of-factly as she struggled to stay on her feet. "I am from Skane. I go to my brother Pelle in New York City."

Anna smiled a limpid thank you to God.

"Ah, you are sick," Kristin expressed with compassion. "Lay back on the pillow. I will get tea. That will give you strength. But first, I take the baby."

"Her name is Alma...*tack sa mycket.*"

"Alma! What a fine young lady you are and such a smile, too," Kristin cooed to the child, and Alma responded with delighted giggles.

Kristin, holding the door of the reeling cabin with one arm and Alma with the other, continued her amiable chatter.

"My sister and her big family are also in the ship. She will help. We love little children. So you see, my friend, you are not alone. We are all Swedes. We will stick together. I come back soon."

"*Tack, kjare Gud,*" whispered Alma.

When Kristin brought the tea, the sea seemed to quiet down. And after she left to empty the slop jar, Anna opened the porthole to let in a fresh, salt-flavored breeze. She felt so much better. Maybe it wasn't so bad that Father Jepson had paid the extra price for a stateroom. Someone had come. She was not alone. And the tea tasted good and made her sleepy.

Suddenly Anna awoke to the terrifying realization that her baby was not beside her! Then she remembered that Kristin had taken her to strangers. Swedes, ja, but strangers just the same. "I must get up!" she decided.

On desperate, shaky legs Anna stumbled into the large common room in the bowels of the ship. Where was Alma? Anna moved toward a circle of people who were laughing with incongruous joy. "What could be funny here?" Anna wondered, sensing only her own anxiety and weakness.

Then she saw the object of their wonder and delight…Alma, on her tiny legs, taking her first steps.

"She's walking!" one of the older children exclaimed. Everyone clapped, shouting encouraging gurgles at the smiling wonder. Anna began to smile too, and at that moment the baby caught her eye and came toward her, running. Awkwardly, to be sure, but running!

From that day there was no stopping Alma. The whole ship was her playground. Each passenger and each crewmember became her special friend. The storm was over, the sun shone. Anna felt well enough to worry that her baby might fall over the edge and into the teeth of a waiting shark. One bright and beautiful day it almost happened. In an instant, Alma slipped between the vertical bars of the ship's railing and began to fall. Anna screamed. Without hesitation, her hands were there to grasp Alma's disappearing ankles just in time.

"May God be praised!" Anna shouted, trembling with the trauma of an almost-tragedy. She smiled up at the blue sky.

"Lord, you really are here to look out for us. Will you please let us see Lars too?" She knew now she had not left her loving and faithful God in Sweden.

The next day was Alma's first birthday. "Should I tell them?" Anna wondered, "When we can't celebrate it here?" She looked down on her baby's sweet, sleeping face. "Why not?" She decided to get dressed and join their friends.

"It's a nice day, *Fru* Kristoferson," Kristin Andersdatter greeted.

"Ja, a special day…my baby's birthday," Anna smiled, "She is one year old today."

"Congratulations! And she is so advanced for her age," Kristin extolled with sincere admiration.

"How so?" Anna inquired modestly.

"Only one year? I would think two years the way she runs, starting to talk too."

Bursting with pride, Anna felt well enough to stay on deck with Alma all morning. She watched her more carefully than before, not permitting her to venture near the fateful, threatening rail. She didn't know how long they sat there in the sun and spray. At last, Alma slept. Her mama dozed.

"What is that? Singing? Who feels like singing here?"

The little company of friendly Swedes on this boat did. Anna smiled with nostalgia to hear the familiar strains of Swedish children's songs. She too began to sing a song for Alma!

> "Ba, ba, vita lamm,
> "Har du nagon ull?
> I'Ja, ja kara barn,
> "Jag har sacken full!"
> (Baa, baa, white lamb, have you any wool?
> Yes, yes, dear child, I have a sack full!)

Alma clapped and giggled as they sang on, song after song. The final song was a prayer everyone had learned at their mother's knee, and it was sung amid many tears.

> "Gud som haver barnen kar,
> Se till mig some liten ar,
> Vart jag mig i varlden vander
> Star min lychan far."
> (God who loves the children,
> watch over me who is little.
> Wherever I go in the world,
> my happiness is in God's hand.)

These beloved songs were all they had to offer little Alma on her special day. It was not easy to sing in their present circumstances but they did so bravely and with joy.

After the singing, Anna took her baby to their stateroom for a rest. Soon there was a knock on the door. It was Kristin with, of all things, a cake! Never mind that it was only layers of skorpa put together with some carefully hoarded lingonberry jam! And a small white candle on top! What a memorable party it turned out to be after all!

That day turned out to be the best one of the whole voyage. The sea grew angry again and there were many dreary, nauseous days to follow.

But at last...LAND!

Seven

"We are approaching New York harbor!" These words shouted raucously in Swedish by the Captain over his megaphone, sounded sweet in Anna's ears. Yesterday they had begun to watch the dark strip on the horizon grow slowly larger. And now, outlines of tall buildings could be distinguished in the bright morning sun.

"My ordeal is over; I will soon see Lars. He will hold me close and all will be well at last!" Thankful tears stained Anna's face.

At last the ship slowly puffed its way through the harbor. Castle Gardens lay mysteriously shrouded in mist. Anna could just make out four domed towers of the main building. "A castle!" she exclaimed, "They are welcoming us into a castle! How rich America must be!"

Castle Gardens, in reality, proved to be something less than a castle, and the reception of this new ship of Swedes something less than a welcome. It was more like a prison, a self-enclosed country for those who had no country.

It was late morning when they arrived. Anna, her restless baby squirming in her tired arms, still weak and on 'sea legs', was heartlessly shuttled from building to building, from room to room. She could understand nothing said to her, and it seemed they were treated more like animals than persons deserving of dignity.

The cacophonous blend of sounds was deafening...crying children, blaring megaphones in a multitude of strange languages, the scraping of belongings being dragged across unpolished floors, the noise of loud voices all chattering at once, their divergent nuances blending into one roar.

In the midst of all this confusion Anna searched only for a tall, straight figure, and the jovial, familiar face of her Lars. He had assured her he would be there when the ship arrived, so that he could accompany her through the difficult inspection procedures, and help her with baby Alma.

"Lars is not here," she finally acknowledged, crumbling into the last seat on a bench, "And I don't know how I shall cope. God, help me!"

The immigration process was lengthy and trying. First came the dreaded medical examinations. A doctor watched them climb the staircase in the main hall. This was known as the 'ten second physical', in which the unfit could be quickly separated. Anna thought she would never make it, feeling woozy and weak, and half-carrying, half dragging her adventurous toddler.

Anna did make it, for she was young, healthy, and strong. She looked with compassion on those who were turned away, who stumbled piteously upon the stairs, or, fainting, tumbled downward. A little grandmother with her son, a pregnant woman, and a pale gentleman who had become very sick at sea, coughing blood and gasping for breath...all these would be sent back to Sweden. America had no welcome for those who could not work hard.

Those who scaled the stairs without difficulty watched with dread as the blue uniformed doctors approached. Each immigrant was scrutinized with judicious care...eyes, feet, gait, face, and teeth. Suspicious cases were marked with chalk on their backs and detained. A circle with a cross in the middle meant inevitable deportation. Anna shuddered, crying inwardly to God for her friend Kirsten's mother, whose acceptance seemed doubtful. At that point they became separated, and Anna never knew what happened to these dear, dear friends.

Stage Two was where so many names were changed. The inspectors simply could not comprehend foreign pronunciations. Thus Americanized names were written down. Anna was thankful their names were not too difficult. Alma could only be Alma. Anne in Swedish could only be pronounced Anna. And for Kristoferson, the inspector wrote Christopherson. Then, at last they were free to approach the door marked TO NEW YORK.

Anna sat down on a bench. She refused to board the ferry for Manhattan because she must wait for Lars HERE. If she were to leave Castle Gardens she would be lost. Here he would be able to find her. This she tried to explain to an officer who knew a little Swedish. He had cold blue eyes and a cynical smile under his brown mustache.

"And what if he doesn't come? He may have deserted you. You know it happens more than I like to think. Then what will you do?"

"Sir, you are wrong. My husband will be here, you will see," asserted Anna bravely. If the officer had sown any seeds of doubt she did not permit him to see them.

26

Her greatest fear was not that he did not intend to come...otherwise, why would he have sent her the ticket? But she worried that some accident or illness may have overtaken him in this maze of confusion that was New York City. For a moment she flushed with horror that he could even be dead!

It was getting late. The rosy, smoke-tinged fingers of sunset surrounded the tall buildings of Manhattan to the west. Alma had at last succumbed, and slept fitfully on the empty bench beside her mother. Half-waking, she listened to Alma's peaceful, even breathing, interrupted occasionally by a startled jerk or a weary sigh Anna shooed the flies from her pretty face. Conscious of her desolation and helplessness, she could only whisper, "Please God, bring Lars soon!"

Anna looked up. A tall man was bending over her, smiling.

"Lars! Oh, Lars, Lars...I waited so long. God be praised!" She flew into his arms. Lifting her tiny body from the bench, they were blended, one person once again in that first sweet embrace in America.

Next Lars lifted the sleeping Alma upon his strong shoulders, baggage in the free hand, and they started for the ferry.

"My darling," he began, "Can you forgive me? You see if I had come this morning I would have lost my good job at the piano factory. All day I have been worrying about you."

"Shush...it doesn't matter now for we are together," was Anna's quick response. She laughed merrily, her first delicious laughter in such a long time. What did anything matter, now that all the pieces of her troubled world had come together in Lars?

Before they left Castle Gardens Lars arranged for a dray to bring Anna's trunk to his address, the Grondval's flat.

Eight

A nd so, what would have been terrifying, the outrageous sight of tall buildings and mysterious strangers, became to Anna fun and adventure, all because Lars was by her side.

Lars took his family to the cold water flat near Central Park that was the home of his cousins, the Grondvals, where he had been staying.

"*Valkommen!*" Mrs. Grondval greeted warmly, "We are honored to share our home. Please, make our home your home."

Anna had somehow forgotten how weary she was, and Alma was ecstatic. She giggled and splashed with total and delicious abandon in the wooden washtub in the kitchen, supervised by a delighted Kari Grondval. Kari was middle-aged; her only child had died long ago in Sweden.

"Ja, what fun to have a young one in the house, eh Bengt?" Her husband chuckled while he waited patiently for supper.

Anna filled the blue enameled coffeepot with water, her wonder-brimmed eyes fixed upon the steady stream pouring effortlessly from the spigot. "My, my, "Anna wondered, "Isn't it amazing? Water coming out all by itself with no pump!"

Many other features in the Grondval's flat delighted Anna, especially the gaslights, and the gas stove, upon which one could cook coffee without first splitting wood. And the joy of being able to read in the evening without straining one's eyes!

"I can write letters to Sweden…perhaps I shall begin tonight."

Dear Brother and Sister-in -law,
HILSEN TIL ALLE. And a special greeting to your little ones!
 I am tired, but I must write about the goodness of God in bringing us safely to America. Alma is sleeping now, but has been running about happily all day, exploring every nook and corner of Cousin Grondval's flat. Oh yes, she learned to walk - and to run - on board the ship! That is all I want to say, or even remember, about our voyage.

The flat is in a large building, called a tenement, and fairly new. It is on the third floor on the front, looking south, so we will be able to look out and see all the people and carriages hurrying past. The parlor has a nice bay window with lace curtains, and Kari has many plants, just as we do in Sweden. The floorboards are new and clean and decorated with pretty rag rugs Kari brought from Sweden. She has no loom here, but she has braided some rugs for the kitchen, a large room opening from the parlor. It too has a sunny exposure. And it has a gas stove! How simple in the mornings! You don't have to chop wood to make a fire. Coffee is ready in a blink of the eye!

All the rooms connect - like the cars of a train, so there are no halls, except outside the flat, of course. And what do you think? There are, only a short distance down the hall, wash rooms - one for men and one for women - with sinks large enough to wash clothes in, each with its own faucet of cold running water! Oh, Jon and Lisa, you would be amazed…water running without a pump! And I hope you won't think it indelicate of me if I mention the water closets…toilets that flush. What a convenience!

The Grondval's bedroom opens from the kitchen and ours from the parlor. We have a lovely large room with commode and mirror, beautiful china pitcher and bowl, a large bed, and a little bed Kari got especially for Alma. It is so nice here!

Kari and her husband are truly kind and gracious to us. They truly enjoy the fun of having a child around the house. Last night Alma was wildly happy. How she loved her bath after all that time on the ship! Oh my, but Lars was tickled to see her again!

Lars is so dear and wonderful to us both, Soon we shall have our own pretty flat, maybe in this very building - so that I can be near to Kari.

I truly miss all of you. How I long to see you once more! In a lesser way, I miss the trees, flowers, and green grass of home. But tomorrow we are going to Central Park, only a block away, where there are trees, grass, and plenty of flowers and beautiful birds…and with fancy benches upon which to sit while we watch them. I am told it is an enormous park.

It was worth the long, hard voyage to be near my beloved Lars. Jon, please know that his only thought is for my happiness. He has a fine job in a large factory called Steinway Pianos. When you think of my Lars, please think of him kindly.

I love you! So goodbye for now. May God be with you!
Your Anna

Lars and Anna's new flat was on the second floor of the same tenement building in which the Gondval's lived.

What *lycklika*! (good fortune) Anna exclaimed when Lars told her these rooms were available. "Kari will still be close by to help me!"

They had three light and cheery rooms facing the east. As Anna opened a window to let in the warm, late spring air, she thought she could detect a faint whiff of lilac and honeysuckle wafting in from Central Park. The sky was intensely blue, the air was clean, and the chimneys were inactive now, for the warm spring sun made the burning of coal unnecessary.

"Our home looks pretty; don't you think so, Lars?"

"Ja, it reminds me of our first home...now so far away."

"Well, no wonder. There's my big trunk, and look what came out of it, our own bright rugs, our pretty dishes, and the pictures. And doesn't Uncle Berg's teakettle look grand and charming since I polished it? I'll bet he never did think it would be on a gas range!"

"Just to think..."

"Lars, the lace curtains you bought me are just so elegant there in the bay window with Kari's red geraniums."

"My little Anna, did I ever tell you that you have a gift for making everything sing together in harmony?"

As Lars sat in the rocker he had made, gazing at the cleanliness and order of his surroundings, his big heart was filled with generous and tender thoughts toward his wife. So much so that he patted her on the shoulder and gave her a little squeeze. Anna then gave Lars an adoring smile and sighed. It was so good when they were together.

"If only you could be at home more, dear husband. You work so hard and have so far to walk, since we can't afford the trolley." Just thinking about him being gone from her brought poignant longings.

She smiled in anticipation of quiet evenings, and of nights of closeness under her mother's hand-made quilt. How pleasant it would be now that they were alone together in their own home. The Grondval's had been very kind, but small strained places were beginning to show beneath the curtain of smiles and polite words. Like the tears in Kari's eyes the time Alma broke a wedding plate. Lars had given her money but they all knew that nothing could replace the tender memories of Sweden that plate evoked. And sometimes all four of them would become overwhelmed with waves of homesickness they could not explain and seldom discussed. These four brave Swedes huddled together in the little tenement flat against a world that seemed peculiar and alien. All winter they had supported one another, and irritated one another, all at the same time.

For days Anna stayed in her rooms fixing, fussing, cooking soup, and baking bread, except when she ran upstairs to have coffee with

Kari. But the day finally came when she had to go outside the tenement building.

To be sure, Lars shopped for her on his way home from work, but today she just had to have some eggs. She had already started on the *kringla* batter, and she had already tried to borrow some from Kari.

"I am sorry, Anna, but I just used my last egg," Kari sighed.

There was only one thing left to do…put on her shawl and Alma's sweater and head for Mr. O'Leary's store on the corner. She tied some money in her handkerchief and resolutely set out.

"Uff, how I dread going! How am I ever going to make him understand?" She moaned softly (in Swedish, of course).

Alma skipped delightedly down the stairs and along the sidewalk, humming her individual little tune of anticipated adventure.

When they got to Mr. O'Leary's store, Alma gazed longingly at a jar of peppermint sticks, but her Mama paid no attention. She was trying too intently to make Mr. O'Leary understand what she needed to buy. Anna lay a quarter on the counter.

"*Aggs*," she stated in a loud voice, as if to be sure he understood.

"Eggs?" He understood!

Anna nodded. "*Ja, ja et dussin.*"

"Eight dozen?" Mr. O'Leary looked surprised. What in the world did this tiny Swedish woman want with eight dozen eggs?

"*Ja, et. Var sa god.*" (be so good)

"But ma'am, I need more money…two dollars."

"*Nay…et dosen ar sa,*" she insisted, pointing to the quarter.

"Well, I know your husband. I will let you charge." He proceeded to take eight dozen boxes of eggs from the cooler.

"*Nay, nay!*" Anna shouted, "*Bare ET…et, et, et!*" (only one). Whatever could this man's problem be? If only she could remember the English word for *et*. She knew that she had heard it.

Suddenly inspiration struck. She held up one finger.

"Aha!" smiled the grocer. Why didn't you say that in the first place?" He was so thrilled by this breakthrough in the language barrier that he handed Alma a peppermint stick.

At last they strolled homeward contentedly. "Well, that wasn't so bad." Anna asserted with a smile of new confidence.

Nine

It was morning, and mornings were not easy for Anna these days. Today her legs were as uncertain as jelly and she moved as in a dream to the stove...maybe we need the lamp...still dark outside...get the coffee...back to the table...get the rye mush...get the milk on the windowsill.

"Oh, Lars it smells sour!"

"It is warmer these spring nights. I'll bring some ice tonight. Anything else you need?"

"More milk. Maybe a soup bone and some yellow peas. Lars?"

"Ja, my love. What is it?"

"Nothing. It's nothing, only the day seems so long when you are away...and sometimes...

"Ja?"

"Sometimes I have feelings I can't explain. Fear? Homesickness? Longing?"

Lars arose and hugged her gently by the stove where she had been stiffing the mush. She turned toward him, spilling some wistful tears.

"It is only natural for one in your condition." Lars whispered. "I understand and I love you."

"Thank you, dear Lars."

What a gift he had given her in his love! And now, even to have expressed it in words! Most Swedish men thought that tenderness meant more when it was expressed only infrequently. 'I love you' must be special, never commonplace. But for Lars, it was easy to express affection. It was for every day. And so, in this early-dawn moment, his warmth enveloped and comforted her deliciously.

Anna felt better. "Forgive me, Lars. I'm forgetting how long your day is, how hard you work. I was only thinking about myself"

He just waved and smiled, and softly closed the door.

After Lars left, Anna had to heat water to wash the dishes.

"It is so convenient," she mused. "I don't have to pump it." She began to sway in the doorway.

"I wonder why everything seems so hard then, I have to sit down-just for a little while."

Alma woke up just as her mama dropped wearily into the warm rocker in which Lars had been sitting. "My, but what a perpetual motion machine that child is!" Anna thought, "My, but I am just not right today!"

"Alma hungry Mama. Have peppermint?'

"No my pet. Mush."

After serving the little one's simple breakfast, Anna began to feel waves of pre-natal nausea slowly envelop her body. "It will pass," she said, speaking from experience.

"Alma, be a good girl and play in the parlor a little while. Mama needs to rest." With that, Anna picked up the basin and stumbled into the bedroom.

"Alma is being so good," Anna noticed after awhile, "I'll just take a tiny nap."

Two hours later, when Anna awoke, the house was still quiet. Golden sunbeams danced through the lace curtain and played tag on the old quilt. Anna luxuriated in the stillness. She began to feel good. The morning sickness was gone and her strong old self was back.

"Alma? Baby, where are you?"

Anna heard only the ticking of the clock.

"Mama is up!"

Anna looked with horror at the clock. Could it be she had slept for two hours?

"Alma, I'm coming!" But Alma did not answer.

Running desperately into the parlor, Anna saw that the door was open. Baby Alma was gone! She was not in any of the hallways. Anna, hoarse from calling, dug her fists into Kari's door. "Kari! It's me - Anna!"

The door opened quickly, plunging a disheveled Anna into the familiar, orderly room.

"Anna, whatever is the matter?"

Anna could only rasp, "It's Alma...she's gone!"

The whole story of her sickness, her nap, her carelessness, tumbled out with desperate tears. Kari tried to be consoling and calm. She talked to Anna as a patient mother to a child. "Alma is alright. She is a lively child, curious about the world. No one would harm a remarkable child like her. No, they would befriend her, you'll see.

Come. First we will knock on the door of every flat in this building. Dry your eyes. Pull yourself together. Trust in God's protection."

It took until noon to talk to everyone in Kari's broken English. All the neighbors were sorry, but they had not seen Alma.

Kari declared, "She must have left the building."

All afternoon they searched, Mr. O'Leary's store, the street, Central Park. It was getting dark.

Soon Lars will be home. "Lars will know what to do," Kari assured Anna.

A heavy lump pounded against Anna's heart. "How can I face Lars?" she sobbed, "When I have lost our child?"

Kari did not know what to say. Hugging each other, the two women walked in mechanical silence up the stairs to Anna's flat. They must wait for Lars.

"Oh, dear God in Heaven! What has this new country done to us?" Anna cried.

The clock ticked on. Anna began to pace from one end of the flat to the other, wringing her hands and biting her lips until they bled. In her mind, tortured by fear, she visualized terrible things that could have befallen her baby...trampled by horses, drowning in the Hudson River, huddled frightened and cold near a trash bin, or even-God forbid-stolen by an evil man. Kari hurt for Anna, for she knew what it was to lose a child.

Finally Lars came and Kari told him the alarming news. As usual, he remained unruffled. "Have you been to the police station? No? I will go right away. Kari, please take care of Anna."

"Funny we never thought of that," Kari observed.

Anna could no longer speak or even sit erect. The icy fingers of her fear closed in on her like a dark curtain. The two women sat in the twilight silently, waiting.

"Kari," was Anna's barely audible whisper, "Read something from the *Salmebok*. Oh, why is Lars taking so long?"

Kari read from the 91st Psalm: "In the Lord I will put my trust. He will give His angels charge over me, to keep me in all my ways. He who keepeth thee will not slumber."

"*Tack*, Kari. Kari?"

"Ja?"

"God gives His angels to watch after Alma. Now I have peace."

Anna dropped her head on the table and slept, awakening after what seemed to Kari a very long time to a familiar sound.

It was the firm thump of Lars' big feet on the squeaky wooden floor of the hallway. One set of feet? For a moment it seemed his mission had been in vain. But just then the door opened, and Anna saw his big smile. Why not, when little Alma, safe and sound, slept peacefully upon his shoulder?

"A policeman saw her outside the building this morning. And all day she has been fed, and spoiled, and fussed over by all the officers in the precinct. Some lucky little girl!"

"May God be praised!" was all that Anna could say, over and over again.

Ten

The beautiful spring days turned slowly into the insufferable heat of a New York summer. Tenement living was nearly unbearable, day or night, there was no cross-ventilation, no yards, and no shady porches to sit or sleep upon, only the red-hot iron fire escapes steaming in the sun. The weekly wash was reeled out to scorch, suspended limply between the brick buildings,

The only oasis to which the tenement dwellers could flee was Central Park. Every day Anna and Kari hurried with their housework after the men had left, and headed for the park.

Alma loved to play in the pools and stand under the waterfall, while Anna and Kari sat knitting on a cool bench in the shade. They took off their shoes and stockings, feeling the slithery coolness of the grass between their toes. Sometimes they would try wading with Alma in the shallow, sparkling water of the pond, giggling like schoolgirls. Then they spread the blue checkered cloth under some trees and laid out the contents of the lunch basket...skorpa, diced herring sandwiches on rye bread with pickles, some fresh fruit and coffee in a jar wrapped with newspapers to keep it warm.

"Tastes good, doesn't it?" Kari remarked.

"If only we didn't have to go home." Anna sighed.

"Ja, the heat even feels pretty good out here, but in the flat...uff, uff, uff da!

While Alma napped on the cool green grass under a big elm tree, Anna and Kari rested. Anna was careful to keep an eye open in case Alma decided to run off again.

"No fun being in the 'family way' in summer, Kari," murmured Anna sleepily,

"Well," encouraged Kari, "I do believe it is beginning to cool off some. But what to prepare for supper? I won't have a fire, not even a gas one, not today."

"But how could you cook coffee then? Lars could never do without his coffee."

"I made extra this morning and set it out on the fire escape. Oh, it will be hot alright!"

"How smart of you, Kari!"

"I have plenty. Come up and I will fill your pot."

"Kari, you are too good."

"Better still, why don't you and Lars come up and have a little cold supper with us?"

"*Tack sa mycket*...but tonight I feel like an elephant."

Kari laughed. "So, I look like one too is what you're thinking?" Anna asked and she began to laugh too.

The four adults, and Alma, had fun together that evening. At sunset a nice breeze began to filter through the windows.

Lars was feeling especially jolly. "You know what I did today?" he inquired mysteriously, "You'll never guess. We quit early at the factory. Ran out of materials."

"Ja, so?" Anna raised her brows in surprise.

"So I went swimming at the beach off Long Island, high ocean waves spilling all over me, cool and salty." Lars tingled with excitement, remembering his afternoon. "And then, so as not to get hot again, I took the trolley home."

"That's the way to live," commented Bengt, "Not bad in America, eh?"

"We had fun too," noted Kari as she poured the sun-heated coffee. But Anna became silent, puzzled by her conflicting feeling, happiness for Lars' good fortune, tinged with a touch of jealousy and self-pity.

As if Lars sensed her mood, he reached out for her hand, noticing that it was a little swollen, the gold wedding band immovable.

"I don't feel so well," Anna suddenly remarked, "I'd best go home...you stay, Lars, if you want to."

"What? Let you walk downstairs alone in the dark? Come, little Mama."

Anna tossed and turned all night while Lars slept peacefully by her side. As she listened to him snore, it occurred to her that maybe he didn't care that she was sick, hot, and uncomfortable.

Rosy-pink dawn was beginning to break out on the horizon. Hot haze seemed to envelop the room, while the dresser lifted before Anna's eyes and the bed rocked like a ship at sea.

"I'm so dizzy," she observed. And then it stabbed her abruptly in the back without mercy. Her startled moan awakened her snoring husband.

"Oh, Lars, my time has come!"

"Already? Are you sure?"

"How can you say that? Get Kari and the Norwegian woman."

He bolted upright and pulled on his pants. "I'll hurry. I'll run two steps at a time!"

"Don't do that. You might fall. It will take hours, I should know." With that, another pain seized her like a vise.

Lars shot out of the door like a bullet, leaping wildly up the stairs to Kari's flat.

Kari was making coffee for Bengt. The news did not surprise her. "I could see last night that she was ready," she stated matter-of-factly.

"Well, why didn't you say something then?" Lars stammered.

Kari said nothing, giving him a look that said, "You men! So blind to what is obvious."

"I can't leave her. I can't go to work today. I may lose my job, but no matter. I cannot leave my Anna!"

"She'll not want you to lose your job, Lars. Don't talk foolishness. Besides, you would just be in the way. Go to her now, until I come with Mrs. Oie. Then go to work!"

"My, how that woman can order someone around." Lars muttered as he hurried down the stairs.

Mrs. Oie, the Norwegian midwife, lived on the first floor. "Lucky she was home," Kari exclaimed as she saw the door start to open.

It was not as if Mrs. Oie was not expecting this call, for only last week she had examined Anna, telling her that all was well and in readiness. "Soon," she had smiled, "He will come soon."

"He? How do you know?" Anna had wondered, hopefully.

Mrs. Oie had some explanation for her prophecy, something about the position of the baby, but Anna did not dare to believe it. After all, she was a Norwegian. Swedes could understand Norwegians, but they could not always believe them. Still, Anna did trust this smiling, bustling, rotund, middle-aged midwife. Something about her practical cheerfulness made Anna feel better.

As soon as Mrs. Oie arrived she took charge of everyone. "Kari, take Alma to your flat. This is not for the eyes of a child. "And you," she ordered, gesturing toward Lars, "Out, out! You have a day's work to do!"

"I don't want to leave you, my darling," whispered Lars into Anna's ear.

She replied, "But you must, Lars, we need your job, silly one." Lars kissed the perspiration on her brow, and then her pale, drawn lips.

"*Jag alskar dig!*" (I love you) he called, and then gently closed the door.

Mrs. Oie saw another contraction coming. "Just in time. Men! You have a good man, Anna. But this is women's work."

Mrs. Oie had brought a chunk of ice from her own ice box, with which to keep Anna comfortable on this sweltering day. And when she herself was nearly overcome with the heat, she would plunge her fat arms into the tub of ice water until her cooled blood circulated. She kept changing the ice water soaked cloths on Anna's brow and wrists.

Around noon Anna felt like 'bearing down'. After only two gigantic pushes, the baby appeared. A girl!

"I'm glad it's a girl," Anna sighed, "She'll be company for Alma. And I'm glad it's over. Thanks be to God!"

"Well, Anna, she's perfect. And you had an easy birth, as birthings go. What are you going to call her?"

Anna did not answer Mrs. Oie, for she was already asleep.

"Poor soul, all wore out. I'll tidy up before I get Kari and the little one."

"After Mrs. Oie let Anna have a good nap, and started the baby nursing, she ran up the stairways as fast as her fat little legs would go. Soon two women and a child were hurrying downstairs.

Alma looked at her new little sister with wonder. "Where she come from?" She wanted to know.

"God sent her," Kari explained, thinking that was absolutely all a child should know.

Alma giggled. "God surprised me. He sure did!"

"She is your sweet little sister, Alma," her mother explained with a warm smile.

While Anna was in labor Kari was busy making *kjerrina* soup and trying to stay cool. She put into the soup what she had, a little cured meat, cabbage, potatoes, onions, and carrots. She couldn't keep much food on hand in this heat, and she needed to get rid of what she had fast.

The soup turned out to be delicious. Anna said so after her third spoonful. Then she said she was too tired to eat more. "I'll eat some more when Lars comes," she promised, "What a day he must have had worrying about me!"

Lars came home early. The thought of swimming had not even crossed his mind. He opened the door cautiously, fearfully. "Anybody home?"

"Silly question," Mrs. Oie mumbled, "I see now it is time for me to leave." After making sure Anna and the baby were comfortable, she waved a cheery "Good-by, Anna. I see you tomorrow," and went to the door. Perhaps the midwife's abruptness had something to do with the failure of her prophecy that the child would be a boy. Lars wondered why she had nothing at all to say to him.

"What?" he almost shouted, "What has happened? Anna, are you alright?"

"She must be," he concluded thankfully, hearing friendly laughter from the bedroom.

And just then he heard another sound, a small cooing sound like the mew of a kitten. "The baby is here!"

Soon Lars was trying to embrace both mother and baby with his long arms and work-worn hands.

The joy in Anna's heart was akin to the joy she had felt on that day when she looked up from the bench at Castle Garden, and all of a sudden his strong arms had surrounded her. Like then, she now felt safe and protected.

"Thank you, my dearest, for another beautiful daughter," he whispered hoarsely, "so lovely...so sweet...I want to name her after you. She will be called Anna-Lovisa."

Little Annie thrived in the persistent heat of summer, but the days in the tenement were long and weary for her mama. It was hard for Alma to understand why it was too far for Mama to walk in the sun to Central Park carrying the baby. And it was hard for her to understand why Baby Sister got all of Mama's attention now; especially when she herself needed it, being hot, bored, and peevish. She ran away again...and again. Mama could no longer go look for her. However, Mama didn't worry so much. She was too busy. Besides, she knew that her Papa would find her at the police station again.

It happened so often that Alma thought it was a game, a way to get the attention she craved. She wondered why her Papa stopped thinking it was funny and why he didn't even seem glad to see her. She wondered why he spanked her, when he had not done so previously. But she never ran away again. That was the end of it.

One Sunday in August Papa walked with his family to Central Park, carrying little Annie on one arm, and a picnic basket in the other.

"Hurrah for me!" Alma squealed, "Mama is well again, and I can play in the fountain!"

They all had so much fun they decided to come to Central Park every Sunday. Mama and Papa sat on a park bench and talked, while Annie slept on the grass in a blanket and Alma splashed in the water.

One Sunday they saw a lady pushing a baby in a luxurious woven perambulator. She spoke kindly as she passed, "It's lovely in the park, isn't it?" When she saw Lars' and Anna's hospitable smiles, she stopped.

"What a beautiful baby!" she exclaimed graciously, "Do you mind telling me how old she is?"

Lars answered her in good English. "Just the age of my baby," she said, inviting them to peer at her chubby little fellow in the pram.

"What a nice lady," Anna remarked after she had left. "How I wish I might have spoken to her in English!"

"And how I wish," Lars added, "that I had the money to buy a fine perambulator for our little Annie."

Just then their attention was diverted to a photographer in the park. Alma saw the large black camera on its tripod first. Then Lars saw the sign: PHOTOGRAPHS TAKEN OF YOUR CHILDREN. REASONABLE.

"Say, why don't we get him to take a picture of Alma? She looks so pretty in her striped pinafore carrying her little pail."

"Oh, Lars, that would be wonderful if it doesn't cost too much."

"It costs a dollar."

"Well," Anna considered, "that is a lot, but we could send a picture to Sweden, and show everybody how much she has grown."

Alma posed grandly for the picture, and the photographer promised to bring three finished pictures to this same spot the following week.

"Ja," Lars remarked, as he handed the photographer one of his precious silver dollars, "We do have to trust people here in America."

Eleven

The following Sunday afternoon the Kristoferson's arrived early in Central Park, to wait for the little man who had taken Alma's picture.

While they were sitting on a bench watching Alma play, Lars brought up a serious question: "Anna, how would you like to leave New York City?"

"Lars! How did you guess?   I prayed that we need not spend another summer in this hot, sweltering city."

"Ja, and it's not a good place to bring up our children. I never did think about staying here permanently, Anna."

"What, Lars? I thought you adored New York. You always say so."

"But I don't mean it. Well, at first maybe…"

"What are you saying, Lars?"

"Oh ja, at first I was intrigued by the excitement and variety of this city. It seemed an enchanted place where dreams come true, a place for adventure and opportunity."

Lars paused. Anna remained silent. How could she explain to him that she had felt none of these things about New York? That New York was only her cozy flat, her babies and their needs, and her only friend, Kari …that, outside of these simple realities, New York was frightening, confusing, and thousands of people whose languages she would never understand.

"Ja," Lars continued, "I was young and restless…full of dreams."

Anna laid her hand upon his. "You are still young. Are you saying you have given up your dreams, my love?"

"They were only vapors, only the morning mist before the sunrise. None had substance. But now…" He hesitated.

"But now?" She coaxed him to go on.

"Now my dream is to be a good husband to you and a good father to my girls. I just want to be able to care for you, in every way. But I have failed."

"Oh, no Lars! You have been the very best."

"I have failed," he continued, as if he had not heard her. "My dream is mist, and my pockets are empty.

"But my heart is full," she replied, "Isn't yours too?"

"Oh yes, Anna, full of love for you. But for a man that is not enough. I must accomplish something with my hands, something that will last. And I must provide for my family."

"But if we go away, Lars, where would we go?"

"I don't know yet. But I've heard there are lots of Swedes in Minnesota."

"Ja, Lars. I have some cousins there."

"Mama! Papa!" Alma called, "I see the man! The picture man!"

Sure enough, true to his word, the little photographer appeared with three pictures of Alma. Lars was amazed with their clarity and life likeness.

"Oh, Lars," Anna begged, "I would be so pleased if tonight you would write a letter to my brother Jon that we could send with Alma's picture."

"Why me?"

"Because I want him to know you better, now that we are so far away."

"That makes sense." he laughed, "if you will write a letter to your cousins in Minnesota."

That evening, Lars penned the following letter:

Kjare Brother-in-law Jon,
We are well and hope you and your family are the same. We plan, if all goes
well, to journey west from New York next spring, perhaps to Minnesota,
I have news for you. We have a new little one in our home, a girl named
Anna-Lovisa, born July 17th. We are sending you a picture of our daughter,
Alma-Inge, and you will see she has a pail in her hand. She will soon be out in
the country and be a milkmaid!
Beste halsa, Lars Kristoferson August 30, 1881

"Lars? You finished the letter?"

"Ja."

"I finished mine to the Minnesota cousins."

"Good. Now all I need is to save up the money so we can leave in the spring."

"It will happen Lars…you will see."

"You know what my best dream really is, Anna? It is to own land and be a farmer."

Twelve

In the spring of 1882 Anna knew that they were not going to spend another summer in the New York tenement. Soon they would be on a train slowly chugging its way westward to Minnesota.

"Min-ah-so-dah...Min-ah-so-dah," chanted three-year-old Alma in rhythm to the clacking wheels.

The train had left Grand Central Station that morning, and in the long shadows of late afternoon they looked out upon the lush landscape of upstate New York and the mighty Hudson River. Anna exclaimed in sheer wonder at the magnificence of it all. She had never dreamed the 'land of promise' could be so beautiful, for all she had seen was the teeming, sordid city. She quietly folded her hands in a prayer of thanksgiving. God had made a way.

After that day in Central Park when Lars had confessed to Anna his wish to leave the city, she had written letters to two cousins living in a small town in Minnesota, the Eckbergs and the Perqvists. She remembered these cousins had left Sweden before she was married to Lars. She had not known them very well, for they lived in the country, many miles from Solvesborg. The last time she had seen them was at her mother's funeral and she could no longer recall their faces with clarity. She remembered they had sailed for America, and settled near the town of Willmar, Minnesota. Her brother had heard from them one Christmas, and she recalled at the time marveling that anyone could leave Sweden for the strange land of hardship cousin Perqvist portrayed.

And here she was on her way to Minnesota! So many questions crowded her mind. Anna wondered what kind of people her cousins would be. Both families had written her back, and the Perqvists had offered to meet their train, and let them share their home until Lars could build one. The Eckbergs had also offered assistance, but wrote that Mrs. Perqvist would feel very offended if the Kristofersons did not stay with them. She would feel that their home was not 'good enough' if they chose to stay with the Eckbergs. "Dear cousin, The

44

Perqvists are very sensitive," Mrs. Eckberg wrote, "and I wouldn't want to hurt their feelings." To the Swedish settlers, showing hospitality to a relative, however distant, was more than a duty: it was a privilege.

After her prayer, Anna chattered happily to Lars, who pretended to be asleep, and to her little girls, dressed in their best blue striped pinafores, bouncing up and down on the red velvet seat opposite their parents.

"I wonder if Minnesota will be as pretty as what we see out the window. I wonder if our cousins will like us. It was nice of them to offer to let us stay with them, wasn't it, Lars?"

"Relatives should stick together, especially in America," he replied, "But soon, my love, you shall have your own home. Ja, I will build you a house before winter comes."

Anna smiled adoringly into his handsome face. "I feel like I can put up with anything, just so you are there, Lars. Just so nothing happens to you."

"I'm indestructible," Lars laughed, with a wink at his girls.

"And now," proclaimed Anna, feeling cozy and safe, "We shall eat some more of the nice lunch Kari fixed for us. It's time for supper!"

The sausage and rye bread, the cheese, and the cookies all tasted so good. Lars bought hot coffee from one of the vendors who were forever tramping through the coach, shouting loudly about what they had for sale. "Sandwiches, soup, coffee, lemonade!"

This train seemed to Anna to be truly luxurious, so much more than the little train that connected Solvesborg with Ystad. Lars told her the train was safe too, because it had the fabulous new air brakes. It had two coaches, a Pullman sleeper, a dining car, even a parlor car for the ladies and a smoker for the men. While Lars went to the smoker car to puff on his evening pipe, Anna and the little girls went to the parlor.

The chairs in the parlor were of the softest red velvet, comfortable and elegant. The golden chandeliers were visions of splendor, and the oriental carpet felt soft beneath their feet. The Kristofersons had never seen anything so fine. Opening on the ladies parlor was a boudoir, with a brass sink, a gilded mirror, and a toilet that disposed of everything between the rails below. Anna wondered if this might not offend the young couple she had seen walking hand in hand beside the tracks. And there was even a table for changing babies, very handy, for Annie was not yet trained. Anna changed her, and rinsed the diaper in the brass sink. "I will just hold it out the window and it will dry in no time," Anna stated with practicality.

When night came it was fortunate that there was room for each of them to have a seat to themselves as Lars could not afford the Pullman sleeper. They had to scrimp and do without for months just to pay coach fare. Anna bustled about, tucking blankets and shawls around the girls. Soon they were asleep. Now she and Lars had time to talk, their cheeks gently touching and their arms encircling one another in the darkness.

By the time their train neared Willmar, a whole week had passed. Pretty good considering the train kept up a steady forty miles per hour and stopped only at the big towns. They had to change to another train when they reached Minneapolis, which was the end of the line for the new luxury train. There they boarded a funny little gray-painted coach with wooden benches, a branch line that took three hours to get to Willmar.

When they arrived at their destination the girls were hungry, bedraggled, tired, and very crotchety. Annie was crying pitifully and Alma was like a little wild animal. Anna was so weary that Lars had to hold her up. She didn't even care that her best black dress was now soiled and rumpled, and that her flower-trimmed straw hat was now ruined.

Anna felt drained by the effort of keeping her children content, for the train ride was long, and the little ones constantly bounced, or fussed, or needed help with some vital function. The sparkling new Passenger Express, which at first had seemed so luxurious, had become a kind of prison.

"If we could have afforded the Pullman," Anna whispered, "we'd feel more rested." Her head dropped to Lars' shoulder.

"Rested? Did you say rested?" Lars was smiling, lost in thought. "Ja, I am rested."

Anna sighed. She looked at him closely, this man for whom she had crossed the Atlantic. Never had he seemed so full of abundant vitality. Never had she seen him so confident.

"Ja, I do love that man," she sighed again, leaning upon his energy for the strength she needed to gather their few belongings together, to pat the little faces with a wet cloth, and to comb the rumbled heads.

"WILLMAR!" called the conductor loudly.

"We're here!" Lars stood up.

"Oh, Lars, do you think anyone will be looking for us?"

"Don't worry, Anna," he reassured her with a chuckle, as he hoisted Annie to his broad shoulders. "All will be well. You will see."

A large lumber wagon was pulling up to the platform, with a rather shabby middle-aged couple, and two young ladies dressed in solemn black sitting behind them.

"That must be the Perqvists!" exclaimed Anna, thinking to herself that they didn't look as prosperous as their letter had indicated.

Karl Perqvist was very gracious, hurrying to meet them as they were helped from the train.

"*Valkommen* cousin Anna, and *valkommen* to your family," he greeted warmly, shaking hands with Lars. "We are honored to have you share our humble home. It isn't much, but we have plenty of food. Our home is your home!" He smiled, spreading his arms widely.

"*Tack sa mycket!*" Was all the Kristofersons could reply.

Just as Mr. Perqvist started to go with Lars to the baggage car to unload their trunks, Mrs. Perqvist and her girls appeared shyly behind him.

"*Ja sa*, and this is my wife, and my daughters, Selma and Amanda." The teen aged girls curtsied self-consciously, while Mrs. Perqvist stiffly extended her hand.

"*Valkommen*," she greeted politely, through narrow lips. She did not smile, and Anna did not know the reason: her teeth were missing in front. So Anna had the distinct impression that Svenborg Perqvist did not like her very much. And yet they were going to live together in a tiny sod shanty!

The big lumber wagon, with its heavy load of eight people and the Kristoferson's trunks, was hard for the old workhorses to pull. They padded on lugubriously with measured tread. The three-mile ride to the Perqvist farm seemed interminable to Anna. Even the delight of being able to speak Swedish to someone once again did not make their conversation less formal and stilted. What there was of it was mostly initiated by Lars, who remained optimistic and energetic as he sat up front beside Karl Perqvist. The women and girls sat on the rug-covered wagon bed, leaning on the trunks and boxes, and remained mostly silent as the wagon bumped along the rough and rut-filled roadway.

At last they approached the farm, just as the late spring sun disappeared gloriously into the prairie grass. The sod house was silhouetted black against the rosy panorama. Lars remarked to Perqvist in Swedish that the sky was singularly splendid.

"Such beauty we have never seen in New York!" And then, calling back to Anna, "Didn't I tell you America was something? Now you see!"

Lars had been impressed during the ride by the vast farm fields of wheat and corn pushing upward out of black loam soil.

"This is rich country," he exclaimed, smiling with restless excitement. Hope filled his heart, the hope of a new beginning.

Karl drove his load into the farmyard at last and they all climbed out.

"*Valkommen til vart hemm*...it isn't much." Mrs. Perqvist apologized for her humble home as Lars bent over to enter the door after her. Anna noticed that, even though the walls were sod, and the floor was hard packed dirt, the house seemed amazingly neat and orderly. The hard dirt floor was nearly covered with bright rag rugs. The sod walls were decorated with hand-woven hangings and Swedish proverbs carefully embroidered on linen. Lace curtains hung in the tiny windows and red geraniums adorned their wide sills. The large common room boasted both a stone fireplace and a cast iron cooking stove, new and shiny.

Svenborg went immediately to the stove, her pride and joy, and fed it sumptuous handfuls of corncobs. Soon a cheery fire crackled beneath the blue-enameled coffeepot.

Anna helped set the table while the men tended the horses and unloaded the wagon. Perqvist told Lars to set the trunk, which contained their clothing, in the bedroom. They would store the rest of their things in the grain barn until they obtained their own place.

"You are more than welcome to stay with us as long as you need a home," he offered kindly. Karl Perqvist was a pale, stooped little man with a thin voice. He was shy in the presence of Lars, who towered above him, straight, tall, and self-assured.

"*Tack, tack*, cousin," Lars responded, "but before Autumn I shall have my own house built. You are too kind. However, you must not sacrifice your bedroom. We can sleep in the kitchen!"

"*Nay da*, we will not hear of it! Svenborg has our room all made up for you and Anna, with a trundle bed for your little ones. Amanda and Selma slept there when they were small...and now they are nearly grown young ladies," he reminisced wistfully.

"Where will you sleep?" Lars expressed with concern.

"Oh, well, we have a nice straw tick by the fireplace…very comfortable. Amanda and Selma have the loft. Say no more. All is settled."

"You have done well, Karl." Lars examined the sod construction with amazement "I've never seen this before. How is it possible?"

"On the prairie we must use what we have. Lumber costs much money. But some day…Perqvist seemed defensive, and rather sad and pathetic.

"Forgive me, my friend, I was only admiring your workmanship."

"Lars, I know you are a craftsman in wood from Sweden. So maybe I was a little ashamed of my poor sod shanty."

"Well, you need not be. It is solid, snug, cool in summer, warm, in winter. You should be proud!"

"Lars, I am not a well man. I can do so little. And it seems all my plans come to nothing." Karl looked frightened and vulnerable.

Lars gave Karl's thin shoulders a hearty clasp. "I will help you. That's a promise."

The tall young man shook hands with his smaller and weaker countryman to seal his promise. They each smiled, for each had something to give the other.

Anna had finished setting the table and she wondered what else she could do to help Svenborg, who seemed anxious as she fussed over some 'farmer's potatoes' on the stove, "I make her uncomfortable," Anna felt, "What could be wrong?" Neither woman spoke. Then Anna excused herself to tend to her toddlers.

A blue checked cloth covered the long table. The Perqvists sat on the only two chairs, he at the head, she at the foot, Anna and Lars, with their girls between them, sat on one side bench. Amanda and Selma shared the other bench. The fried potatoes, mixed with eggs, tasted delicious to the weary travelers, for the last of their food had been eaten before they reached Minneapolis. They had not been able to afford to buy much from the vendors, whose loud voices had ever reverberated temptingly throughout the train.

Svenborg had tried her best to make this first meal special. There was green tomato relish and raspberry jam on the table. There were big slices of soft white bread, and a butter cake she had baked in the morning. Rich cream was cooling in the well, ready to whip. A bouquet of spring violets and trilliums adorned the center of the table.

Svenborg had offered them her finest. Even so, a vague cloud of icy melancholy floated between the two women.

49

The two men, chatting amiably in Swedish, had not noticed the cloud. Karl seemed delighted and relieved at the presence of a younger and stronger man on his farm. For indeed, Karl Perqvist was a tired and sickly man. Lars noticed that Karl's veined, work-worn hands trembled as he grasped his coffee cup.

"Lars, your promise to help means a lot to me. I've not been able to finish even half of my spring work, and…" Karl began, stopping to emit a hollow cough.

Lars was sincerely concerned. "Forgive me if I ask about you sickness. Do you know what it is?"

"It is weakness in my back, and this cough. It began two years ago."

"Have you been to a doctor?"

"We don't have a doctor in Willmar yet," interrupted Svenborg.

"Oh, he could go to Minneapolis but of course he won't!" She laughed a tight little titter.

"Never mind," Karl replied with a scowl, "I don't want to talk about it."

"Well, if a person wants to live…" Svenborg persisted.

"*Ja sa*?" argued Karl, "I have seen people going to doctors and they died anyway."

"It was God's will." Svenborg sighed.

"So? You see that woman? Nothing does any good. What do you think, Lars?"

"I think everyone should do his best to live, to live well."

"And what of God's will?

I say what will be, will be," Karl sighed resignedly.

"I don't know about God, or if there is a God. I don't think about it."

"Lars didn't mean that the way it sounded," apologized Anna, with embarrassment. She believed no one should question the existence of God. She fervently hoped that Lars did believe in the depth of his heart.

"Ja, I did mean what I said." Lars asserted simply, with a loving glance at his wife. Then he changed the subject. "Perqvist, I'll be glad to help you finish the spring work. We can begin tomorrow."

"*Tack sa mycket.*"

Thirteen

The Perqvists' bed, with its feather tick, was soft and the guests slept well. Alma and Annie were cozy in the old trundle bed with its new straw mattress. Anna was thankful for the door, with a lock and key that separated the small bedroom from the rest of the house. Surely a sod house with an interior door was a lucky and unusual circumstance. She was thankful also for the little lace-covered window that opened to let in the cool night air, and for the commode and china washstand set, with a pitcher of water for bathing, all hidden behind a chintz curtain in the comer. She could wash the diapers here, as well as other intimate things. Privacy in this house was to be particularly cherished.

Anna wished to bother Svenborg as little as possible and to stay out of her way. Would that uncomfortable feeling ever leave her? How could she change this dismal beginning into a workable relationship? "Well, I will try," she resolved as she closed her eyes, "May God help me!"

Lars began to sense that something was wrong as she lay in bed beside him that first night, deliciously close as the children slept. He longed to touch her, to hold her, for it had been so long. She seemed strangely remote.

"Anna, is something wrong?"

"Sh…it has nothing to do with you."

"Is not all well?"

"Lars, don't talk out loud, please…whisper. I will put my lips to your ear and tell you."

"Ja, tell me," Lars yawned.

"It's Svenborg. I'm puzzled, Lars. She has done so much for us. Yet I feel so uncomfortable with her. Not like with Kari, from the first day we had fun, laughing and joking about everything. Sure, there was sometimes strain, but we could say anything to each other. I can't even talk to Svenborg…not yet at least."

"It will get better Anna. Why, you just met her! Think about what you can do to help her. Just like me with Karl. He needs me...and that makes it better for us to be here, doesn't it?"

Anna got up and sat on the edge of the bed, thinking about what Lars had said. He was right, of course. But whatever could she do to help Svenborg? She and her daughters had everything neat and organized. An extra pair of hands might only get in the way. Maybe she could milk the cow...except she had never milked a cow before. Oh, well, she would think of something tomorrow.

Anna snuggled back down under the covers beside Lars. She stroked his back, ready now to respond to his need for intimacy.

"Lars?" she soothed.

There was no response. Her Lars was snoring.

The summer was slowly passing by, day after sweltering day. The situation between the two women did not improve, even though Anna tried to be kind and to make herself useful.

"Let me help you with the cooking," Anna suggested one day.

"'My girls and I have done everything," Svenborg answered curtly, "Enjoy yourself."

"Enjoy myself?" Anna mumbled, "I need to be a part of this household, and she won't even let me wash the dishes."

"What did you say? I can't hear you." Svenborg almost shouted.

Anna remained silent. The simple reality was that Svenborg had a great deal to do. "Well," she agreed at last, "maybe you could peel the potatoes."

"Gladly." Anna began on the small pail of new potatoes Amanda had dug in the garden. "Svenborg? You know these are good with the skins on. How would it be if I just scrub them?"

"No. Karl likes his peeled."

After a few minutes Anna had finished the job. Svenborg inspected the potatoes carefully then remarked coldly, "Tack...but, my, you peel wastefully. I peel thin. You need not peel potatoes. My girls know how to do it."

Anna sighed and went to the bedroom with her little ones so not to be in Svenborg's way.

The next day, Anna was permitted to gather the eggs. Unfortunately, Alma was helping and broke one.

"Oh, nay-dah," Svenborg hissed, shaking her finger at Alma. "We cannot afford to break eggs. Your mama must punish you now,"

Again they retreated, this time to the woodshed. As they left Svenborg called, "You need not gather eggs. My girls do it!"

Anna and Alma sat down on the log in the shed, tears staining Anna's flushed cheeks.

"Mama spank?" Alma inquired.

"No, my sweet lamb. Why would Mama spank you for just being a child? Mama breaks things sometimes too."

"Why are you crying, Mama?"

"I don't know. Maybe your Mama is just lonesome to have her own kitchen again."

Alma's chubby arms encircled her Mama tightly. "Be better soon, Mama," she soothed.

As time went on Anna's small children were getting on Svenborg's nerves more and more. Anna finally stopped trying to help Svenborg around the house. It seemed to take all her strength just to keep her eyes on her active toddlers, and to stay out of Svenborg's path. Sensing that she disliked them made Alma and Annie try to get attention in undesirable ways. Amanda and Selma liked them, but their mother scolded whenever they spent even a few moments of play with the little girls.

"Don't be lazy," Svenborg admonished, "You are wasting precious time with foolishness." Then she quoted an old Swedish proverb with self-righteous zeal: *"Den lattes bon ar sallan hord"* (The lazy ones' prayer is seldom heard).

Just then Annie reached over to examine the beautiful vase of flowers on the table, it teetered. Then, falling to the floor, it broke into a hundred pieces.

Her face, livid with horror, Svenborg clutched at her heart. Anna waited with dread in her eyes, while Annie sobbed uncontrollably.

"My vase from Skane! My beautiful wedding present!" Svenborg shrieked hoarsely.

Anna sat stupidly silent. What could she say? She had no money with which to pay for the elegant blue bowl-shaped vase, and no amount of money could replace a wedding present from Sweden. It was a situation of devastating tragedy. There was no way Anna could ever make it right.

Nothing more was said. Sobbing bitterly, Svenborg tenderly picked up each piece of her cherished vase. And the grim silence which grew between the two women was like a stone wall that could never be scaled.

Meanwhile, Karl and Lars continued to work together in harmony. Lars had never farmed before, but he was smart and energetic, eager to learn new skills. It felt good to be needed by the frail Perqvist. It felt good to pull his weight. And Karl was truly grateful, for he could never have farmed his sixty acres all alone. He had no money to pay a hired hand. Providence had sent Lars to him just in time.

Karl had to rest for a moment in the shade of the wagon.

"That Lars!" he chuckled, "Never wants to quit. What luck he came to me!" He was thinking that maybe this Sunday he should go to church in Willmar and offer his thanks to a God he feared, but did not understand or love. Besides, he could feel his life slipping away and didn't want to be caught unprepared for the great beyond. It had been more than a year since he had been to Communion.

"Lars, how would it be if we take our families to church on Sunday?" Perqvist ventured that suffocating August day as they drank their afternoon coffee under the big elm tree by the cornfield.

"I'm not a church goer, Karl," Lars answered pleasantly.

"Don't you believe in God?" wondered Karl anxiously.

"Let's just say that I'm not superstitious."

"What do you mean?"

Lars then told a true story of how, all alone, he had slept several nights in a house everyone in Ystad had believed to be haunted by ghosts. "Ja, the Swedes are very superstitious!" Lars laughed heartily.

Karl's eyes grew big as saucers. "You don't say…"

"Ja, it is so. One day my brother dared me to spend the night in that old stone castle overlooking the harbor. It was really just a big house with turrets, old and dilapidated. They said the former owner, now a spirit, walked around in it at night, howling and crying, and vowing to kill the man whom had run off with his wife."

"Well, what happened?" Perqvist's eyes were like full moons in autumn.

"Nothing, absolutely nothing. I just had a good sleep, even if the bed was a rock." Lars laughed again, this time uproariously.

"Maybe you were not the one then, the one he wanted. I mean the one the spirit was going to kill," Karl stammered with trembling lips.

Lars looked at Karl with concern. "Perqvist! You actually believe that nonsense? I suppose you believe in the *Tomten* as well?"

"Lars, you tease me. Let's go back to cutting our oats."

Karl could see there was no use pursuing what was on his heart. Lars would not understand his fear, his pain, and the burden of his sins. Lars was strong and in the prime of life.

Church was not mentioned again in their conversation. Karl simply pushed his burden down deeper, and tried to forget his pain as he exchanged pleasantries with the man who had become his helper and his best friend.

Fourteen

After the incident of the vase, conversation became even more strained between Svenborg and Anna. Anna began to feel that even Selma and Amanda were resenting and avoiding them. It was Anna's private opinion that these teen-age girls did not behave normally. They were prim, stuffy, and never had any fun. Whatever could have happened to the poor dears to make them like fussy old women?

"Ja, those girls are getting to be just like Svenborg...too bad," Anna said to herself

She thought it odd too that Selma and Amanda no longer seemed to enjoy playing with Alma and Annie, even when Svenborg was not there to admonish them. The only time Alma and Annie were praised was when they, miraculously, sat motionless on the bench beside the table, hands folded.

"That's a good girl, Alma," Svenborg commented one morning, smiling a stiff little smile, "Good girls sit still. Good girls are quiet girls. Be ladies."

Even little Annie was learning that she must avoid Mrs. Perqvist and her daughters, or endure the agony of 'sitting like a lady'.

Mostly, Anna took her girls outside to play. She worried about what effect the Perqvist's joyless rigid existence might have on their development, and of what they would do when the days grew cold and they could no longer spend their time out of earshot in the grove by the barn.

Anna loved to play with her children. For lack of toys, she invented all sorts of games to play...running games for Alma, pine cone games, hiding and peek-a-boo games, sitting on the grass singing games, telling Bible stories or Swedish folk tales, or just talking.

"When Annie's birthday comes around I surely won't mention it to Svenborg," Anna promised herself. She had remembered mentioning Alma's. "Ja, so?" was all Svenborg had said. No cake, no song, no word of encouragement. Anna had not expected much, but she was hurt-especially when she remembered all the kind folks on the ship coming over from Sweden.

She reflected that she and Lars did not want to live like this. They loved fun and family warmth, and caring for one another. Something was surely lacking in this peculiar family. Anna wondered what had made Svenborg the way she was. She searched for clues to the darkness and bitterness in Svenborg's soul.

She longed to talk with Lars about this unbearable situation but he always came in from the fields happy, hungry, and too tired to talk after they went to bed. Clearly, the "unbearable situation" belonged only to Anna. Lars was content.

"That Kristoferson!" Anna overheard her say to her daughters, "He is a fine figure of a man-so tall and straight, so kind and polite. If you girls ever marry, it must be to men like Kristoferson. Though you must not think about marriage. You are needed at home to help your Mama and Papa. But ah…that Kristoferson! How can we ever set a table good enough for a man like that?"

As she listened through the bedroom door to Svenborg raving on about Lars, Anna blushed at the startling thought that crossed her mind. "Why, I do believe Svenborg is in love with my Lars! No wonder she hates me. She is jealous. She thinks I am unworthy of Lars!"

In the weeks that followed Anna tried hard to erase this terrible thought from her mind. "Fi, what foolishness!" she told herself.

One particular afternoon, in early September, Anna and her girls were sitting on the grass by the pump, after a game of tag. Suddenly she remembered it was late and told them, "Stay here. I'll see if Cousin Svenborg needs a pail of water. I CAN do something! Perhaps this time she'll let me help."

"Cousin, do you need a pail of water?" she asked kindly.

"No need. Amanda will get it when needed."

"Svenborg, I do wish you would let me help in some way, I feel so useless."

"You feel as you are. I cannot help how you feel. But let me tell you this plainly. This is MY kitchen. But those wild brats are yours. You take care of yours and I'll take care of mine."

Anna was too hurt to speak. Tears filled her eyes as she headed for the door, its top half open to the breeze. Svenborg, grimly silent, turned toward the stove.

Just then Anna observed with horror what Alma was doing. She had jumped over the bottom half of the door and was swinging on it with unrestrained abandon. Anna hoped that she could reach her before Svenborg turned around.

"Alma, stop!" she whispered, hoping Svenborg might not notice.

Then it happened. The whole kitchen door dropped from the uncertain hinges that had fastened it precariously to the sod wall. It dropped noisily onto the flat rock before the door. It dropped on Alma!

Both women screamed. Anna had but one thought: IS ALMA HURT? She frantically lifted the door from Alma's bottom half where it had fallen. Alma sobbed convulsively as her mother swept her into trembling arms. "My baby, oh my baby! What has happened to you?"

"My door! My fine kitchen door!" lamented Svenborg, wringing her hands, "What has that child done now?"

Anna sat down, pulling up Alma's dress to assess the extent of her injuries. She saw some bruises, mostly on the soft places made for spankings, but her wildly threshing legs obviously were not broken. "Thank God!" Anna breathed.

"Thank God, huh?" Svenborg snarled, hands on her fat hips, "For what? For a child who breaks down doors?"

"I'm sorry...so sorry." Tears filled Anna's eyes again. She could take no more. Gathering a child into each arm, she headed for the bedroom.

Soon Lars and Karl came in from the cornfield. "What is this?" Karl yelled with surprise. "What happened to my new door?"

"Alma did it," was all Svenborg would allow herself to say in the presence of Lars.

Lars examined the door, the hinges, and the casing. "I will fix it," he said simply. "It will be better than before."

Before nightfall Lars had finished his professional best on the door. It was indeed better than before. Lars could easily see how it had become unloosed, for the screws were held in sod. He reinforced the sash with several thicknesses of wood instead.

"Lars, you are a real Swedish carpenter," Karl praised, thinking of a few other jobs he might ask Lars to tackle later on.

After watching Lars repair the door, Svenborg's mood changed from darkness into light. "Well then, come to the table. *Var sa god,*" she invited heartily. The men joked amiably. Selma and Amanda even giggled a little. But Anna sat red-eyed and silent. Lars noticed this and wondered what was wrong.

He meant to ask her after they went to bed that night. But he started to snore before it crossed his mind again.

Fifteen

The first faint essences of autumn were breathing gently across the southern Minnesota prairie. Black clouds of crows hovered over the cornfield, conversing cacophonously about their imminent get-away plans. Gentler birds lingered in the treetops of the grove, sensing the ominous approach of winter cold. There had been a few frosty nights and mornings in which the warm breath of horses could be seen, and dew frozen into sparkling diamonds on the grass. Soft haze brooded over the meadow, and the sky seemed more brilliant cobalt than before. The Perqvists' single maple was beginning to glow under the sun, and the tall poplar windbreak resembled the gold spires of cathedrals in Sweden.

The men in the fields had little time to take note of this entire splendor for the urgency of the task at hand, getting in the crops before the first killing frost. Karl worked slowly, wearily, with aching joints and bent back, Lars worked with the steady gait of a young gelding that never seemed to tire. He was always ready for one more shock of grain, one more load, and one more hour at the plow.

"Say, Perqvist, we better work tomorrow, even if it is Sunday. What do you think?"

"No," Karl answered with finality; "God made the Sabbath for man...for a no-good man like me."

Lars, sensing how much Perqvist needed to rest, said no more. "Poor Karl hasn't got his health," he noted quietly.

Anna got up early on that bright Sunday morning because she wanted to read her Bible and *Sahmabok* before the others got up. She tiptoed softly to a chair by the small bedroom window and opened the precious hymnbook that had been given her years before by Madame Yjerst. She opened it to the 142nd Psalm. Tears ran down her cheek as she read the words of David: "I poured out my complaint before the Lord. When my spirit was overwhelmed within me, God knew my path."

God's immediate answer to the cry of her heart was soon to encourage Anna. For as soon as he opened his eyes, Lars blurted out, "Anna, today you and I are going to have a talk about the things that

60

are bothering you. Don't tell me it's nothing, because I can see that sad look in my sweetheart's face,"

"Sh...softly...they might hear us."

"We shall go for a long walk in the cornfield, just the two of us alone."

"But who will take care of Alma and Annie?"

"I will ask Amanda and Selma to watch them," he declared, as if everything were simple.

"Impossible! Those girls have never done anything for our babies. Svenborg does not want them to," Anna whispered very carefully and quietly.

"They will," Lars smiled, "for I shall pay them...besides, Svenborg never refuses anything to me."

He was putting on his clothes while Anna smoothed the bed. They could hear the Perqvists rattling around in the kitchen.

Anna smiled as she dressed. How silly of her to be arguing with Lars over God's quick answer to her morning prayer!

After breakfast, Lars smiled broadly at Selma and Amanda. "How would you girls like to earn fifty cents each?" he invited.

"Fifty cents! For each of us?" They could hardly believe their ears. Nor could Anna believe Lars' outrageous extravagance when they had so little. A dollar was more than a man could earn in one day!

"Will you girls take care of Alma and Annie today? Mrs. Kristoferson and I are going on a Sunday outing."

"Ja, sure," Amanda answered, "We'll take good care of them."

Then Lars turned to Svenborg. "And would it be alright if Anna fixes us some sandwiches and a jar of coffee to take along?"

Svenborg raised her eyebrows. She was overwhelmed and shocked by Lars' unusual suggestion, thinking, "Why would he want to spend the whole day with that mouse?"

"I will make the sandwiches," she clipped, "Anything for you, Lars." She made polse and rye sandwiches, and poured the leftover coffee into a jar wrapped in a woolen rag.

It was a day glorious with promise, warm sunshine with just a hint of frosty crispness in the air. The maple tree at the end of the lane beckoned Lars and Anna like a flaming torch of freedom. They walked hand in hand, with the springy step of youthful lovers. Suddenly, it seemed as though they were back in Solvesborg, dancing in the village square. It was so right, so perfect to be walking thus together. As soon as the Perqvists' sod house was out of sight they burst out laughing, and their arms entwined tightly around each other's waists. For a moment in time, the sod house and the dismal Perqvists became a distant dream. Two lovers basked in the wonder of the present.

Anna had almost forgotten why they had come to the road beside the cornfield. She hated to bring it up. Such unpleasantness could wait.

"Hearing you laugh again is music to my ears," Lars observed joyfully.

"It's hard to think of anything now but the pleasure of just being with you. Oh, Lars, where have you been? When I needed you so?"

"Where have YOU been, my darling? My songbird has gone away and an old lady who never smiles has taken her place."

That brought the flood of tears. The beautiful dream in which they had lingered faded into the daylight of reality. Now they must begin to talk about what was going on in their lives...the hard things.

Pouring forth with a torrent of hot tears came the agony bottled up within Anna's tender spirit, Lars had not realized until this moment the enormous difficulty his wife was facing in her day to day existence with Svenborg.

"Strange," Lars considered, "I have never seen this darker side of Svenborg. Perhaps she has concealed it from me all along."

"Of course Lars! I'll bet she's in love with you!"

"How could she help it?" he teased with a wink, suppressing laughter. It seemed like such a ridiculous idea to Lars.

"Well, she HATES me. Everywhere I go I feel the hatred of her cold gray eyes upon me."

"Oh, *nei-dah*, Anna," he soothed, "you must be imagining something."

"That hurts, Lars." Then she told him everything that had happened...how Svenborg had talked when she offered to help and when Annie broke the wedding vase, as well as everything else she could recall that had caused her pain. The deep wounds and the smoldering anger. The guilt for seeming to be an unlovable person. The loneliness and the sadness. All these feelings came rushing out of Anna's soul like a cloudburst of lightning. Having said it all, she felt much better. When Anna was all finished, Lars said quietly, "I never knew you were suffering so much."

He put his strong arms around her and let her sob. The catharsis of her tears and the comfort of his love brought new life to Anna. Somehow she knew that now everything would be alright.

They sat down under the big elm tree by the creek to eat their lunch, a sweet, silent communion passing between them. Afterward, they lay in the tall grass, giving expression to their deep love not possible in the crowded sod house.

"Anna, I've been thinking," Lars ventured after a long silence, still cradling her close to himself, "Here I've been happy working for Perqvist, feeling good because he can't do without me, feeling his friendship and approval when all along you have been miserable because Svenborg doesn't need or want your help, is annoyed with our babies, and doesn't even like you!"

"She wishes I would go away."

"She has no reason to wish that. But there must be some reason for her being the way she is."

"I have puzzled over that too. What could it be?"

"Who knows? Someday she may tell you."

"Meanwhile, Lars, we must find a way to get away from here-get our own place."

"I promised you your own home before winter. Oh, Anna, how I have failed you! I've been so busy helping Karl I haven't had time to find work in town, so as to save money to build our own home."

"Perqvist said the crops have been good for the first time in years. And Lars, that has been all because of you!"

"Ja, that is a satisfaction,"

"Don't you think Perqvist would pay you something?"

"I helped a friend…a friend who has given us his best."

"Ja so," agreed Anna, "but at least we should feel proud and not beholden to them. Why can't Svenborg see this?"

I will talk to her."

"Be careful, Lars. She will be meaner if she thinks I complained to you."

"She will listen to me," he said with finality.

It was time to return to the sod house. Hand in band, Lars and Anna strolled slowly, reluctantly, into the golden western sky.

Lars had a plan. "I will be able to work in town," he explained, "at least part of the time, now that the fall work is nearly over. I will save every dollar and soon I can build your house. Anna, you'll see. But first I must talk to the Perqvists'. He too must know what has been going on. I will not allow her to torment you any longer."

As they approached the house, Anna said wistfully, "Why didn't I speak my mind before?"

"Ja, why? Why are we Swedes like that?"

Just then, Alma and Annie ran out joyfully to meet their Mama and Papa.

Sixteen

After breakfast on Monday morning, Karl rose from the table with unaccustomed vigor. "Ja, the Sabbath helped me some, Lars. Shall we go?"

"Just a minute," Lars began, with a solemn authority in his voice that made Karl sink back into his place at the table. "I need to bring up a matter that concerns the four of us. Girls, I wonder if you would be so good to take Alma and Annie out to play?"

They obeyed without question. "Ja," Anna said to herself nervously, "When Lars speaks softly, everybody listens."

Svenborg went to the stove. "More coffee?" she offered briskly. After she filled the cups she sat down meekly, eyes fixed upon Lars in wonderment.

Lars plunged into this encounter with what he hoped was a non-threatening remark. He tried to sound casual. "Ja, I've been thinking...you both have been so good to us...sharing your home, sharing your best food, giving us your bed. We cannot thank you enough."

"Where are you going with all that sugar stuff?" Anna mouthed silently, anxiously. "Come on, Lars."

Lars did not notice Anna, but continued, "But now I think we must make plans to build our own home."

"What?" Svenborg interjected, "*Nei-dah*! You would leave us? Just when Karl is weakening? His life ebbing away?"

"I would still help him as much as I could, Svenborg, even when we move to town,"

"Move to town!" Svenborg's large gray eyes darted about wildly.

"I thought you would be pleased, Cousin," Lars continued kindly, "You know the Swedish proverb about two women in the same kitchen?"

"Anna never bothers me in MY kitchen!" Svenborg took care of that proverb!

"And our children," Lars continued, "are now at an age to cause a lot of trouble for you. Your girls are nearly grown ladies. And I can see that you like to keep things nice."

Tight, simmering rage began to rise slowly within Svenborg. She wondered how she could speak plainly without offending Lars.

"I don't mind the children," she began slowly through narrow lips, "but Kristofer (as she often called Lars) I have to tell you the truth. I don't mind the children...ah...if you..." Svenborg's voice became a hoarse, hissing sound.

"Ja, if what?" Lars insisted, looking directly into her averted eyes.

"If...if you see to your wife disciplining them," was her barely audible answer. She hung her head, her hands folded in her apron.

"Ah, so this is the problem? You know what I think, Svenborg? I think my wife is the most wonderful mother in the world, in Sweden or America!" Lars' face reddened and his piercing blue eyes flashed.

Svenborg felt threatened. "You would think that, of course, but I could give her some pointers!" she snapped, "If she would listen. I raise two good girls. My girls never run wild in the house; never pull down things, never break doors." She ended her speech with a tight little laugh, and an old Swedish proverb about children being quiet and sitting still in the presence of grownups.

"Well," Lars answered sharply, "I seem to recall another proverb that says children should grow up happy and have fun!"

Encouraged by her husband's boldness, Anna quoted another proverb:

"Ack hur lyckig ar barndom's tiden, men ack hur snart, hur snart den hasten bort." (How happy are the days of childhood, but how quickly they pass away)

Tension was high and stinging. Lars wondered if he should just let it go, now that they had uncovered the source of a strained relationship. He disliked angry words, and tended to avoid them at all cost.

But Anna would not let it go. She would have her say.

"Svenborg, so far it has been you and Lars talking. I just want to say one thing to you." Anna's voice was soft and nearly breaking with emotion. "I am a PERSON...with feelings and needs. And my children are people...with feelings and needs. They deserve a chance to grow up happy. The days of childhood are so short and so precious. That is why we must move out as soon as possible. And until then, we must try to get along together."

Svenborg was suddenly seeing herself as the innocent victim, the persecuted martyr. Tears stained her face. "I have done nothing wrong," she sobbed, "I have given up everything for her...my room, my privacy, my pretty wedding vase. And now I am the one pointed at!"

Karl could no longer keep silent. A man whose life was ebbing away must speak plainly. "Woman," he addressed his wife with vigor, "Stop those crocodile tears! You know you never wanted Anna here. You wanted Lars, and you were jealous because she was the wife of such a man. And I also wanted Lars...because he could help me. Last year there were no crops to speak of. This year we are prosperous. So what can we do for Lars? I will share my profits with him. What can you do for Lars, Svenborg? You can be nice to his family...be good to Anna and patient with their little ones. And let her do some things around here so she feels it is her home too."

Karl's face became florid and his breath was emitted in short panting sounds. Three pairs of eyes turned to him with alarm.

"Careful, my friend," Lars began, his strong right arm supporting Karl's frail and stooping shoulders.

But Perqvist was not finished. He had one more thing to say to Anna. "If things don't work out, Cousin, you talk to me...if things around here don't change right away."

Amazingly, Karl Perqvist had become the head of his home, and his wife was silent.

There was no more to be said and the men went out to the barn. Lars gave Anna an affectionate kiss, and Karl gave Svenborg a stern look.

The next morning, Svenborg asked Anna an astonishing question, "Anna, do you know how to bake bread?"

"Ja sure," Anna answered without having to think.

"Well," continued Svenborg, with unaccustomed friendliness, "My girls and I are going to walk to town today to buy winter clothes. I wonder if you be so kind to bake a batch of bread while we're away."

"White or rye?" Anna was too surprised to say anything else.

"Whatever you like," was the quick reply. And before Anna had time to recover from the shock of these words, the three Perqvists were strolling briskly down the lane.

"Alma, what do you think? For one day, this house is ours!" She took her little girls' hands and danced joyfully around the kitchen like a silly schoolgirl. Then she got onto the serious business of making the most delicious bread that had ever been tasted.

Meanwhile, out in the field, Karl and Lars were loading the last of the corn into the lumber wagon. "*Tack Gud.* We are almost done with the fall work." Karl heaved a big sigh. "Thank God? I thought it was thanks to ME, Perqvist," Lars teased good-naturedly.

"God surely must have sent you to me then. I was at the end of my rope."

"Well, I don't know about that. But as far as anything I did goes, *Valkommen!*"

"After we take our first load to Willmar tomorrow, I will pay you. You deserve a share of the harvest. Without you there wouldn't be any."

"No, no," Lars protested politely. You have been supporting my family for months. I ask no more."

"You must let me thank you, my friend…I…I…" Karl began, his voice breaking.

Lars put a large, strong hand on each of Karl's stooped shoulders, as a quiet communication passed between the two men.

That evening, everyone enjoyed the good, fresh white bread that Anna had baked and the fragrant cinnamon rolls. She had also cooked a kettle of yellow pea and potato soup, flavored with salt pork. Almost everybody, even Amanda and Selma, said it was the best they'd ever tasted. Except Svenborg of course, who said it was "not too bad".

Seventeen

In Willmar the next morning, Karl was given a fresh burst of energy by the good news that his wheat was worth one hundred fifty dollars. After the elevator manager carefully counted three fifty-dollar bills into his open hand, Karl turned, and silently slipped one of the bills into Lars' pocket.

"Fifty dollars!" Lars exclaimed with mock protest, "I've never seen a fifty dollar bill in my life! I wouldn't know what to do with it!" He held the bill out to Karl.

Perqvist's hands were both in his pockets. "Don't be so sure. Seems to me I saw some big lots for sale on the other side of town for fifty dollars.

"Let's go look at them then," Lars smiled, putting the fifty dollars back into his pocket. Perqvist had finally accepted the Kristofersons' need for a home of their own.

The lot Lars purchased was indeed a fine one...two acres, with apple trees, a cow and a horse, together with a small barn and hay. There was even a flaming maple tree in the yard, almost as large and beautiful as the one in the Perqvists' yard. All that was missing was a house. The sod shanty that had been used by the former owners had been so damaged in a windstorm it had to be torn down. Lars, the master carpenter, would build a house. Plans began to form in his mind as he surveyed his newly acquired property...plans to begin as soon as possible...plans to seek work in town. He explained all this to Perqvist as they drove home in the empty wagon. "I've been thinking Karl, maybe now that the crops are in and you won't need a field hand...that maybe now I can look for a carpenter job in town, and start working on my house in my spare time."

"Ja, Willmar is really booming," Karl agreed.

"Maybe I can look tomorrow, when we bring in the oats?"

"Ja, sure, Lars. I wish you luck." Karl sighed deeply.

Lars looked at his friend with concern. "I won't forget you, Perqvist. But my wife is again in the family way and needs her own home."

"Ja, sure, I understand," Karl assured him.

"But what about the future? What are you going to do?" Lars spoke out of deep compassion for his suffering friend.

"I lie awake nights...puzzling, thinking, even praying," Karl confessed, "and if I'm lucky I think I'll come up with something."

Lars nodded.

"I'm not getting any better, that's for sure," Karl continued, "I have to face that...and no one to carry on for me. So I think maybe I will sell my farm. I could buy a little house in town. If my health holds out I could do odd jobs for awhile. By the time I die, maybe Amanda and Selma will marry and be able to care for their mother."

"It's for sure they'd have a better chance in town," Lars ventured, while he was trying to think of something more suitable to say. Perqvist looked so bent over and forlorn.

"Perqvist, let me help you build your house in town... just as soon as I finish mine."

"Would you? A wooden house?"

"Not sod."

Karl let go of the reins for a moment, and the two good friends shook hands.

After Anna's bread baking day Svenborg began to treat her with an amazing new respect. Anna did not know that Svenborg had also seen the new doctor on that shopping day in town, or that it was his evaluation of her health that had mellowed her.

It was as Svenborg feared. She was not a well woman. And so she began to realize that no one, even one such as herself, can exist as an island, needing no help from others. No matter that she disliked Anna. Just as Karl needed Lars, she needed Anna. Anna was still young and strong, while she was feeling old and tired at forty-eight. Dr. Black, who came to Willmar once a week from Minneapolis, had heard a heart irregularity and advised Svenborg that she must rest more and be relieved of some responsibilities. Svenborg was so frightened she might die, even before Karl, that she began to put her personal feelings toward Anna aside. She began to see herself less perfectly as the invincible queen of her humble kitchen. She began to wonder how she would ever cope when Lars and Anna moved to their own home in town.

Anna was puzzled by this change in Svenborg. At times, Svenborg seemed grateful to her for taking over some of the cooking and cleaning chores. Sometimes, however, she would unexpectedly lash out at her cousin, complaining bitterly that some trivial thing was not done 'her way'. Occasionally, Svenborg treated Anna like a sister, confiding in her. Many days Svenborg was merely silent and sad.

Meanwhile, Anna had let go of her fear of Svenborg. She spoke to her boldly and plainly "Cousin, I don't mean to criticize, but why is it I never know what to expect of you?" Anna ventured one morning when Svenborg was in one of her dark moods.

"You just don't understand me, Anna," she pouted, gazing out of the tiny window at the drizzly day, "You see I have had a hard life."

"Ja, how so?" encourage Anna, pouring her a fresh cup of coffee from the stove.

"Back in Sweden…" Svenborg hesitated, needing to talk and yet feeling the stabbing pain of long repressed memories. "Well, never mind." There was an interval of silence, in which Anna poured herself a cup of coffee, took a sugar lump, and sat down on the bench opposite Svenborg.

"Perhaps if you tell me about it you will feel better," Anna encouraged, "I'm listening."

Svenborg was beginning to realize she didn't dislike Anna quite as much as before…even if she was married to that wonderful man, Lars Kristoferson. She looked into Anna's face for the first time seeing honesty, warmth, and gentleness. Something about this small, unpretentious woman disarmed her in a strange new way. It was hard for her to believe that she wanted to tell Anna some things she had not even dared to think about for a long time.

"My father was not the good man everyone thought he was," she began hesitatingly, "He did unspeakable things to me…I mean, really unspeakable…things no one ever talked about for the shame of it. Then he died, and I was glad. So you see, all these years I have had to live with the sin of willing his death! Oh, I was punished for sure! Soon my mama died too and I was left all alone, except for my two brothers. But they didn't want me. They married me off to Perqvist."

The shocked look on Anna's face seemed to inspire Svenborg to continue pouring forth her bitterness and pain.

"Times were hard. You never knew how hard we had it in the country, Anna. We never owned our own land. And when the famine came, we nearly starved to death. That's when we came to America,

71

the Land of Promise, they said it was. Uff dah! Some land of promise! It was work, work, work, sun up to sun down, and nothing to show for it but a poor sod shanty. Well, what could I expect with a no-good man like Karl Perqvist?"

Anna swallowed hard, thinking how she might have a few positive words to say to this dismal, bitter, and unpleasant woman. No wonder she was so unpredictable and hard to live with. No wonder her daughters were so solemn, so utterly lacking in normal youthful gaiety! Svenborg was suffering from soul-sickness, and Anna determined in her heart she would try to find some way to help her.

"I'm so sorry," Anna fumbled.

"Well, how could you understand when everything has gone so well for you?"

"Do you think that?" Anna sat up straight and spoke with startled conviction. "Well, you are wrong. Let me tell you, Cousin, you are not the only one who was left alone without father or mother at a tender age. Or who tasted poverty or fear. Yes, even guilt. I, too, had these things happen to me." Anna searched Svenborg's face, but her cousin's eyes remained averted. She did not believe that Anna could understand.

"Our lives have been so different …you could not know. Svenborg stammered defensively.

"Ja, there was a difference," Anna continued thoughtfully, "a great difference between you and me. It was love that came to me from my parents and my brother, and the forgiveness given to me by my Savior. That is why I have peace in my soul. Jesus gives me joy deep inside, even in the bad times when I maybe don't show it much, even when there are tears."

"Ah, fi-dah! It's because you were lucky and got a good man," responded Svenborg bitterly.

"You have a good husband too. Karl is patient and kind. He can't help that his health is failing."

"You are criticizing me," pouted Svenborg defensively.

"Oh, no, my cousin. I have no right to judge you. Forgive me if it seemed so!"

Svenborg stared down at her coffee in the pretty cup with the roses, slowly drawing circles in the blue-checked cloth, and thinking, "Ja, ja, I have said enough."

But Anna wanted to respond to this unexpected opening of Svenborg's heart. "Deep hurts lie there," she mused silently, "and I need to help." She prayed for guidance.

Just as Svenborg began to gather up the coffee service, Anna spoke again, earnestly searching her cousin's anxious, furtive, and averted eyes.

"Cousin Svenborg," she began gently, "would you...would you permit me to speak my mind? Not criticizing you, of course. If you say 'no' I won't say anything."

Svenborg was curious. What in the world was Anna about to say?

"Ja, just go ahead."

Anna sat quietly, hands folded on the table. She spoke slowly, deliberately, praying silently that her words would help, and not offend.

"As I listened to you, Svenborg, I seemed to hear a woman who sees life as bitter and hard. My life has been hard too. No one is given an easy life in this world of sin and suffering. But it seems to me that you desire your life to be as bad as possible."

"Why? What a crazy thing to say! How dare you speak to me like that?" Svenborg arose from the bench on which she was sitting. She stiffened angrily.

"Just a minute. Please sit down and let me finish! You talked about feeling guilty about your father's death, even though it was not your fault that he abused you, and even though your thoughts could not have killed him..."

"How could you know that? Were you in my father's house? I know I hated him and cursed him just before he stumbled on the porch and died, I hated him almost as much as I hated myself for causing him to be so..."

"That is what I mean, Svenborg. I'm wondering if you're afraid to be happy because you feel you need to be punished."

"I have done nothing wrong. You just said it was not my fault. So why should I be punished? You think I've done something wrong?" Svenborg bristled.

"No. Nothing wrong!" Anna wondered how she could reason with Svenborg's conflicting and confusing thoughts. "But you yourself just said you feel guilty about your father...and something about living with your sin."

"Ja, I did say that, come to think. It's my cross to bear. We have to suffer enough to enter Heaven. Isn't that right?"

73

"No, Cousin, it is not right! We could never suffer enough to pay for our sins - not in a million years!"

"You think I am bad then? I thought you said what happened was not my fault." Svenborg was confused and angry.

"Oh dear me, Svenborg! How am I ever going to make you understand me? Listen carefully, and I'll try. You are not responsible for someone else's sin, like your father's sin. But we are all sinners. We have all gone astray like lost sheep. All our sins have to be paid for. But we can't do it ourselves, not by suffering, or work, or being good, or anything. Cousin, didn't you ever hear about Jesus suffering in our place on the cross? Did you know He died for us so that the heavy burden of our sins could be taken away?"

"What do we have to do then?"

"Only one thing... just accept His forgiveness. It's free! Madame Yjerst told me that."

"Madame Yjerst? No *prast* told you that?"

"It's true. It's in the Bible. You can ask the pastor of the church in Willmar, Svenborg. He knows about grace, too."

"Why should I believe you?"

"Then go to church."

"You are a fine one to say 'go to church', Anna Kristoferson! You whose babies are not even baptized!"

"They will be...soon."

Anna was disappointed that she had not been able to make Svenborg understand God's forgiveness. "I am no better than she is," she thought as she cleared the table, "except that I know I am forgiven. I wonder what terrible thing her father did that would leave such a scar."

That Anna was never to know. Svenborg never mentioned it again. In the days following they talked only of common things. But they talked. And they were becoming friends.

Eighteen

Lars found a job in town finishing the interior of the banker's big new house. The banker and his wife were delighted by Lars' careful craftsmanship as he worked on the beautiful oak cabinets. And when Lars shared with them his need to build his own small home on his newly acquired land, the banker offered to loan him money so he could get started immediately. And so, by starting work early in the morning, Lars was able to begin building his own house while working on the banker's house at the same time.

These fall days were hard on Anna, for Lars left the sod house before daylight on horseback and did not return until long after the sun had set.

"Thank God, Svenborg is nicer to me now...and even when she isn't, I don't care, because I'm not afraid of her any more. I just speak my mind," she told Lars one evening after they had gone to bed.

"That means everything to me," he replied, "now that I have to be gone so much. My darling, can you be patient just a little longer?"

"I really can't say, Lars. With the baby coming, I'm just not myself. It's not because of Svenborg, but I'm sad and lonesome for you. And I hate being shut up in this tiny house with people who are so gloomy and grumpy,"

"I know," Lars agreed helplessly. How he longed to hear once again the rippling music of her joyous laughter!

As the days of autumn grew shorter and the scarlet and golden leaves had all fallen from the trees, Lars worked even harder on the sturdy frame home he was building for Anna. He had the stone foundation firmly in place, and had finished the framing. When the days became colder, he would be able to work on the interior. Lars toyed with the idea of moving his family into the house before he had finished everything. He discussed the idea with Anna.

"Lars, I really think I would rather wait until all is done. Our babies might get sick living in a cold, unfinished house. Also, I seem to be feeling a little queasy lately."

Lars was surprised and a little disappointed at her reply. He thought she would prefer anything to living another day in Svenborg's house. He thought she would want to be near him as he worked.

"Well, it might be too hard for you to camp out in a drafty shell of a house. I just thought..."

Anna saw the hint of sadness that crossed Lars' handsome, craggy face. She reached out to touch his beard, "I'm sorry, love. What is happening to us? What is happening to me?" Tears flooded her eyes.

He kissed her silently. He understood, for twice before his Anna had been 'in the family way'.

"I will finish your house soon. And I promise it will be nice." Lars assured her with a warm smile.

Christmas came, and the brown grass and the leafless maple tree were covered with a blanket of shimmering white wonder. *Julaften* came, and Anna's house was still not finished...almost, but not quite, for Lars was building the beautiful hand-crafted cupboard that would be her belated Christmas gift, the cupboard that would be just like the one she had left in Sweden. He was also building a table and four sturdy chairs.

No one felt like celebrating Christmas in the sod house. "What's to celebrate?" Svenborg challenged, "Christmas is for children...and I was never a child."

"Sometimes that Svenborg just takes the heart right out of me," Anna confided to Lars.

"Only a little longer, my Love. We shall move into our own home before St. Stephen's Day (January 13)" reassured Lars, his eyes reflecting pained empathy.

Anna began to smile again, as each evening Lars shared with her the progress he had made on the new home she had not yet seen. It was an unpretentious house, a house of wood, not sod, a house sturdy and strong, built by a master craftsman. It would be their first real home in 'the land of promise'. Anna's eyes shone as she visualized her completed house with smooth wooden floors, white plastered walls, full-sized windows, and sun filtering softly though the starched lace curtains she had brought from New York. She imagined unpacking the unopened trunk, arranging her pretty dishes and tablecloth, and placing her bright rag rugs on the floor.

"Only a few more days," she sighed, leaning bleakly but hopefully against the sod wall.

The day before moving day Lars bought a red carpet-covered settee and chair at the furniture store. It was an admitted extravagance, but he wanted to surprise Anna. He also bought an enameled iron bed with good springs, and a mattress, for the downstairs bedroom. They had their rocking chairs, brightly painted Swedish chests, and many other things to bring out of the Perqvists' shed that had come on the train from New York. Upstairs in the new house were mattresses for Alma and Annie, filled with fresh, clean straw. It was a sturdy, pretty little house, on a good foundation, with a solid stone chimney. Lars surveyed his creation with pride.

Anna's first sight of her new home came on moving day. This is what she had preferred. She loved surprises and Lars hoped with all his heart that this surprise would truly delight her.

"Oh, Lars!" she squealed with the joy and excitement of a child, "It's perfect! It's beautiful!" Anna exclaimed over everything, while the little girls ran from room to room, giggling wildly with a sense of new freedom.

"Papa! Papa!" Alma shouted with abandon, "Is this really our house? Our very own? Without Cousin Svenborg to frown at us?"

"You can be sure, our very own."

"It smells GOOD!" piped up little Annie.

"You know what the best part is Lars?" Anna asked mysteriously, "Not the new settee, or the stove, or even the wonderful bed. It is that you made me a new cupboard just like the one in our little cottage in Sweden. That is what I treasure most."

Lars smiled with deep satisfaction. Anna's praise was worth more to him than all the wealth in the world.

After Anna had finished her pleasant task of putting everything in its place, she thought it would be fun to celebrate by having company. She invited the nice lady across the street and her grown daughter, Emma. Lars had met her when he first began to work on the house. He told Anna how kind Mrs. Stafford had been to him…encouraging him, bringing him soup, coffee, and freshly baked bread, and always asking him about his family.

Anna prepared her special meatballs for this company dinner. And she baked fragrant, steaming *Julebrod* in her clean, new oven. She had wanted to have lutfisk too but Lars told her that, since Mrs. Stafford was an English lady, she most likely would not appreciate lutfisk. Even so, it was Christmas dinner in January. It was the Christmas they had missed in the sod house, and Anna tried to make it as festive as she possibly could.

The house looks beautiful," Mrs. Stafford complimented, "with your bright rag rugs and lace curtains, and everything so new and clean. You have a knack, Anna...and Lars, you are a master craftsman."

"Oh, no," Lars corrected her modestly, "my father and my brothers are master craftsmen, but I left Sweden before I had attained my status."

"What does that matter? It's what you do that counts," Mrs. Stafford protested," We are not in the old country!"

Anna wished so much that she could understand everything that Lars and Mrs. Stafford were talking about. "Lars," she said in Swedish, "will you ask Mrs. Stafford if she would teach me English?"

He did, and Mrs. Stafford graciously replied, "Of course, my dear. It will be my pleasure."

In spite of the language barrier, Anna understood everything important, that her neighbors accepted and loved them. And they thought her Christmas dinner was delicious.

After the Staffords had gone home, Lars mentioned that they must have the Perqvists over soon.

"Uff-dah, ja I know it can't be avoided. But, may God forgive me. I want to keep putting it off." Lars chuckled softly.

"What is so funny? Actually, today it was more fun having people over I couldn't even talk to, than having over that sharp-tongued woman!"

"I do understand, my love," Lars reassured her, "Oh how I do understand!"

"Now you bring up that subject just when I am almost starting to forget Svenborg!"

Anna lit the lamp and no more was said about the Perqvists.

"It's starting to snow again," remarked Lars, "Good thing the Staffords only have to walk across the road."

"Ja, so," yawned Anna sleepily.

The snow continued to fall softly upon the roof of the cozy new home, and upon every branch and twig surrounding it. It fell in a divine benediction upon the little family who sat beside the warm and crackling fire, safe and secure in their very own house.

Nineteen

The Kristofersons settled into their new house with deep contentment. The cold winter days seemed to pass quickly because there was so much warmth within their little home. Their home was filled with peace, fun, and love. There was rippling joy as they gathered around the kitchen stove to pop corn and tell Swedish folk tales to Alma and Annie, singing together the lilting songs of Sweden. Lars went to his inside-finishing job each day while Anna played with the children in soft, new-fallen snow. They made a snow elf near the front window. Often she had tea with Mrs. Stafford in her elegant house, learning new English words every day.

It was almost spring when Anna finally got around to inviting the Perqvists to Sunday dinner. Dressed in their best black clothes, the Perqvists sat proud and straight in the lumber wagon. Svenborg forgot to say "*God dag.*" Instead she apologized for the mud that had splattered on their clothing.

"Uff dah! What ruts!" she exclaimed, "We were lucky we didn't get stuck...then you would have seen muddy clothes! After I worked so hard to clean them too."

"Ruts tell us the frost is coming out and spring is just around the corner," suggested Lars with a twinkle.

"Well, that just reminds me of work," put in Karl drearily, "of work I can't do anymore."

"Just let me know when you are ready to plow and seed, and I'll help you, my friend," Lars promised, "The days will soon be long again and I can come after work. And on Sundays too."

Anna sighed. Svenborg glared at her. And she addressed Lars, "She'll be jealous of your time, Kristofer - especially now."

Lars spoke firmly, obviously not pleased with her attitude. "Anna and I will discuss this matter, Svenborg. I will not come out without her approval. I do put my family first."

Svenborg said no more. She did not praise Anna for the fine roast pork dinner she had prepared, nor for the neatness and attractiveness of her home. She commended only Lars…for his fine craftsmanship, his cleverness, and his strength. She pointed out to Karl all of Lars' fine qualities, implying he could never do what Lars had done. Finally, her frail, stooped husband silently disappeared out of the back door, like a sad, whipped puppy. Lars followed him, leaving the women and girls in the parlor.

Svenborg smiled, a nearly toothless smile. Anna did not return her smile. Not because she had lost her front teeth, but because the corners of her mouth turned down and she did not smile with her eyes.

"You look dreadful!" Svenborg began with a tight little laugh, "But, you know, you can ask me how to keep this from happening again. I have the secret of bearing only two girls."

"Ja so?" Anna was curious, for she had never heard of such a thing as birth control.

"Ack, ja," Svenborg volunteered with a sardonic giggle, "Perqvist has not touched me in that certain way since Amanda's birth."

Anna was surprised and shocked, but said nothing. She knew the Perqvists slept together by the chimney, but was too shy and polite to say more. "Poor Karl," she thought, "Perhaps his sickness has made it impossible…and then, he must endure her mean tongue as well. Ack, poor man!"

That night Anna told Lars, "I can see that Karl is failing more and more. He needs you to help him, and I will not stand in your way, even if it means not having you home as much."

"*Tack sa mycket*, my love," Lars answered with a kiss, "It is only right that we help one another in the new land."

"Ja, that is the neighborly thing to do…the will of God,"

"You look tired, Anna. And do I see a little sadness in those pretty eyes? Maybe it was Svenborg saying something to hurt you?"

"Ja, but never mind. It's just that she is a truly unhappy woman and can't help herself."

As the warm spring days merged imperceptibly into a steaming and sizzling summer, Anna grew round and restless. Now that the haying must be done, Karl could not do it alone. And so, every afternoon after working since dawn as a builder, Lars mounted old Fannie and went out in the country to help his friend. When Anna expressed concern that his strength would give out, Lars only laughed.

"I guess you never get tired like I do," she sighed wistfully, "or need to be with us as much as we need to be with you."

"Anna, dearest Anna" he began, remembering her condition. What was there to say? They had already agreed he must be a good neighbor to the Perqvists.

Anna began to worry and fret. It helped some to go out under their big elm tree by herself in the cool of the morning to pray. "Lord," she pleaded, "I have no one but you to depend upon. Please help me, one day at a time, until my trial is past." She tried to think of the happy day when she would have the baby and be thin again.

Karl's hay had all been put in the barn at last. Now the corn was growing tall, almost audibly, through the long, sweltering nights. And Anna's time had come.

Small pains had kept her awake most of the night, and her water broke just as Lars opened the door to go to work.

"Get Mrs. Stafford...and hurry!" was all she said, but something about the expression of her face catapulted Lars into action. He bolted across the street and pounded on Mrs. Stafford's front door, ignoring her elegant bell pull.

Mrs. Stafford had assured Lars and Anna months ago that she would help Anna when her time came. They had asked her if she knew of a good midwife in Willmar. "Well, my goodness," she had said, "I was a midwife and trained nurse in England. Of course I will come to Anna myself!" Anna had loved Mrs. Stafford the moment she had seen her smiling, motherly face. And Mrs. Stafford felt the same about Anna.

"I didn't want Lars to disturb you...and the pains were not yet hard."

"Well, I see I am just in time," Mrs. Stafford said with bustling efficiency.

Just then, Anna called for Lars. She wanted him in the bedroom with her. She wanted to grasp his strong hands when the 'bearing down' pains came. They were both glad when Mrs. Stafford allowed this, unlike the bossy Norwegian midwife in New York. It became a very special time of intimacy and sharing for Lars and Anna. It was lucky, Lars thought, that he was permitted to have this almost unheard of privilege...so that he could support Anna, and at the same time feel himself a part of the miracle of birth.

The baby came quickly. Lars could see that it was another girl.

"A girl? Once again?" exclaimed Anna weakly, "Oh, Lars, are you disappointed?"

"No, only happy my darling, my wonderful, brave little wife...never have I loved you so completely!"

"Thank you, Lars," she whispered, "for being with me...and all praise to God!"

Mrs. Stafford had finished bathing and dressing the new little girl, "She's a big one, Lars. What are you going to call her?"

"Is it up to me? Would it be alright with you if we named her after your daughter, Emma?"

"It would be an honor. My Emma was born twenty-five years ago in London. And today, it seems I'm living it all over again."

Anna smiled and nodded. "Well then, chuckled Lars, Emma it will be!" Then he laughed audibly out of a relieved and grateful heart,

"What a beautiful namesake my daughter has!" beamed gentle Mrs. Stafford.

Just then Alma and Annie woke up and crawled down the narrow staircase in their long, batiste nightgowns.

They looked for their Mama. She was not in the kitchen as usual, preparing their breakfast. They peeked in the bedroom.

"Is Mama sick?" Alma asked anxiously-

"Oh, no, my pet," answered her papa, "but she has a wonderful surprise for you! Meet your baby sister. Her name is Emma."

"Where did she come from?" little Annie wanted to know.

"I know," answered Alma, "because I felt Mama's tummy."

"Oh, my," Mrs. Stafford said, "I wonder if children should know such things. It is a new Idea to me."

"We are not superstitious here...no ghosts, and no storks," Lars explained.

"Of course you are right," agreed Mrs. Stafford, "I just hadn't had the chance to think about it."

Lars asked Mrs. Stafford if she would stay until he had a chance to walk down the street and ask his employer for the day off. Anna and the children needed him today.

Twenty

A few days after Emma's birth, Anna and Lars had a visit from her other cousins, the Eckbergs. Mrs. Eckberg apologized for not having visited them when they were living at the Perqvists.

"I am so sorry, Cousin Anna. The fact is that Svenborg told us never to come to see them after we'd had them over to dinner last year. I feel bad about this, and I don't know what the Christian thing to do is." There were tears in Lena Eckberg's eyes,

"Why did Svenborg say such a thing?"

"Who knows? She turned against us when we moved into our new house from our sod one. And that was when she told us that you and Lars were going to stay with them and not us."

"I think I understand" Anna said kindly, "Svenborg cannot help the way she is."

"Oh, Anna, it must have been a great trial for you to live with her. We should have insisted!"

"Oh, no everything is alright...now." Anna said no more.

Lena brought a hand knit sweater and cap for baby Emma, and exclaimed warmly and repeatedly, "What a fine, healthy baby, a beautiful girl...a blessing from God!" And all of the Eckberg children wanted to take turns holding her.

Lars made coffee for the guests, and they left with a cordial invitation for the Kristofersons to visit them soon.

One bright blue day in early fall, Anna thought about how much she had liked her cousin Lena, after their brief visit a few weeks ago.

"Lars, do you realize we have not yet visited our cousins, the Eckbergs? They invited us and we promised to come.

"Why not today?" Lars answered.

"It's too far to walk, six miles. Maybe you could borrow a lumber wagon and another horse to go with Fannie?"

Soon Lars obtained a horse and wagon and they were on their way singing, "*Prastens lille kraka skulle ut ach aka.*" It was their first outing after the birth of little Emma, and the girls were almost silly with joy, Meanwhile, Lars ruminated quietly about his good fortune...the woman he loves, healthy children, his new home built, plenty of work, and above all being able to wake up each morning feeling strong and vital, and not at all like poor Perqvist.

"Ah, Perqvist," he sighed. "I should be out there helping him."

Lars did not wish to dwell on anything unpleasant this joyous day, but he was curious about something. "Say, Anna, what was it Svenborg didn't like about the Eckbergs anyway?"

"Who knows? Perhaps she is jealous. Or maybe, it is because they are Baptists."

"Hmm…more likely she envies their prosperity. Eckberg is a hard worker."

"Ja, that is like Svenborg. Eckbergs have a fine house and five children."

"Well, there it is!" A two-story white square house loomed suddenly over the hill. Behind it stood a large red barn.

"I can't believe it!" exclaimed Anna, "Is this palace really my cousin's?"

"It says ECKBERG on the mailbox," Lars pointed out matter-of-factly.

Lena Eckberg's greeting glowed with warm sincerity. "I am so happy you have come! Every day we have been waiting to see you. My, how your little Emma has grown! She's blooming like a rose…and just look at that sweet smile!"

Lena chattered like a contented chickadee, while Anna smiled and patted her cousin's shoulder. Soon Lena had to hurry to the kitchen to put a few more potatoes in the pot, and a few more chips into the oven. It was almost time for the hearty noon time dinner. Anna and the baby went with Lena to the kitchen, while Lars, Alma and Annie went to look for Eckberg in the barn.

Nils Eckberg, tall, blond, and bronzed by the sun saw them coming. He met them with a cordial smile, and extended a large, work-worn hand.

"*Valkommen*, Lars! Let me show you around the place before we go in to dinner."

Lars viewed everything with inspired wonder…the large herd of milk cows, the substantial buildings, the fat sheep, the flock of chickens and geese picking contentedly in freedom, the cornfield and the wheat and oats, the nifty harrows and plows, clean, sharpened, and standing in readiness. And to think Eckberg had two teen-aged boys who helped him with everything! All this was the fulfillment of every immigrant's dream.

"A farm...my own land...independence...this is what I really want." Lars spoke resolutely within himself.

"Come," Nils suggested, "let's sit awhile on the swing by the pump, maybe your girls would like to play with my children in the house. We can talk about the old times in Sweden."

"No," replied Lars quickly, "I want to forget about Sweden. I want to talk about what you have done here in Minnesota."

"Well, ja, God has been good to us..." Nils began. Just then Lena came running out from the back porch.

"Dinner is not quite ready." she announced cheerfully. "So maybe Alma and Annie would like to come with me, ja, girls? I think my Krista will let you play with her toys. Come?"

Lena led two happy tots to her sun porch, where her children, three year old Krista, eight year old Marta, and ten year old Harald, were noisily and happily playing with their toys.

"Now you be good children and share with your nice cousins who have come to visit us, while I show dear cousin Anna the rest of the house." She waited a few moments to be sure Alma and Annie were feeling accepted and 'at home'.

Anna's eyes were wide with excitement over this lovely new home. There was a large parlor with a cheery bay window filled with pink and red geraniums, also a formal dining room. Both rooms were well furnished. Anna caught sight of the lovely red velvet settee and matching chair. There was a polished reed organ with a mirror above the hymnbook. In the dining room she gazed longingly at the expensive china cabinet. "Lars could make one like that," she murmured, "If he could afford to buy the curved glass."

Anna sighed, looking down at the shiny floor, adorned with blue-patterned oriental rugs.

"Is it well with you, cousin?" Lena was concerned, having heard Anna's sigh.

"Forgive me for just a little wistfulness. Oh my! I don't know what to say...to discover such prosperous cousins in the new land! I must write to Sweden. My brother will be so pleased!" Anna recalled that she and Jon had heard about Nils Eckberg going north to Smaland, marrying there, and then going to America long before she and Lars were married.

"Ja, Anna. We have been on this farm seventeen years. It was very hard at first. We too had a sod house until five years ago. Of course Nils had to build the new barn first, and the silo. My, my, he was so pleased when at last he could build us this fine home, with God's help, of course. God is the One who has blest us."

"Were you and Nils already Baptists when you were in Sweden, Lena?" Anna's eyes grew wide with wonder.

"Indeed. That's why we came over here. As dissenters, we were persecuted by the State Church. We met secretly in homes. Then we were told we were breaking the law. Our Pastor was put into prison."

"What law?" Anna gasped. She had never heard of such a thing.

"When we were in Sweden, only pastors of the State Church were permitted to preach or teach the scriptures, to serve communion, or to baptize anyone. We celebrated the Lord's Supper in our homes. We had baptisms in the lake. These things were absolutely forbidden."

"What did they do to you?"

"We were so blest. God heard our prayers. They gave us two choices: prison, or going to America, this great land of religious freedom. At the same time, many were coming from Smaland to America because of the potato famine. We ourselves experienced hunger. But more important was our hunger for the freedom to worship God!"

"Oh, my," Anna exclaimed, "We never knew what happened...only that you had settled in Minnesota. How I wish we might have known each other long ago!"

"Ja, I feel like we are sisters already. Anna, do you know the Lord Jesus?"

"I do. Long ago at Madame Yjerst's I gave my heart to Him."

"That's it then! That's why we are so close even though we just met!" Both women laughed spontaneously, like carefree schoolgirls. They agreed that a mysterious bond of joy exists between believers.

"Come to our church in Willmar," Lena invited.

"I'm sorry, Lena. We can't go to church. Lars is not a believer."

Lena grasped Anna's hand. "The Bible says that if two of you shall agree, trusting God for the answer, He will answer our prayer. Let's pray for Lars' salvation."

Lena led them in a simple, fervent prayer. Tears filled their eyes and they said no more.

Just then the men came in from outside. It was time for dinner. Anna helped set the table with Lena's best china, and she brought the savory platters from the kitchen wood range.

The two teen-aged Eckberg boys, Anders and Pelle, came in from the field they had been plowing. They smiled shyly through faces blackened by the rich soil.

"Uff dah! You two wash up extra good for our nice company!" Lena shooed them out to the pump. Soon they returned with glowing faces and clean blond hair. Lena invited everyone to sit down at the dining room table, with its pure white linen and lace cloth.

The Eckbergs and Anna bowed reverently while Nils prayed…not the familiar Swedish table prayer, but his own words, fervently asking the Lord to bless, not only the food, but each person sitting around the table, naming each visitor. He closed with thanksgiving for Jesus' death upon the cross for the sins of all. There were tears in Anna's eyes as she realized that Nils was a friend of God.

There was much to talk about besides the delicious dinner and the rhubarb pie. Lars was trying to understand how all this abundance could be possible. He asked many questions, and Nils answered with humility and graciousness, Anna and Lena exchanged recipes and news about neighbors and people in town. Then they washed the dishes while the men sat at the table until coffee time.

On this day a dream and a goal began to grow within Lars Kristoferson. The Eckberg homestead stood out tall and proud on the Minnesota prairie, the quintessence of an immigrant's faith in the promise of America. It became a beacon of hope for Lars. If Eckberg could do it, maybe he could too.

All too soon, the time came for the Kristofersons to say good-by to their warm and friendly cousins. They must reach Willmar before dark.

The shadows were long against the rich crimson blend of sunset, but the ride back to town seemed short to the Kristofersons as they reminisced happily about their good day,

Each one had received something unique. The girls had each been given a pretty rag doll by the Eckberg children, along with the rare gift of having someone new with whom to play. Anna had the secret bond of prayer she had shared with Lena, together with three jars of Lena's strawberry jam. Lars had begun an enduring friendship with a fellow Swede. Most of all, this visit had given Lars hope, the hope that he too might taste the sweetness of success in this new land, the hope that perhaps he too might some day own a fine farm. A farm! For the first time, Lars saw this as the cherished object of his restless soul's quest.

Twenty One

It was the sixth day of Christmas, and the little willow bush Anna had covered with strips of green tissue was still standing in the comer, except most of the candy was gone from the woven paper heart baskets that had adorned the tree.

"Too bad there are no evergreens to be found on the prairie," Anna sighed as she sat knitting beside the window.

It was a quiet afternoon. The sun was warm, causing the icicles to glow with rosy iridescence as they dripped down from the eaves to the front porch. Anna watched them from the lace-curtained window as she rocked, knitting Lars' socks, thankful her little girls were napping. Alma didn't usually nap, but today she had a slight cold and wasn't feeling her usual perky self.

A knock at the door! Anna peered out the window to see a portly gentleman in a black coat standing there.

"My," she thought, "who can he be?" She pondered what she would say...excuse, please? I speak not much English. Come back when my husband home? This much she had learned from Mrs. Stafford.

Cautiously, she opened the door to a warm smile and words in Swedish, cordial and disarming. "*Jag ar Pastor Svendson, av Willmar Svenska Lutheran Kirke,*" he began with a bow.

Anna was speechless with delight at seeing this kindly man. God be praised! A Swede! A man of God! She motioned him to come in, smiling broadly.

He sat on the red settee, with its white crocheted doilies. She sat in the rocker with her knitting. They must have chatted for at least an hour before she remembered to put the coffee pot on. The time just flew, for she had many things to discuss with this kindly Swedish *prast*...Yes, she would like to go to church, but Lars was not a church goer. No, it would probably do no good to talk to Lars, but she would like him to try. Oh, yes, Lars had determined in his heart never to go to church, good man that he was...No, she did not care to go alone.

Lars needed her on Sunday mornings. He worked all week, her Lars, and such a good husband and father. The children? No, they are not baptized, not yet. Well, it would be hard to bring them to the church font. Could he do it here? In their home? Yes? Tomorrow? Would Lars mind? No, he would not care. Could the Pastor ask him? For soon Lars will be coming home.

"No, I really must go now," the Pastor said, rising. "*Tusen tack* for coffee. I shall come back tomorrow evening for the baptism. Perhaps then your husband will be home. May God be with you."

Ja, sure. Tomorrow is Sunday and Lars will be here. *Tack sa mycket.*"

"A nice man," Anna said to herself as she closed the door. "Like a father, so comforting to me. Perhaps next time I can tell him what is really in my heart."

The next morning Anna told Lars this was to be a special day.

"How so?" he asked, curiously, smiling with a twinkle of fun and mischief.

His smile faded when Anna explained what this was all about.

"The *prast* is coming? Maybe I should go ice fishing."

"Please, Lars…for me?"

"Ja, for you I would suffer any torment," he teased, pinching her affectionately.

The Pastor arrived at 4:30, dressed ceremoniously in his black robe and high white ruffled collar, a large gold cross around his neck.

Anna had covered the small table in the parlor with her most elegant embroidered linen cloth. She had filled her prettiest china bowl with water from the pump, placing it on the table with a lace-trimmed towel. The girls were dressed in their best dresses - washed, combed, and well behaved. Even little Emma seemed to love the smiling Pastor and take delight in the water in Mama's bowl as it splashed over her face.

Over each child, Pastor Svendson said the solemn words: I BAPTIZE YOU IN THE NAME OF THE FATHER, THE SON AND THE HOLY SPIRIT.

Then he read a long Swedish prayer from the big black book he carried. He asked Lars and Anna to promise two things, "to renounce the devil and all his works and all his ways", and to "bring their children up in the fear and admonition of the Lord." Anna's 'Ja' was loud and clear, but she thought Lars had remained silent.

After the baptism, as they gathered around the table for the supper Anna had prepared, Lars was silent no longer. He and the genial pastor had become instant friends talking about Sweden, about trees and ships and crops, about hunting deer and pheasants, and about ice fishing through the frozen lake.

Pastor Svendson joked with the children and complimented Anna again and again on her excellent raspberry tapioca with cream and her buttery Christmas cookies.

Everyone laughed and enjoyed themselves, especially Lars and the Pastor.

As they were getting ready for bed that night, Anna whispered to Lars, "Ja, it was a special day. Huh, Lars?"

"Very special, my love. Ja, and I'm not sorry I missed fishing. That Pastor Svendson is an interesting man. We might go partridge shooting come spring."

"Oh ja?" Anna smiled, secretly thinking, "Ack, maybe the Pastor will get Lars to come to church and talk to him about his soul. To him Lars would maybe listen."

As she did every night, Anna opened her *salmabok* to read a little and pray for her dear ones, and especially for the strongest desire of her heart, for Lars to know God.

Twenty Two

On Tuesday and Thursday afternoons Mrs. Stafford walked across the street to give Anna systematic lessons in the English language. After her lesson, Anna would serve tea to her British friend, instead of coffee, with *smorbrod* (open-faced sandwiches) and tiny cakes.

Anna was a fast learner, and Mrs. Stafford was a patient and gentle teacher. She wanted to make sure Anna learned to speak English correctly. She would sometimes express a kind of subdued contempt for the way many Americans 'butchered' their language, an improper language that, to her dismay, Alma and Annie were beginning to speak.

"Not HE COME OVER, but HE CAME OVER," Mrs. Stafford would instruct them. She would often admonish the children not to say WE WAS, but instead to say WE WERE. "Please don't say 'iffen' or 'ain't. These are not words!"

"Why would people say things just opposite of the right way?" Anna wondered.

"I think it's rebellion in the heart of man," Mrs. Stafford answered solemnly, "It comes from original sin."

"I really doubt that," Anna thought, but didn't say aloud. She didn't know enough English to explain about the dialects in Sweden, and how people who had gone to Upsala University spoke.

Lars and Anna spoke quite differently from the country people. How could it be a sin to speak in the manner in which one was raised? Anna didn't agree with Mrs. Stafford on this point.

It seemed Mrs. Stafford could read Anna's expression. "Perhaps I spoke harshly out of pride," she said. Mrs. Stafford was a humble woman.

Somehow, Mrs. Stafford's dedication and cultured ways reminded Anna of Madame Yjerst, her teacher of long ago. Even her house, with its beauty and order, seemed a link with Anna's pleasurable school days in Solvesborg. Mrs. Stafford had become, to her younger neighbor, not only teacher and midwife, but mentor, friend, and counselor as well.

Even the children seemed to listen when Mrs. Stafford spoke, sitting quietly on the small chairs their father had hewn for them out of wood scraps. Little Emma was Mrs. Stafford's favorite. Perhaps that was because she was named for her own daughter, a young spinster who worked nights as a nurse. And since Miss Emma slept days, the children had to be very quiet when they visited.

Perhaps Mrs. Stafford delighted in Emma because she was such an intelligent and well-behaved toddler. She had already begun to speak, and looked up at Mrs. Stafford with wide blue eyes, set in a tiny, serious face. This look Mrs. Stafford found irresistible. She determined to oversee the education of this bright and unusual child. "Emma is just unique," she would say.

On one particular day in the early summer of 1885, Anna was glad her girls were napping. She had something of great importance to share with her friend.

"Yes, I thought so." Mrs. Stafford did not seem surprised.

"Well, I suppose you just know about these things," smiled Anna.

"I have a feeling your next girl will come in early October. Right?"

"Oh, no! Not another girl! Lars must have his boy this time! "

"Don't count on it. Girls run in families - like curly hair or blue eyes. Not a thing you can do about it."

Mrs. Stafford's words were not reassuring. "I still can hope for a boy!" Anna insisted.

"That you can!" answered Mrs. Stafford with a smile.

As Mrs. Stafford left Anna to walk across the street, she met Lars coming from work.

"May I have a word with you, Mr. Kristoferson?"

"Of course, madam." Lars tipped his hat and bowed.

"Anna has told me the news. She hopes for a boy for your sake." Lars grinned.

"So this is what I have to say to you. It may be a girl. If so, don't break Anna's heart by mentioning that you are disappointed, even if you are. Or now, by always talking about how you are expecting a son. Good day, Mr. Kristoferson."

She didn't even wait for Lars to reply, but quickly and crisply crossed the unpaved street to her porch.

Twenty Three

One morning in early October Anna awoke in the soft double bed beside Lars. She noticed a little sparkly frost on the comers of the window, and then thought what a pretty frame it made for the maple tree, glowing red with iridescent splendor in the rising sun.

Lars snored as she stroked his beard, ever so gently. "Poor man! So tired. I'll surprise him this morning and make the fire myself!"

She edged carefully out from under the goosedown comforter. "Oops! What was that?" She winced, rubbing her lower back as she put on her slippers and robe. She inched softly across the floor, trying not to awaken Lars. "Uff dah! How clumsy I am!"

She took a few pieces of kindling from the woodbox and carefully laid the fire in the cookstove. As she reached up for a match, it suddenly hit her.

"LARS!" That was a real one, and Anna knew what it meant. "Get Mrs. Stafford! It's started!"

Lars slowly opened his eyes. He yawned. He slowly stretched his long arms and legs. He smiled.

"LARS!" Anna yelled.

"How unlike her," he mused.

"Lars, you know how quickly my babies come. HURRY!" She noticed a small puddle of water on the floor beneath her. "Ja sure then, my water broke. It won't be long, this one."

Lars suddenly lurched into high gear. In no time he poured himself into his clothes and boots, bounding across the street to Mrs. Stafford.

She was already up, and not surprised. "Well, Mr. Kristoferson, remember what I told you."

"I will. But maybe I won't have to," he grinned hopefully,

Anna went back to bed after she got the fire roaring and had wiped up the floor. It seemed her hard labor had started right away.

Lars went to the kitchen and put the kettle on. Then he sat down, leaning his elbows on the red-checked tablecloth while he waited for the water to boil. Just as the pot began to spout steam he heard a cry -

like a kitten it seemed, small and faint. "Wonder what that could be," he said to himself.

Just then Mrs. Stafford ran breathlessly into the kitchen. "Hot water!" she yelled, "I must sterilize the scissors!" She poured some of the steaming water from the pot into a small pan. "She is here so soon! And such a wee one. Help me, Lars! Warm these blankets!"

For an instant Lars stood stupidly in petrified silence. Then he sprang into action, aware only that his wife and baby might be in danger. That kitten cry was his baby, and it didn't sound a bit husky. And poor Anna! Had she been too weak even to scream in pain? Did Mrs. Stafford call the baby 'she'? Shucks, what did it matter?

Lars warmed the blankets and hurried into the bedroom. Anna was pale, but smiling faintly. "It was a quick birth, not so bad at all," she whispered. "But my baby! Is my baby alright?" Suddenly her voice became intense, "SHOW ME MY BABY!"

"Just a moment, Anna," Mrs. Stafford wrapped the tiny, bluish girl in a warm blanket and brought her to Anna.

"A fine girl!" Mrs. Stafford said cheerfully. "She will get stronger when she takes nourishment. See if she will suck, Anna. Let her suck now, before your milk comes in. There is healing power in the fluid that comes before the milk."

Amazingly, the tiny mouth soon sucked contentedly at Anna's breast. And the little face became a healthy pink.

"Well, I declare," Mrs. Stafford smiled, "She is a wee one - but she is strong!"

"Lars, are you disappointed?" She had to know.

"Do I look disappointed? No, no. I look like the luckiest Swede in America!"

Good for you, Mr. Kristoferson," beamed Mrs. Stafford. So, what are you going to call the little mite?"

"We have already picked out a name," he stated positively. "She is Betsy Matilda."

Twenty Four

Days, months, seasons, and years flashed quickly by with a sure and steady pace. The little white house hummed with incessant, orderly activity. Anna's days were so crowded and demanding that she had little time for introspection, for reflecting upon the meaning of her life, of her marriage, or even upon her relationship with God.

Two more little girls, Hilda and Alice, were born in the little house on the corner. Now there were six little Kristofersons.

"What a phenomenon!" exclaimed Mrs. Stafford one day over tea, "Six little maidens! Will there ever be a change in this incredible pattern?"

"My girls are perfect, and every one is wanted," Anna answered. She was slightly offended at Mrs. Stafford's attempted humor.

"Forgive me, my dear. But have you ever thought to pray for a boy?"

"Oh, yes, I always do. But too late."

"How so? How can a prayer be too late?"

"I pray when I'm well along in the family way. How could God change what is already inside me?"

Mrs. Stafford laughed heartily. "Well, my goodness! Better you start praying right away. Or is it already too late?"

"I certainly hope not. When Alice is not yet one and still nursing," Anna sighed.

Anna's days were long. She arose before dawn, baby Alice crying to be changed and fed. Then she built a fire in the shiny black range and put the coffeepot on, thankful that Lars had filled the woodbox and pumped a pail of water before he went to bed, ja. But she had a good man! He even milked Rosenhaugen, the aging little red cow he had bought at an auction. In Sweden, milking was women's work. Anna smiled at the thought of Lars' big hands delicately pumping Rosenhaugen's teats.

After a breakfast of gruel and potatoes, sometimes eggs too, Lars went off to work at various construction jobs in the village. The children left for their various activities. Alma walked down the street to Dressmaker Lund's little shop. Annie and Emma walked three blocks to the schoolhouse. Betsy and Hilda went out in the big yard to play. Alice was too little to go anywhere at all.

Anna was thankful for the expanse of their yard, the sheltering trees, and the rich, green grass. She treasured her flowerbeds and the vegetable garden behind the children's sandbox, and the barn in which they could play on rainy days. There was fresh hay in the loft and a ladder for hiding and jumping games. There was a swing under the maple tree in the front yard. It was a good home for a thriving family of healthy young Swedes.

Anna loved to watch her children play, and sometimes she would join them in their games. She had only one strict rule: Do not leave the yard – except when running an errand for Mama.

Each girl blossomed into her own unique individuality. Alma, at twelve, was almost a young woman and could be trusted with many responsibilities. She was clever with her hands, and her special endowment of energy became channeled into such things as sewing and helping her Mama with the task of knitting long woolen stockings for chilly winter days. It was for this reason that, when Alma had completed the eighth grade, it was decided that she should spend some time with Mrs. Lund, a professional seamstress with a shop on Main Street.

Ever since the previous winter, Alma had spent every day helping Mrs. Lund, a true perfectionist, as an apprentice. For a long time, she had hated every minute spent with Mrs. Lund.

"Mama," she confided one evening, through her tears, "You know how much I love to sew. But there is just no pleasing that woman! Haven't I learned enough to quit now?"

"I will talk to Papa tonight," Anna promised with a hug.

Anna went down the street to meet Lars so they could talk privately as they walked home together.

"Alma is young," she explained, "She needs encouragement, not to be told every day that nothing she does is good enough."

"Ja, vel," Lars considered thoughtfully, "But is this not the way of masters? My master in Ystad would never be pleased. Yet I learned well."

"You did. But Alma is a tender young girl."

"I will talk to her," he promised.

Anna never knew what Lars had said to their eldest daughter. But there were no more complaints, only fresh smiles blossoming on Alma's face.

"I wonder," Anna said to the cow, "Did Lars talk only to Alma?"

Quiet Annie looked to Alma as her role model. Yet she was secretly proud of her own abilities, especially her cooking skills and helping her mother with the cleaning.

"Annie will be a fine wife and mother some day," Lars often remarked. He praised her constantly for her cakes and puddings.

Emma, serious and reflective, was cherished and beloved by Mrs. Stafford. She was often across the street helping this gentile lady keep her elegant house immaculate. Anna was glad for any small way they could help repay Mrs. Stafford for the infinitely valuable contributions she had made to all of their lives. Emma had learned many lessons from Mrs. Stafford – cheerfulness, gracious manners, and, above all, putting the needs of others before her own. She learned to speak English correctly, and she was taught to memorize many passages from the King James Bible, words that were never forgotten.

One afternoon Mrs. Stafford invited Anna and her children to tea. Emma was asked to serve. She smiled shyly and glowed with pride when Mrs. Stafford praised her for the special flair with which she had accomplished this elegant and ladylike task. To Mrs. Stafford, 'tea' was a ritual, a sweet and solemn reminder of gentler and happier times.

After tea, Mrs. Stafford began to tell about some of her experiences in America. Six pairs of eyes were fastened upon her, full of wonder and expectation.

"When we first came over from England my husband was a merchant in Boston. Then, like so many others, he had a desire to come westward."

"Did you come by train?" asked Alma.

"Only part way. The rest of the way was by wagon train. That was the only 'train' around here in those days, my dear."

"Tell us more...please, Mrs. Stafford," Emma begged.

"Perhaps you think it odd that I have not spoken much about my experiences. Oh, my dear children, it is only because so much of it is painful, even to remember, much less to relate to others."

"Dear friend," Anna spoke with tenderness, "We would not for the world want to cause you any pain. Please forgive the children for their curiosity."

"Someday I will tell you the whole story. But this must be a happy day. It is such a pleasure to have you all in my home!"

Twenty Five

O f all the Kristoferson girls, Hilda was the most fun, and the one most likely to get into trouble. It had rained for a week and the street was delicious with reddish, chocolaty mud. As the bright sun reflected itself in the puddle mirrors, little Hilda stood transfixed. Wouldn't it be fun to wade in those puddles? To put the basswood boat Papa had made into the winding rut canals? But Mama had said no. "Stay in the yard, especially today when it is so muddy."

Just then, Hilda caught a glimpse of her five-year-old friend, Lillian, who lived across the street next to Mrs. Stafford's house. Lillian bounded out of her door dressed in high rubber boots. Soon she was splashing in the puddle next to where Hilda stood longingly at the edge of her yard. "Hilda, halloo! Come play with me!" squealed Lillian with delight.

"Mama said stay in the yard." Hilda looked downward, strangely solemn.

"That sounds silly," Lillian reasoned, "Maybe she didn't mean RIGHT in the yard. My Mama said I can play in the mud. My Papa bought me new boots. "See?" She lifted her right foot proudly.

"Well, maybe I go ask."

"Don't ask. What if she says no? Just come!"

Hilda slowly obeyed the older girl, one bare foot cautiously in front of the other, almost touching the yummy, squishy mud. Suddenly she heard something. Were her sisters watching from the barn? Was Mama tapping on the window? She looked back. Seeing no one, Hilda took one more furtive step.

"Well, come on, slowpoke!"

Suddenly Hilda was in the puddle and all was forgotten but the wonderful red clay sloshing through her toes. She waded with wild abandon, muddy water spilling all over her pretty blue calico dress." Uh Oh!" she exclaimed, "Now Mama will know!"

"Get your boat," Lillian suggested, seeing it near the street.

Hilda forgot about her dress in anticipation of trying out Papa's wonderful gift. The boat floated splendidly in the big puddle the girls called their 'lake', and down the wagon wheel ruts they called 'rivers'. Time stood still for an hour in this land of enchantment.

A shrill whistle beckoned them to reality. "It's my Mama. She blows a whistle when she wants me to come. And you'd better come with me so my Mama can clean you up before your Mama sees you!"

"Wipe your feet on that old carpet by the door," Lillian's mother called out cheerfully.

All at once Hilda screamed. Blood was pouring from the side of her foot.

"My goodness! You've cut yourself!" exclaimed Lillian's Mama. "Must have been a piece of glass on the rug." She swooped Hilda up on her arms to carry her across the street to her own Mama.

"No, no!" Hilda protested, "Let me down – here. I can walk home all by myself."

Lillian's Mama could see how determined Hilda was. "I really should go with you and speak to your mother. I'm SO sorry! What a brave little girl you are!"

Hilda hesitated, looking up at Lillian's Mama pleadingly. She seemed to understand. "Would you like to come in and have me bandage your foot, Hilda?"

Hilda thought for a moment, and then realized what she must do. "No, thank you. I need my Mama. Goodbye." Hilda hopped across the muddy street and up to the back door.

Anna had been baking cinnamon rolls in the kitchen. When she saw the blood she dropped her rolling pin on the floor. She lifted Hilda carefully on the counter next to the washstand, gently placing the little bleeding foot into the basin. "Sit still," she commanded, "While I get some rags." Anna had sterilized some old sheet remnants in the oven and kept them in a jar for just such emergencies. First, she tied a rag around Hilda's ankle to stop the bleeding. Then she washed the wound with her strong homemade lye soap. "I have to put iodine on it too," Anna insisted.

"Will it hurt? More than it hurts now?"

"Yes, it will hurt. Let's see what a brave girl you are. Look out the window! See the robin in the maple tree?"

Hilda tried to be brave and concentrate on the robin, but her foot hurt badly. When the bandage was finally on she sobbed as though her heart would break, knowing she deserved the pain because she had been disobedient. "I'm a very naughty girl," she reasoned in her heart.

Even so, she lied. When Mama asked her what had happened, she blurted, "I fell over by the chicken coop."

But Mama already knew the truth since her little girl had red mud like the street all over her dress. While Hilda napped, Lillian's mother came over and explained everything.

Anna wondered what she should do. The moral training of her children was of supreme importance. She decided not to do anything right away. "Wait and see," she reasoned, "I think Hilda will tell me herself when the burden becomes too heavy."

Hilda's foot did not heal well, in spite of Anna's care. It became infected. Hilda could not step on her foot without crying out in pain. Everyone in the family pampered her, taking turns carrying her about, and bringing her special delicacies and little gifts. The more kindness showered upon her, the worse Hilda felt. The more she was loved, the greater became the burden of her disobedience and deceit.

One morning as her Mama prepared Epsom salts for her daily foot soaking; Hilda could stand it no longer.

"Mama?" She began, plaintively.

"Does it hurt, my little one?"

"Not my foot, but here." Hilda pointed to the middle of her chest.

"Suppose you tell me about it. Would that help?"

Hilda nodded. Hot tears trickled down her cheeks.

"Mama, I played in the mud puddle in the street."

"Oh, my, did you forget about our rule then?"

"No, Mama."

"So what did you do?"

"I disobeyed."

"Ahhhhh...and what else did you do?"

"I lied. I really cut my foot at Lillian's."

"I see," Anna replied gently, "and what do you think God calls these things?"

"Sin?"

"Ja, and He wants you to ask Him to forgive you. Will you, Hilda?"

Hilda folded her small, chubby hands and whispered softly, "Dear God, I'm sorry I disobeyed Mama and told a lie."

Anna held her little girl close.

101

"But Mama, how do I know if God forgives me when I can't tell if He's smiling?"

"God loves you very much, and He forgives all our sins because Jesus died on the cross for us."

"Oh." That settled it for Hilda, even if she didn't understand all about Jesus dying for her.

"Mama?" she added, "I'm sorry to you too. Forgive me?"

"Of course, my little Hilda, I do forgive you." Anna held her daughter tight with tears of joy.

Hilda didn't mind the hot water today, as Mama soaked her foot.

"Mama? My foot is better today."

"Ja? Good. Soon it will be fine."

Mama looked up at the blue sky through the kitchen window. "Thank you Lord," she prayed, "You always give me wisdom when these things come up."

Twenty Six

It was one of October's special bright sunny days, cloudless and crisp. The crimson flame of the maple was etched in splendor against a blue sky. How fitting for the celebration Anna had planned.

It was Betsy's sixth birthday. This week she had started school, her tiny feet trudging a bit behind those of her sisters. A lump filled Anna's throat as she watched her walk down the street on that first day of school. The Willmar Public School was a fine white two-story structure with eight rooms, one for each grade. Alma had graduated from this school with honors. Annie, Emma, and Betsy were now the schoolgirls, and Hilda would begin in another year.

"How quickly my girls are becoming young women!" Anna reflected. She began to stir busily about her spotless kitchen. "Ja it will be nice," she planned joyfully, "a little party when Lars and the girls come home."

She took down the large blue-striped crockery bowl and began measuring sugar and lard into it. She sifted the flour, and then hurried to the barn to retrieve two brown eggs out from under Little Red's warm feathers. "Too bad, my friend," she soothed the chicken, "not setting time, not now. For I must bake my Betsy a big soft cake with whipped cream and jam on top. *Tack sa mycket!*"

On the way back to the house Anna stopped at the well to pick up a jar of cream that was suspended there in a box.

The table was spread with the lovely white woven cloth from Sweden, and the blue candelabra held six white candles. The last of the chrysanthemums from the garden were carefully arranged in Anna's only cut-glass bowl.

"Oh, Mama!"

"*Kjare* Mama!"

"*Tack sa mycket* for the party!"

"For my birthday!"

"Happy birthday, Betsy!"

103

The joyous cries of the children blended together in high excitement. It was hard to wait, but wait they must for Papa to come home.

"Maybe Papa will bring me a present," Betsy ventured hopefully.

Emma frowned. "You must not think of such things, Betsy"

"Ja, it's enough to see Papa. Maybe he can't buy me anything. I still love him!" Betsy agreed with her sister with a small, sad sigh.

"Good girl!" Mama then changed the subject. Now it was time to talk about school, and especially about how Betsy had fared on her first day.

"I helped her find her room," Emma put in quickly.

"She really likes her teacher," Annie volunteered hopefully.

"Ja, so?" interjected their Mama, "But how about if we hear from Betsy herself?"

Anna hugged her little schoolgirl playfully. "Betsy, can you tell us something you learned today – something that made you happy?"

"I didn't learn much I didn't know before…but I got two new friends!" she answered, beaming brightly.

"Ja. That is good," her Mama encouraged.

Just then they heard the familiar sound of the kitchen door.

"Papa is home!"

Lars came in with an unexpected look of gravity in his face. He kissed Anna and embraced the children in silence. Betsy was disappointed, for he did not seem to notice the pretty table or even remember it was her birthday.

"Lars, what is it?" Anna sensed something was wrong.

"I got a letter today from Sweden," he said simply. His voice faltered and he handed the envelope to his wife. She read the letter in hushed silence.

"Oh, Lars! I am so very, very sorry. I loved your Mother!"

For a few moments no one could speak. Even the children shared this grief for a grandmother they had never known. Papa was sad. They could tell he was bravely trying not to weep openly.

"Ja, ja," Anna reminisced, "She was so good to Alma and me when you left for America."

"I wish that I could remember her," Alma said, as she brushed back the tears that trickled down her cheeks.

"She loved you so. She often held you on her lap…rocking, rocking…singing, singing."

"What did she sing about, Mama?" Alma wanted to know.

"Mostly about Jesus."

Lars had to get up and go out to the barn for awhile. "Ja, ja, so it goes," he murmured as he closed the door. After a few minutes Lars came back to the house. His eyes were red, but he smiled at Betsy and gave her a silver coin. Her birthday must not be spoiled by his sorrow.

They had an extra special supper of milk porridge and potatoes, and afterward they ate the festive cake Anna had made with such great care.

"Ja, Mama," Lars complimented wistfully, "Your high bush cranberry jam tastes almost as good as Swedish lingonberries."

In the weeks that followed, Anna tried to bring Lars out of his silent stoicism. She encouraged him to talk about his mother and remember his life in Sweden. She sensed that Lars was trying hard to forget – to bury all his past, and even this real and present grief, beneath a blanket of denial.

One evening, when the lamps were lit and the children all cozy in bed, she and Lars sat side by side on the red velvet sofa with their individual and secret thoughts."

"Lars?" She began, finally determining to be open.

"Ja. Vel?"

"Let's talk about *Sverige*. Let's talk about '*hemlangten*', about our homesickness. *Jag langtar hem.*"

"*Jag, inte*…not I, Anna. When my ship sailed I did not look back. I looked only forward.

"If that is so, Lars, why do you have so much pain? Why have you mourned so bitterly and so long, even though silently, for your mother?"

Lars arose, shocked by his wife's perception and her courage to express it. His voice rose. "What makes you think that?"

"I know these things, *Kjare* Lars, for we have become one."

Lars was disarmed. His strength ebbed. Stoic control became a broken dam as hot tears flowed, and sobs shook his large, sinewy frame.

Anna held him tenderly. At last he was still.

"If only I had asked my Mother's forgiveness," he whispered. That was all he could say, but after that night Lars' shattered heart began to mend.

Twenty Seven

Another summer had nearly passed. For Anna it was a summer so busy she had scarcely any time to reflect upon the meaning of her life, a life punctuated only by the immediate, and by the constant intrusion of the commonplace. Anna's was a life in which order was being replaced by constant interruption. 'The tyranny of the urgent' became a broken dish, spilled porridge, potty training, or dirty clothes that cried out daily to be scrubbed on the washboard. Another pail of water from the pump...Run! Chop some wood for the fire! Ten loaves of bread must be baked every other day!

And now it was Sunday. Anna had almost given up hope they could ever go to church together. God had seemed so far away. It was this spiritual discouragement that now made every task so heavy. "And Lars will never change," Anna decided bleakly, "because he will never give up his stubbornness."

She had tried. She had even gone to Pastor Svendson and he had promised to help. Indeed, right now he and Lars were out on the prairie partridge hunting. Anna sighed. "Not much chance that will help."

The Pastor and Lars were good friends. They talked of politics and the Swedish king, and old Swedish folk tales they recalled. They hunted and fished together, and even drank ale together, chatting amiably while they smoked their pipes.

Pastor Svendson told Anna how much he enjoyed the stimulation of Lars' keen mind. "He could have gone far in Sweden," the genial *prast* had once remarked. That observation made Anna flush with sudden anger. She cast her eyes downward, and after a moment retorted, "Gone far? What does that mean? Lars is not a failure in America, and must never be told that he is. He needs your encouragement, Pastor...not to be told he would be better off in Sweden."

"Oh no...I did not mean..."

"You see, Pastor, we get letters from Sweden about one of Lars' brothers getting rich, and another is a professor at Upsala University, and so on. Lars hardly ever writes letters to Sweden anymore."

"I understand. Perhaps one tends to hope for too much, to dream too large for the hard life here."

"You are an understanding man, Pastor," Anna pleaded softly, "Please tell Lars he is not a failure."

"I will, I will indeed…if the subject ever comes up."

"What a funny smile the Pastor has," mused Anna as he cheerily waved goodbye.

Anna was taking her aromatic cardamon bread from the oven as he stamped his feet on the porch.

"Lars?"

"Who else?"

"It is late. Did you shoot any partridges in Perqvist's meadow?"

"Anna, just wait till you see!"

She spun around to behold her largest washtub overflowing with large birds.

"Lars! No! No! How can I clean all those tonight? And what will we do with them?"

Lars walked silently into the house. His shoulders drooped and his steps were slow.

"Oh, Lars! What have I done? I'm sorry…So sorry!"

She tried to explain, to apologize, and to give him a portion of the encouragement he craved. But it was too late, and he would not listen. What she had said could not be undone that day. She could only clean the partridges and put them into the icehouse.

That night two strangers lay side by side in the iron bed, under the old down comforter. Each one pretended to be asleep. Each one huddled beneath a dark, protective curtain…each one vulnerable and afraid.

"It is like that terrible night long ago in Sweden," Anna pondered, "that night he told me 'the news'. Like then, I feel I do not know him, that I can't find him. Where have you gone, Lars? What do you do in that private world from which I am excluded? Where is your laughter? Where is our joy?"

"I have disappointed Anna," he was silently reasoning, "the last thing I ever wanted to do. I was a child to think she would jump up and down over those partridges! But ah, it is not just that. I promised her a good life in America. But what have I done? Odd jobs. Helping Perqvist. No new shoes for the children. No red meat for two weeks. No new dress for Anna. And then, those letters from Sweden. Would it have been different had I stayed in Sweden? I was proud and restless. I thought I could do anything. Where is that young man today? Is there nothing left of him?"

Just then Anna turned her back to Lars, lying as close to the edge of the bed as she could squeeze, thinking "I wonder why Lars has been gone from us so much. He hasn't even had steady work. Where is he when he doesn't come home? He never says...never talks to me as before. And we used to talk over everything...sitting in Central Park, whispering in bed in the sod house, lying together in the deep grass. Ah, something is wrong!"

Lars, meanwhile, pretending to be asleep, was thinking, "I wouldn't dare tell Anna where I've been going after work...playing cards with those cronies in the saloon, laughing, drinking a little, and forgetting myself for a few hours. I am breaking her heart. And I don't know how to stop!"

Anna also pretended to sleep. "Lars is a man. He needs to have something to look forward to. If he could have some hope...like getting his own farm. Or having his own son? Tonight I must pray: Oh God, forgive my sins. You seem so far away, but if you are still there, please grant me one request - a son for Lars!"

The partridges in the icehouse were good eating, every day for a week, stuffed and roasted, fried, and boiled in soup. All the Kristoferson women smacked their lips and praised Lars for his accomplishment. And Lars praised Anna's superb cooking.

Twenty Eight

One day Anna brought two of her partridges across the street for Mrs. Stafford and her daughter. She had prepared them with her special cranberry stuffing.

"My, how delicious!" exclaimed her neighbor as she took a bite.

"How did you cook this stuffing?"

"I used the high bush cranberries behind my barn, the same way we use lingonberries in Sweden. It helps cover up the wild taste, doesn't it?"

"Yes, and to think your Lars brought home all those wonderful birds!" What a fine man you have, Anna."

"Hmm..." Anna mumbled. Her eyes dropped in shame.

"Whatever is the matter, my dear? You seem troubled. Are we not close enough so that you could confide in me?"

"Oh, yes, Mrs. Stafford! If I could talk to anyone it would be to you. But I feel this is just something between Lars and me."

"I understand," Mrs. Stafford began gently, "but I still think it might be better to talk to somebody. Perhaps to the Pastor?"

"Oh no. Not him! He is Lars' best friend!"

The kindly older woman decided to try the role of counselor. "Is not Lars good to you?"

"Oh, yes. It is all my fault."

"You are tired? Overworked? And you feel you and Lars are not as close as before?" Anna, are you pregnant?"

"I could be...and all those other things are true."

"I'm here to help you, dear Anna."

"I thank God for you, Mrs. Stafford."

"Anna?"

"Yes."

"Thank God for your husband."

Mrs. Stafford's wisdom suddenly made Anna feel ashamed, for she remembered her friend did not have a husband, and only one child, now grown.

"You are right, Mrs. Stafford. I have not appreciated Lars these days...only thinking about myself. The night he brought home the partridges I was angry because he was late, and I didn't want to clean all those birds. Instead of praising him I just growled."

"You know, my dear, it helps if we begin each day with praise and thanksgiving to God. For everything. And in everything."

"That's what I'll do," Anna agreed with a smile. She thought it remarkable that Mrs. Stafford could always be so thankful in all her circumstances. She had always wondered what happened to Mr. Stafford, and thought that tragic circumstances may have prevented her friend from talking about him.

"Sit down, Anna. Now is the time for me to continue the conversation we began that day when all of you came to tea."

"I wondered why you stopped just when it was getting so interesting. You were telling us how you came out here by wagon train in 1861. The children were fascinated, and now they aren't here."

"I had to wait for a time when the children were not here to tell the rest of the story." A dark shadow of pain and sadness crossed Mrs. Stafford's lined face.

"Why?" Anna wanted to know.

"Anna," she whispered hoarsely, "my daughter and I are survivors of the Sioux Indian Massacre of 1862."

Anna gasped. "Oh my friend, I had no idea."

"It's been nearly thirty years, but it is as vivid to me as though it were yesterday. The Indians came right into our house and killed my husband. And they carried away our eight-year-old son. I never saw him again. I always wonder if he might still be alive, living with the Indians as one of theirs."

"Oh, that is terrible. I don't know what to say." Anna grew pale and shuddered.

"We lived out west of town then, on a farm. Byron, my husband, did not do the farming himself, but started a bank and a store in Willmar, which was just beginning to grow. We were building this house when it happened. A few more weeks and we would have been in town when the uprising began...and we would have been spared."

"I have heard about the Indians," Anna interjected, "and their anger over the loss of their land. But I never knew that anger was turned on you!"

"Emma and I fled, hiding in the cornfield. They set fire to the house, my husband's body still in it, except they took his scalp with them. And my dear son Peter was with one of the Indians on his horse, riding furiously into the western sky."

"Oh, my dear" was all Anna could say through her tears.

"Anna, it has been years since I have spoken of this. I was not able. I kept it like a hard, bitter lump inside me for so long. But you know? I think I feel better having told you, my dear young friend."

"It must have been very painful for you to go on living after that day."

"I had to go on...for my Emma's sake. I sold the farm and my husband's businesses. I had enough money to finish the house, making it as much like homes in gentler, more civilized places as I could. Soon the railroad could bring me fine furniture and beautiful dishes from the east. Yes, I have tried to make this home a refuge, a sort of fortress of beauty and gentleness. I had thought of going back to Boston, or even to London. Why did I stay? The truth is I MUST stay because my son may be somewhere near, and I may see him again. It may be just a dream, but often I look out my window and imagine I see a tall, handsome Indian brave walking right up to my door. At first I am terrified, but then I see his face. It is my darling Peter!"

"Perhaps one day your dream will come true."

"My mind tells me it will not. But my heart and my faith tell me, WITH GOD ALL THINGS ARE POSSIBLE. I shall always hope."

Anna received a new insight that day...about the preciousness of each day, of each moment, and of her need for a thankful heart.

"Anna, do you know what the hardest thing for me to do was?"

"No, Mrs. Stafford."

"It was learning to forgive the man who killed my husband and stole my son."

"Did it take a long time?"

"A long, long time. I was so bitter, so full of hate. I lived for revenge and I lived in a big dark hole. And all the while I was calling myself a good Christian woman. After all, who could blame me? A monstrous thing had been done to me, and rage and bitterness were justified. However, one day when I was reading from the Prayer book, I made a decision, a decision to forgive my enemies as God has forgiven me. Oh, I didn't feel very forgiving. But as I prayed the Lord's Prayer I knew I had to do it. I said these words: Lord, I forgive the Indians who killed my Byron and stole my Peter just as you have forgiven me. From that day something began to change within me.

111

The heavy burden of my bitter heart was lifted. I had peace. I could go on living."

"Oh my friend! I can't tell you how much it's meant to me that you shared all this. I too will never be the same."

"I'm glad I told you, Anna, though I won't speak of it again. And I'm so pleased you can now understand a conversation in English."

"That's all because of you!" Anna smiled as she hugged her dearest friend.

As she walked across the street to her own house, Anna's troubles seemed so insignificant after what Mrs. Stafford had just told her.

Twenty Nine

Anna and Lars moved closer to the middle of their sagging mattress. They no longer felt so isolated from one another. Perhaps that was because Anna tried to praise and encourage Lars every day...and to thank God for him. Like a watered plant, his ego had begun to thrive again. One night he whispered in her ear, "Anna, do you know how much I love you?" Their tears blended together in the darkness as they kissed. Lars began to accept the person that he was, to value his work, and to count his blessings.

Soon he began working at a good job, finishing the inside of a well-to-do merchant's home. He no longer stopped at the saloon but came directly home after work, playing with the children while Anna cooked supper.

And there was indeed a new baby on the way!

One day Lars talked with his employer about the availability and price of farmland.

"Around here," the merchant confided, "There are no more homestead lands. Farms are expensive. The soil on the prairie is rich. Also, it is getting settled fast. But I could get you a nice eighty or one hundred acres for a small down payment."

"How much does the land sell for?"

"About ten dollars an acre, more or less."

"Uff dah! Out of the question. Vel, there goes my dream of being a farmer." Lars laughed, somewhat bitterly.

"Don't give up, Kristoferson. You could homestead in North Dakota. Or you could buy cheap land up north."

"How much?"

"Less than one dollar an acre, I presume. Try writing the Nelson Land Company in Staples."

"That I will," determined Lars.

All winter Lars' silence meant that he was thinking, planning, and scheming of a way to make his dream a reality. He did not wish to

113

share his thoughts with Anna, not just yet. He had always disliked men who talked about what they were going to do before they did it.

Meanwhile, Anna was getting all sorts of ideas of why he was sitting silent in the rocking chair, smoking his pipe. When she spoke he often ignored her, or gave a monosyllabic answer unrelated to what she had said.

She sat on the settee, knitting stockings and mittens, a woman's endless job. Her thoughts clicked busily with the needles. "Lars has no idea of how much I must do or how tired I am. I see he's put up his curtain again. Shut me out...just when things were going so well between us. Ah well, at least he is coming home, that I appreciate. But I can see something worries him. Whatever can it be?"

She was hurt by his failure to communicate his thoughts. Then she herself withdrew under a shawl of sadness, wondering if she had done something to make him want to shut her out.

Lars thought it was natural for a woman to be moody when she was 'in the family way'. For an instant a smile crossed his strong, handsome face with the thought, "Is it possible this one is a boy?"

Thirty

Anna's seventh pregnancy was unexpectedly difficult. She found each day increasingly harder to manage. A warm, oppressive summer heat intruded when it was only spring. Anna felt as heavy as the humid atmosphere, her short figure as awkward, clumsy and slow as Perqvist's ox.

Nevertheless, there was so much to be done! The garden must be planted, cultivated, harvested, and canned. The baby chicks needed her attention. The cow must be milked and the butter churned. Even with splendid help from her older girls, Anna felt strained and unable to cope.

"What does Lars want a farm for?" She exclaimed one morning to the cow, "I could use some of his help with this little farm. He always has to help poor Perqvist, still living after all these years. Well, I am sick too!"

With that, she kicked over the empty milk pail. "Never mind me, Bloomster. Just feeling sorry for myself again!"

On just such a day the Pastor chose to call. He looked very dignified as he appeared at the door in his long black coat with its wide ruffled collar. This was the way a proper *prast* of the Swedish church was dressed when he came to call. But when he went hunting with Lars...that was a different matter.

Anna quickly put on a clean white apron and welcomed him warmly. Her small parlor was always neat and presentable for the children were not allowed to play there. They had the barn, the big yard, and the unfinished upstairs, but the parlor was for company and proper adults.

"First I put the coffee on," Anna began, "and then we talk. I'm sorry I don't have much to go with the coffee."

The Pastor smiled his funny little smile, thinking, "Why do Swedish women always have to apologize for something that is nothing?"

After the pleasantries Anna came right to the point of what was on her mind.

"Have you talked to Lars yet?" She inquired eagerly.

He knew exactly what she meant. A look of pastoral reserve came over his face as he made his position clear.

"Mrs. Kristoferson, please do not be offended when I tell you we cannot discuss your husband. He is my friend and I cannot betray his trust. You see, it is a wonderful and rare thing for me, a *prast*, sent to America by the Church of Sweden, to have a friend."

"Oh, my…how so?" Anna's eyes opened wide with amazement.

"You see, I represent God to the immigrants. They see me as larger than human, for without me they are without salvation. I bring them the Word of God and the sacraments, and I usher them into Heaven when they die.

They see me as a *prast,* not as an ordinary man like themselves. Except for Lars! He alone is not impressed by my priestly robes. I cherish him!"

Anna served Pastor Svendson his coffee and cookies without a word…except to say "*Var sa god*" of course.

He thanked her, and then continued, "So you see, I could not talk to Lars about his soul. He does not see me as one who has authority." Then, seeing the look of disappointment and sadness in her eyes, he added, "Don't worry. Lars has been baptized."

As she poured the Pastor another cup of coffee, she realized she would never again speak to him about her husband.

"Good coffee," he remarked politely, continuing, "The reason I came today is to remind you that your two youngest children have not yet been baptized."

"Ja, I know. As you see, I am with child again. Perhaps we could have all three *dapt* at the same time. If this one is a boy, perhaps Lars would go to church for the sacrament."

"Oh, I don't think that would make any difference," the Pastor replied, "Lars will not go to church."

After reading a prayer, he bowed graciously at the door.

"You know what I think?" Anna said to the cat as she watched the wind blowing the Pastor's robe as he walked away, "I think the Pastor doesn't want Lars to go to church. Then he might lose his best friend. Well, I for sure won't bring it up again."

Thirty One

It was late August. The grain was high and Lars was out helping Perqvist for a few days. Anna had told him she would be fine. He might just as well stay out there all night, even two nights, and save the walking. By early afternoon she was sorry she had told him this.

"Emma!" she called, with a sharp urgency in her voice. "Tell Mrs. Stafford to come quick!"

Emma understood and ran as fast as she could across the street to the home of her special friend. Mrs. Stafford walked briskly to Anna's side. "When did it begin, Anna? I thought we had two more weeks!"

"It started this morning and now I'm sure."

"Did you tell Lars?"

"No, because I've had false alarms before. He is out to Perqvist's for a couple of days."

"Never mind. We don't need him. This is women's work."

"But who will take care of the children?" The three older girls reflected in their faces their concern for their Mama.

Alma put her arms around her mother and whispered, "I'll take real good care of the little ones, Mama."

"Take them over to my house," ordered Mrs. Stafford, "My Emma is at home and she will help you."

Alma wanted to ask for permission to stay but Mrs. Stafford was very firm. The children left reluctantly.

Mrs. Stafford helped Anna to bed, made some tea, and got everything in readiness for the birth. "I have some new medicine," she said, "I'll put it in the tea and it will take the edge off your pains."

"Is it safe? My pains aren't too bad yet."

"Anna, did you forget I went to that training session for midwives last year in Rochester? I know the latest things to do. Why, Dr. Mayo himself gave me this bottle of medicine."

Anna nodded. It was comforting to be in such capable hands.

Mrs. Stafford fluffed the feather pillows. "It helps to relax," Dr. Mayo said, "and to breathe deeply with each contraction."

"Contraction?" asked Anna, "What new kind of misery is that?"

"Oh, it's just a new name for labor pains."

The labor was going well. Anna felt more comfortable and relaxed than she had before, due to the new medicine. In fact, she was beginning to feel deliciously giddy and detached from the world when two big ones struck like the power of a mighty waterfall tearing through her innards. She heard a deep involuntary groan coming from somewhere deep within herself. Then she lay still, disconnected from all feeling.

The strong cry of healthy baby lungs revived her. This time it was not the plaintive cry of a sick kitten, but a roar, loud and insistent.

"Hurrah, Anna! It's a boy! It really IS a boy!"

Anna was so excited she ignored her weakness and sat bolt upright in bed. "A boy? Are you sure?" Seeing for herself the beautiful boy in all his slimy, unwashed nakedness, she was convinced.

"God be praised! God be praised!" Anna laughed hysterically, hot tears of joy bathing her cheeks. She slept well that night, thinking of Lars' happiness when he should return from the Perqvists'.

"Oh, Lars has a surprise waiting for him alright," Anna chuckled to her friend.

"He has indeed," Mrs. Stafford agreed, "I wonder how it happened."

"It's simple. I prayed. God answered."

"Well, I won't deny it. My own faith has been strengthened today."

"Mine too," Anna murmured sleepily.

Mrs. Stafford agreed to remain at Anna's side until Lars should return. The next morning she went over to get the children. She insisted they tiptoe softly, even though they were bursting with excitement when they heard the news of their new little brother.

Anna was awake and heard their quiet steps and muffled whispers in the kitchen. She called out cheerfully for them to come to her.

Never had anyone seen six little girls so beside themselves with joy...babbling all at once in Swedish monosyllables, tumbling upon one another as they jumped in the air and rolled on the floor.

"A brother! A real baby brother!" They begged Anna to allow them to walk out to Perqvists to get Papa. She finally consented that Alma and Annie could go.

They ran three miles out to the country, acting silly, and discussing whether they should play a trick on Papa and tell him he had another girl. But as they neared the farm sensible Alma decided, "No, it would be cruel and wrong to lie. Papa must be told the truth. He has waited so long to hear this news." Annie agreed.

Before the girls reached the house they saw two men working in the field. Lars ran out to meet them, apprehensive that something had happened to Anna. "I should not have left her," he worried.

"Papa, we have a surprise!" Annie began, grinning broadly.

"Ja...a BIG surprise!" her sister added.

"Guess what it is!" They both chimed.

"I can see by your faces that Mama is alright and that's all that matters."

"Guess again."

"A baby?" asked Papa.

"But what kind?"

Papa hesitated. "The usual kind?"

"No, no...the unusual kind!"

"You mean...?"

"Ja, ja, ja...a boy! A big, healthy, loud-bawling baby boy!"

"You wouldn't fool your Papa? Can it really be true?"

Realizing that his girls were always taught to tell the truth, he called loudly to Perqvist, "A BOY Perqvist! A BOY!"

Papa beamed from ear to ear when he said *tack* to Mrs. Stafford.

But when he went into the bedroom, seeing his perfect little son nursing at Anna's breast, and seeing her triumphant smile, he buried his head in her lap and wept uncontrollably with pure happiness.

Lars decided to name his son Karl, after the king of Sweden. Mrs. Stafford suggested that the English equivalent of Karl is Charles, so in time little Karly became known up and down the street as Charley.

It was time now, Lars decided, to confide in Anna about his secret plans. When he had finished telling her about his conversation with the banker, and about the cheap land up north, she understood why he had often been silent and taciturn. She understood now that he loved her more than ever.

"What do you think, Anna? Should we try our luck? It is the only way we can have our own farm. That, or maybe homestead in Dakota Territory." Lars sincerely sought his wife's counsel.

119

"No, Lars, not Dakota. Up north might be best…if we have to go."

"You are not happy about the idea?"

"It's just that there are so many things to consider, confusing things to question…moving from this nice town, this neighborhood…where we have relatives and good friends. It would be hard to move from a town where there are schools and churches to a wooded wilderness. Oh, Lars! How painfully long you would work to clear the forest, a real farm so far in the future. And your only son is just a baby."

"You don't want to go then?"

"I didn't say that. You always do what you want to do anyway."

"That's a hurtful thing to say, Anna. Don't you realize I'm not the same reckless young man who made a decision to go to America alone? I'll forget about the farm if you ask me to." His blue eyes searched her brown eyes intensely.

"Oh, Lars, my beloved…forgive me for all those discouraging words. I only want what's best for you. I am your wife. Do what you must do, Lars. If you don't do this you will be miserable, and the children and I will be miserable too."

"But what about you, Anna? What about your happiness?

"I'm happy only when you are happy. That's the way it is for a woman."

"I love you, Anna," he whispered with a tender embrace.

The next week Lars took the train to Staples, with his savings in his pocket. He bought a sixty acre farm from the Nelson Land Company.

When his train returned to Willmar three days later, the whole family went down to the depot to meet him. Little Charley was in his new buggy, a gift from the prosperous Eckberg cousins.

As Lars stepped from the platform Anna thought it had been a long time since she had seen him so excited and radiant. His pockets were bulging with hazelnuts.

"Papa, you are a squirrel!" exclaimed Hilda, who had heard about squirrels in school and watched them climb the maple tree with acorns in their mouths.

The children were as excited as Lars, while they listened to his glowing report of a country where deer and bear roamed free among the pines and sugar maples…a place where blueberries grew in abundance, raspberries and cranberries too, and chokecherries and currants for jelly. It was a place with everything one could desire, including all the logs needed to build a house, and a beautiful river on which to skate in the winter, swim in the summer, and fish all year round.

"I can't explain it," Lars said thoughtfully, "but when I stood on our land, on the rise on which I want to build our house, I was overcome with the feeling that I had at last come home."

Anna nodded, wiping away a tear. "*Hembygnen*," she whispered.

"When are we going?" shouted the children in antiphonal chorus.

"In the spring," their father answered. The children moaned because they were going to have to wait so long. Only Emma remained silent.

"I don't want to go," she stated firmly.

"Why not, silly?" inquired Hilda.

"I don't want to leave Mrs. Stafford, or my books and my school."

There was much to be done before spring. The house must be sold, and so Lars painted it and fixed it up to look as nice and inviting as possible. It looked so pretty and homey that tears filled Anna's eyes whenever she thought about moving, which was all the time. She tried not to complain because she knew how much it meant to Lars to hope for his own fine farm, perhaps some day as fine as that of the Eckberg's.

And so Anna tried to concentrate on the positive aspects of the move. For instance, she reasoned that Lars would now be separated from the men at the saloon and other cronies, including Pastor Svendson. Perhaps now he would begin to believe in God, as she did, even go to church. With that thought, however a negative realization intruded. There were no churches in the woods.

Anna wanted their last Christmas in Willmar to be extra special...even if there were no fir trees and Lars would not go to *Julotta*.

She put a white linen cloth on the table, and the red candles. Then she put a small branch of the pine tree Mrs. Stafford had given her to plant, on the table.

"Mama, couldn't we take the whole tree?" little Alice begged.

"Oh, no. It must be left to grow." Then, seeing the child's poignant, quivering mouth she comforted her with thoughts of the wonderful tall *julatre* they would have next Christmas in the northern forest.

Anna had made a pair of red woolen mittens for each of her little ones for Christmas. Lars bought each a red-striped peppermint stick and a sweet, bright orange. These gifts would be presented to them on *Julaften*, after their very special supper.

As in Sweden, the birds were remembered with a shock of wheat, mounted on a pole. This was a gift from the Perqvists. Selma had also made a Christmas goat out of straw with a red ribbon around his neck for the children...just like in Sweden. Svenborg had become a little kinder and more accepting with the years. And Karl stumbled along with the help of his cane, never complaining. The girls had become women, unmarried spinsters. Amanda and Selma had learned to do everything, even fieldwork, and their father had become quite dependent upon them.

When the Perqvists came to call, bearing their gifts, Karl told Lars how much he would be missed – and not only for the work he had done for them. "You are my only true friend," Perqvist said, his voice breaking. And Svenborg told Lars over and over how glad she was to have the new house of lumber he had helped them build, even though it was not the large and grand home she would have liked. The sod house had been slowly dissolving since the last torrential rainstorm, and was now a pile of dirt, a hill from which their dog could survey the domain under his protection.

"Uff dah!" Svenborg would often say, "Just to think we lived in there!"

Lars asked if he might help with the Christmas preparations. This gesture touched Anna deeply, since this was not expected of a Swedish man. He meticulously prepared the lutfisk, soaking it in caustic lye until it was absolutely perfect, lye he had made of wood ashes from the kitchen stove. Then he soaked it in pure, clean water until no lye remained. Lars was very proud of his white transparent lutfisk, smacking his lips at the thought of eating it with cream and melted butter.

Lars also gathered the eggs, milked the cow, and made butter and cheese, so that Anna and the girls would be free to bake the *Julakaka*, and the dozens and dozens of assorted cookies that were a nostalgic reminder of their beloved homeland.

Just before Christmas Lars took some of his meager savings to buy a Christmas ham and other extras, even a pretty shawl for his sweetheart, Anna.

All of these things, and especially being together and filled with love for one another, made this a very memorable Christmas Eve for the Kristofersons in their little white house. The starry, moonlit night pressed its nose against their frosty windowpane and peeked between the white lace curtains to see them crowded close around their small table with its red candles and pine branch in the center eating lutefisk with cream and butter sauce, cranberries, and rice pudding. The winter wind wailed softly above the snow on the window sill to the accompaniment of their laughter, while the winter birds sat contentedly upon their shock of wheat. It was indeed, a *Gladige Jul* for all!

On the second day of Christmas family and friends came to call. The Eckbergs drove up in their big sleigh pulled by black Prince and white Polly, garlanded in cheery, tinkling sleighbells. They were laden with presents, something for each of the Kristofersons, singing warm wishes for the blessings of God throughout the coming year. There was a scarf and small china doll for each of the girls, a blue sweater and a rattle for Charley. And for Lars and Anna, paper, pens, envelopes, and stamps. "Now you must write to us," they urged cordially.

"How I shall miss you!" sighed Anna to her cousin, "You will never know how much being able to share our thoughts has meant to me!"

"If only we had seen more of each other! Oh, Anna, I shall pray you receive from God the desire of your heart!"

"Only you know what that is, Lena," responded Anna tenderly as they hugged.

On the third day of Christmas Mrs. Stafford invited all the Kristofersons over to her lovely big home, where she graciously served them a dinner of roast goose and plum pudding. Then, stuffed and contented, they sat politely upon the elegant furniture in her parlor. She presented each of the girls with an exquisite bone china demitasse cup and saucer. There was a silver spoon for Charley. And for Anna, a china teapot with pink roses painted on it. She had a book for Lars on the history of the British Empire.

"This is too much," Anna protested, "How can we ever thank you, our dearest friend?"

There were tears in Mrs. Stafford's eyes and her voice broke as she said, "Your leaving in the spring will be a real and personal sorrow."

Thirty Two

"Ready to leave at last!" Anna exclaimed as Lars turned the door key in their empty house. "And already it is fall. She did not look back as they padded slowly to the depot, weighed heavily with the most necessary trappings of daily life. Lars had planned to move to Staples in the early spring, but their little white house did not sell until late summer. At last an immigrant family from Smoland was able to buy the house and animals, paying Lars two hundred dollars down and promising to send the rest later. They were staying with relatives and were to move in when the Kristofersons left. The day before their departure, Lars had taken their furniture to the depot to be shipped.

A churning black engine was etched impatiently against the splendor of an October dawn, a whistle blowing short, piercing blasts. "All aboard!" shouted the jovial conductor.

Mrs. Stafford's small, near-sighted eyes peered anxiously into each window for a last glimpse of Anna, her dearest friend.

"There they are!" shouted Emma, waving her thin hand wistfully, hot tears raining on her courageous smile.

As the train began to groan and slowly roll, Mrs. Stafford put a comforting arm around ten year old Emma. "You need my shawl, dear child. My goodness, you are shivering!" She smiled at Emma with compassion, wondering for a moment if leaving the child behind had been the right decision.

"Emma, are you sorry?"

"No ma'am. I'd be sorry if I had to leave my school, and you, just now. But oh, I'm going to miss them!"

"Thank you, precious child, for giving this old lady a year of special joy. You won't regret it."

Mrs. Stafford and Emma had much to give each other. The child had only herself to give. Mrs. Stafford had the means, manners, Christian character, and education to give Emma the finer things of life.

At last Anna reposed quietly. What a simple thing for which to be grateful! What matter that the train swayed wildly, noisily grinding its teeth? Charley sleeping peacefully in her arms, she could lean back and close her eyes after all the turmoil of the last week. After the long wait since spring when they had hoped to sell their house and leave. "If only Lars...ack, no use to look back." A new adventure awaited them in the north woods. No use to look ahead either, with the desolation of winter coming on so soon. Anna sighed deeply, recalling an old Swedish proverb that went something like, "When you don't know what to do, just do the next thing!"

It was mid-morning and the 'next thing' was having to change trains in St. Cloud and see that none of the children got lost. The train stopped with a wrenching lurch. The conductor stomped down the aisle, yelling with the same joviality, "St. Cloud! All passengers for Staples and Little Falls change here. You have a two hour wait!"

"Ack, what trouble they could get into in all that time! Help me, Lars!"

Anna carried Charley and the diaper bag and lunch basket. Lars carried Alice and tried to hold Hilda's and Betsy's hands at the same time, while Alma and Annie walked sedately behind. "We will sit on the benches in the waiting room and eat dinner, even if it is a little early," Anna announced briskly as they alighted.

Suddenly Perhund began to yip in his poignant puppy voice deep within Hilda's covered basket. Her secret was out.

"Good thing you are getting out," the Conductor whispered with a wink, "No dogs allowed on the train."

"Oops, Per! That was a narrow escape. You better be quiet on the next train!" Hilda admonished the covered basket.

"That sounds pitiful to me," Betsy put in, "We just have to let him out for a little while."

"Sure, why not? Then he can be satisfied until we get to Staples."

Lars heard that, but his instruction to "put his rope on" came too late. Before they reached the depot Perhund was free, and ecstatic in his freedom. He was a streak of light bounding across the platform and down the brick-lined main street of this strange town. Hilda and Betsy stood frozen, numb, and transfixed with horror. But only for a moment. Soon they too were running down the street after their puppy.

Lars looked down helplessly at Anna. "I couldn't stop them," he apologized.

125

"What next?" Anna sighed wearily.

"All of you sit in the waiting room and don't worry. I will find them," Lars said with his usual take-charge calmness.

Anna never worried when Lars was in charge. They would wait on the hard benches and pray. He soon returned with a frantic, tousled little girl on each arm. But no puppy! Perhund had disappeared into the milling crowd of wagons, horses, and people.

"'Tis all your fault, Hilda!" Betsy sobbed.

"'Tisn't my fault, tis yours!" Hilda exploded hotly.

Annie dramatically interrupted their quarrel. "Girls, how can you stand there and blame each other when our dear puppy is lost, perhaps lying broken under a wagon wheel?"

Bitter sobs ensued at this voicing of their worst fears. Even little Alice wept uncontrollably.

Anna coaxed the children to try her extraordinary cinnamon rolls and the goat cheese from Cousin Lena. But it was hard to eat while looking at little Per's empty basket.

It was almost time for the train to leave for Staples just as Lars returned from another fruitless search.

"Papa, we can't leave," Hilda insisted, "We must find Per first!"

It hurt Lars deeply to tell the children they must now get into the train and leave Perhund to the mercy of all the kind people in St. Cloud. "Some nice little girl will find him," he reassured, "one who needs just such a puppy. She will take him home and her Mama will love him too. Oh, no, Annie, Per is too smart a fellow to find himself under a wagon wheel." This was Lars' only alternative. This was the only train going to Staples for many days.

There was no arguing with Papa when he looked like that...serious, sad, and firm as a rock. They filed on to the train, nursing silent pain. Anna put the remains of the lunch and some of Charlie's things into the basket in place of Perhund and carried it herself.

They heard the warning whistle. They heard the "All aboard!" Both sounded so far away, Betsy was looking through the murky window, numb and disconsolate, when she saw the man on the platform. "Look, Hilda, that man has a dog that resembles Per. It makes me so sad and lonesome!"

"You dummy! It IS Per! He found our puppy!" Hilda was racing to the door.

"Let me out! My puppy is out there!" she demanded of the conductor.

He didn't hear over the noise. God be praised! For Hilda remembered the 'no dogs' rule just in time.

With unusual sophistication she pleaded with the mild-mannered conductor. "Please, sir, I forgot something important on the platform. Could you hold the train for just a moment?"

"You have three minutes," was all he said as he opened the door.

Hilda pulled on the coat of a certain red-haired man. "You have my Per! You found him!" she shouted, jumping wildly.

"So this is your dog," laughed the man, "I pulled him out from under the train. He's almost scared to death!"

"But he's not dead! Per, you are not dead! Thank you, sir!" She quickly gathered the trembling puppy under her coat and bolted into the train.

"What is under your coat?" Mama looked quizzically at the little girl beside her.

"Sh...Good news, Mama."

"What news?"

"The best news in the whole world. Per is found!" Hilda told Mama. Anna took out the things she had put into Per's basket and he was put in it again, too tired to even whimper. He slept peacefully for the rest of the journey.

Hilda leaned against her Mama's shoulder while she listened to her tell the familiar story of Jesus, the Shepherd who searched diligently for his lost sheep.

"When He found his lamb, was He as happy as I am now?" yawned a very tired little girl.

"Yes, oh yes," Mama whispered, "even happier."

Thirty Three

It was midnight when the train whistled shrilly into the darkness of pine forests, and the sleepy Conductor yawned, STAPLES!

The children were asleep. When roused, they walked like puppets with indifferent eyes, glazed and silent, clutching their few possessions mechanically. Even Perhund slept tranquilly in his wicker basket as the seven weary Kristofersons slipped wordlessly to the platform.

Mr. Oleson, proprietor of the livery stable and landowner was at the station to meet them. He scarcely resembled the man of means and power Anna had visualized. She recalled Lars' glowing words: "I bought my land from Mr. Oleson, and two horses. He owns a log house we can rent while I build. Mr. Oleson is someone I respect, and he thinks…" and so on. Anna had pictured a distinguished gentleman with a pin-striped suit and a tall black hat. That poor crumpled and ragged figure with holes in his hat and tobacco running from the corners of his mouth could not be Mr. Oleson!

But it was. "He must not have a wife," Anna reasoned, "and if he does, she can't be a Swede!"

Mr. Oleson was loud and rough, but at the same time kind and accepting. "A humble man. An honest man." Anna tried not to judge him too harshly.

Mr. Oleson not only had a wife, but ten children as well, all scrunched together, tattered and scruffy, in four rather large rooms above the livery stable. The Kristofersons had no choice but to accept Oleson's kind invitation to spend the night with them. In the morning, he promised, he would hitch up the horses Lars had purchased to the lumber wagon, and take them and their belongings to the log house by Willow Creek.

"The rent is real cheap, only three dollars a month and for one dollar extra I'll throw in the wagon."

"Ja, sure, Oleson. *Tack sa mycket.*" Lars wondered how he could earn money to pay the rent and at the same time build a house and barn on his own land. Lars sighed wearily, a sigh of doubt and worry that soon passed.

A flickering kerosene lamp burned in the cheery kitchen above the stable, and a pot of fragrant soup simmered on the wood range. Mrs. Oleson welcomed them in Swedish. "How tired you must be...and your poor, dear little ones," she spoke with sincere concern. Somehow she had arranged places for all to sleep. Her own little ones were already settled on the floor, so the Kristofersons could have their beds.

"She is a good woman," Anna whispered to Lars, "Maybe not so neat, clean I don't know because it is dark, and I"...Her voice trailed off as Lars was already snoring.

It was still dark in the morning when they started out for the country, Thomastown Township, east of Staples. The nine mile ride to the log house took several hours. Lars sat up in front in the high seat with Oleson. Anna and the children fit themselves in between the beds and bureaus, tortuously, like pretzels. There was not enough room for all the furniture. Mr. Oleson would take the rest of it out on the morrow.

It was slow going on the sandy trail among the luxuriant green pines and scarlet maples. The wagon wheels kept getting embedded in the sand, and Oleson turned the horses wildly to avoid the stumps. Despite these hardships the children were filled with a spirit of extraordinary joy and excited anticipation. Laughter spilled over the tight places where they sat. Even Anna shared in the fun. Bone tired, she had lost emotional control and felt like a giddy schoolgirl again.

"What is the matter with her?" Lars wondered aloud.

"Your wife is happy," Oleson observed, "That is good."

"Anna is always happy when the children are happy," answered Lars with a grin.

"No wonder, my friend. It's a day they call Indian summer," Oleson remarked as he spat tobacco on the sunlit sand, squinting up at the cloudless blue sky, drinking deeply of the pine-fragrant air. "Yup, couldn't be a finer day!"

"You are a good man, Oleson," chuckled Lars appreciatively.

Thirty Four

At last the first glimpse of their new home rose before them. Autumn sunlight was gleaming softly on its roof. Oleson was proud of this recent improvement. "Yup, roof leaked all last winter, so I put tin on...won't leak no more, no way, and sparks from the chimney won't burn it neither." He paused, waiting for praise.

It looked like a substantial house, even for a log cabin, Anna thought, and so pretty too, with flaming sumac surrounding it, but when Oleson opened the creaky door, Anna's bubbling euphoria quickly evaporated. Her mouth fell limply open, and her eyes pulled together in wrinkles of displeasure. She had expected the house to be plain, ja sure, but dirty? This was no ordinary dirty house. Piles of debris covered the floor, and sticky gray cobwebs drooled down from the ceiling.

Nevertheless, Anna contrived a tiny smile, and said reassuringly to the children, "It will be a cozy home when we get it all scrubbed up. 'Tis not too bad."

"Two big rooms downstairs. A roomy loft for the children. Two stone chimneys. Sturdy pine flooring," Mr. Oleson announced as he tapped his foot against the log wall. "It's a good house for the price."

On the days following, Anna and her girls worked hard to bring an air of Swedish cleanliness and homeliness to the musty log house. After Lars had hauled out the dirt and debris in the wheelbarrow, the floor was scrubbed white with lye, and Anna's bright rag rugs put down. Cobwebs were swept away, and the log walls wiped clean. The little windows became transparent again, with crisp lace curtains covering them. The family furniture and few possessions were arranged with charming simplicity. A clean white cloth covered the table, upon which Anna had placed a vase of scarlet maple leaves and yellow asters. Two long benches flanked the table, enough room for everyone to sit and break bread together.

The heavy oak cupboard Lars had crafted with much care survived the trip. Dishes were unpacked to put inside it, along with food staples

Anna had brought; flour, salt, sugar, coffee, and many jars of preserves and pickles. They had even shipped some potatoes, carrots, and squash from their garden in Willmar, together with some smoked fish and salt pork. These were put into the cellar with a trap door in the center of the room.

The locked drawer at the top of the cupboard was for keepsakes and valuable papers. The bottom drawer was for Anna's best linens. "A place for everything and everything in its place," was what she always taught her children.

A large stone fireplace dominated one end of the common room. Its raised hearth was scrubbed vigorously, and the old copper teakettle Anna had brought from Sweden, the wedding gift from her Uncle Berg, was placed in the center. There were hooks inside the fireplace on which to hang the teakettle. A large iron soup pot was already there. Oleson pointed out that it went with the cabin. Anna did not think that black pot could ever be made clean enough for cooking, but it would serve well to heat water for wash day, and Saturday night baths. Besides, she had brought along her precious new iron range, and her spotless blue enamel cookware. She was glad to see there was a smaller chimney with a stovepipe outlet. There her range could proudly stand.

Lars soon had the woodbox filled with poplar and birch logs, some long for the fireplace, some short for the stove. He built fires in both of them, and for awhile black smoke and sparks exploded frighteningly from the chimneys.

"Don't be alarmed," Lars reassured them, "The chimneys haven't been used for a long time, so dust and creosote must burn away. The chimneys are sturdy and the roof is tin, covered with frost.

The roaring soon turned to a quiet lapping of bright flames from glowing coals. The teakettle sang proudly, while Perhund slept, stretching out contentedly near the warm hearth. Then the tiny Swedish cuckoo arose from his room in the clock to announce that it was time for the noon meal.

Anna had forgotten to watch the time. "Oh, Lars, what can we have to eat?" she exclaimed.

"Surely you have something, my dear."

"Ja, sure, we shall have coffee and skorpa with sugar and dried fruit. God be praised! The cupboard is not bare. What we brought will last for awhile. But perhaps not all winter." Anna felt rich and content. Somehow, trusting God, they would survive the winter.

"Girls," she exclaimed, "We have worked hard, and this place is beginning to look like home."

"It IS home!" added Hilda.

"But I miss Emma," Betsy remarked in a poignant moment.

The loft was warm from the blazing fire below, and the children slept well on two large straw mattresses, covered with down comforters.

Charley slept in his cradle near Mama and Papa in the downstairs bedroom. Anna felt her own familiar bed supporting her tired back. It seemed good and comforting.

Thirty Five

Beams of hazy sunlight rippled across the bright crazy quilt and onto Lars' handsome, craggy face.

Anna woke up. "Oh, my, it must be late! And we are not up yet!" She remembered that in October the sun comes up when the workday is half over.

Even Charley was fast asleep, his wispy blond curls askew all over his small round face. Anna smiled. "Ack, what is so beautiful as a sleeping child, so oblivious of all that lies ahead."

Just as Lars was beginning to stir, she heard the sounds of sleighbells! Wagon wheels! Silvery laughter! Swedish words!

Anna grabbed her heavy, dark-blue robe and cap, yelling for Lars to get up. "We have company! And we are not prepared! Whatever will they think of us? Still sleeping until eight o'clock?"

Lars rolled over, laughing and teasing. He couldn't resist when he saw how deeply his attitude had infuriated her. She threw a pillow at his head, and shot out of the bedroom, slamming the door behind her.

There was a smiling family of Swedes standing in their doorway.

"Welcome to Thomastown," the father began, "I am Ole Dahlberg, and here is my wife Lena and our pesky little brood - Karl, Ellen, Axel, and Annie. And, as you can see, one is on the way." he winked jovially.

"My, my, another Annie," Anna mumbled. It was a moment before she could recover from the unforgivable shame of being caught in bed, as it seemed, in the middle of the day, undressed, and with no fire, and no pot of coffee on.

Such as she was, Anna bowed and smiled at the Dahlbergs, reaching out a welcoming hand. Tears filled her eyes. "Forgive me, please. I just did not expect to see friends out here in this wilderness…kind people, Swedes." Quickly she regained her composure.

"*Valkommen*! Come in, come in! I am Anna Kristoferson. We overslept this morning and I am so ashamed. Please overlook the mess," she said, sweeping her hand over the nearly immaculate room.

"Come, sit around the table. I will get the fire going and soon the coffee will be ready."

Quickly Anna forgot all about her embarrassment. The Dahlbergs, with their warmth and humor, somehow made her feel like a queen in her old blue robe and cap, and made her humble home seem cozy and beautiful.

Lars came out from the bedroom in his everyday best, carrying Charley, whom he had dressed and combed.

The girls, hearing laughter, soon exploded from upstairs, all dressed in the best clothes they could find.

Mrs. Dahlberg had brought fresh rolls and sausage to eat with Anna's coffee. They had so much pleasure laughing and visiting about Sweden and Thomastown that Anna forgot all about excusing herself to get dressed properly.

Here were friends, close neighbors, Swedes. And what did it matter they were from Smaland? Anna and Lars felt they had known these strangers for at least a lifetime.

Before they left, the Dahlbergs invited the Kristofersons to come to their home for dinner the very next Sunday.

The children marked the days until Sunday on a tree branch. I can't wait. I just can't wait!" Hilda declared.

"Time goes fast," her Mama chided, "when we have lots of things to do."

There was much work for all the Kristofersons to do. Lars worked in the woods all day, taking Prince and Pet, the horses he had bought, and the lumber wagon to his own land. Here he worked steadily, cutting down trees, some for their winter wood supply, and some to sell in Staples. He would need to earn money to pay Mr. Oleson, and to buy a sack of flour and warm clothes for winter. He also took his gun to the woods to shoot rabbits, partridges, and pheasants. One day he went fishing in the Leaf River, which meandered through his acres.

Every day Lars brought something to eat along with his load of wood, something for Anna to clean and cook. They had little to go with the meat, but she could manage. She made a thick rabbit stew with dumplings, flavored with allspice.

"Mama," Lars complimented after the evening meal, "You are the best cook in the whole state of Minnesota."

"Um...mm" added Charley, smacking his lips.

The next morning Anna noticed that the sack of flour was going down fast. "Ja, we can get by as long as we have flour," she sighed.

Sunday turned out to be one of those rare fall treasures, the sky was the color of Heaven, and a faint breeze sent the red maple leaves dancing gently earthward. The sun was warm, but the air had that familiar tinge of winter and wood smoke. Haze lingered languidly over the pines, softly graying their tops.

"Wear your heavy shawls, girls," called Anna, already enthroned beside Lars in the lumber wagon, with Charley on her lap. "And don't sit on the rabbit stew," she added. They could not go without bringing something.

"The rabbit is small," she sighed, "and better it should be a cake, but it is all we have. How could I bake a cake with no eggs or cream?"

"What did you say, dear one?" Lars was lost in his private world.

"Nothing. Everybody ready?"

"Ja, ja," squealed the girls, each in her individual pitch of excitement.

The much anticipated day had arrived. Here they were on their way to their new friends for Sunday dinner!

Prince and Pet stepped gingerly between the jagged stumps on the winding trail to the Dahlberg farm. It was barely a mile, but to the impatient Kristoferson children, it seemed to take an eternity.

Betsy spied the stream of curling smoke first. "There it is!" she cried, "Over there in the clearing!"

"My, what a big house!" Hilda observed with awe.

"Sided, and painted too," Annie pointed out.

"Even a barn!" piped Alice, "with chickens and cows and a haystack to play on!"

The Dahlbergs heard the squeaky wagon wheels laboring in the sand behind the pine grove.

"They're commin!" Axel shouted. And so, all the Dahlberg children, Karl, Axel, Ellen, and Annie, were soon at the gate to meet their new friends. New friends in the north woods, especially Swedes, were incomparable treasures to cherish.

The children felt shy and inarticulate at first. But drawn to each other with cords of warmth and common interests, like wanting to scamper up the ladder to the haymow and slide down the haystack, they soon began to communicate, with Swedish words, and Swedish squeals of abandoned joy. But first they were expected to bow and shake hands, greeting Mr. and Mrs. Dahlberg and Grandma Dahlberg in proper fashion.

Then, as was understood but unspoken, children were to play outside, away from earshot of grown-up conversation, until they were called to come in for dinner, usually only after the adults had finished eating.

Anna disliked that old custom. At her home, she had always invited the children to sit with company at the table, as long as they behaved themselves and didn't interrupt. If they failed twice to obey these rules, they left the table. Nothing was said. Papa had only to meet the young eyes for one brief, solemn moment. Their love and respect for Papa was profound. Perhaps that was because they too were treated with respect and kindness, never belittled or ignored. While Mama would ask them if they wanted second helpings of what there was enough of, Papa would ask their opinions about what was being discussed.

Anna knew that in many homes this was not the case. Children were not made to feel they were valuable and loved. She was happy to see that the Dahlbergs loved children in the same way she and Lars did.

"Ja, it will be good to have such friends," she thought as the potatoes and cream sauce were passed around the table. Anna was glad the Dahlbergs had such a big round table, so that the children could be seated with them.

"Did you children have fun together in the barn?" Mrs. Dahlberg asked kindly.

"Oh, yes," Alma answered, "It was even fun for ME to slide down the haystack! I'm fourteen."

Anna suddenly realized that her Alma was turning into a woman. Perhaps she should begin staying in the house with the adults.

For dessert, Mrs. Dahlberg served 'sunshine pudding'. Anna asked for the recipe. It was much like the dessert she had made in Sweden with lingonberries.

"It's easy. Take some canned fruit juice, like raspberry or wild currant, and thicken it with flour or tapioca. And don't forget to pour on the thick, rich cream."

Anna looked hurt. Lena should have realized: The Kristofersons had no cow!

When the sun went down that day a friendship between the two immigrant families had begun that was to endure, growing deep roots between all the hard places, through all the years of joy and pain that were to follow.

Before the Kristofersons left, Mrs. Dahlberg gave them a pail of warm milk from Julie, her faithful cow. She promised to bring them milk twice a week; for she felt sad to know the Kristofersons had no cow, which meant no dairy products at all for their growing brood.

"Children need milk," she stated simply, "and butter and cheese too or their bones will grow weak. In the spring we will have a cow for you."

"How much?" asked Lars, proud and always expecting to pay.

"It will be a gift," Mr. Dahlberg answered," a pledge of the friendship we have begun today." He assured Lars with a firm clasp of his big weathered hand.

Anna thought she saw moisture forming in the comers of Lars' eyes. He could not speak. Only the pressure of his hand spoke to Ole of his profound gratitude...not only for the milk supply, but also for the bond of friendship. They were not alone in the wild country.

Thirty Six

There was still time to gather hazelnuts and rosehips for the winter. High bush cranberries too, which Anna made into jars of tart jam. "So like the lingonberries we had in Sweden," she exclaimed in delighted surprise, "Won't it go well with our Christmas lutfisk? That is, if we can get some."

As the days grew shorter, Lars worked harder in the forest. He had already cut nearly enough firewood to feed the hungry stove all winter. Now he was cutting logs into railroad ties by hand with the trusty steel ax he had brought from Sweden. Dahlberg had told him about money to be made cutting ties for the abundant market of railroad expansion. Staples was a railroad town. He could sell them there – as many as he could cut.

Lars had filled a wagon full of ties just as Anna could see the bottom of the flour barrel and had used the last of the sugar for her cranberry jam.

Before dawn Lars hitched up Pet and Prince to the lumber wagon, heavy with sturdy pine ties. He was ready to start out for Staples.

"Good-by!" he called cheerfully to the sleepy children.

"Please bring candy, Papa!" pleaded their small voices from the stairway to the loft.

"I will try," he promised, "if there is enough money left after I buy the other things and pay Mr. Oleson."

"Now, Prince...good boy, steady there." Lars smiled when he recalled how Oleson had to start a fire under Prince to get him going.

"Looks like you sold me a balky one," Lars had observed.

"Why do you think he was so cheap?" Oleson had retorted.

Lars chuckled to himself now, because, after just a few weeks, Prince had become a true gentleman of a horse under his patient tutelage.

"Guess I just have a way with horses," Lars mumbled with a pleased smile.

It was a good enough fall day. Snow had not yet fallen. The air was spicy and sparkling, while a hint of frost hung limply on the tinge of wood smoke. Lars was in good spirits as he weaved along the sandy, stump dotted road to Staples. While bumping along he shared many of his thoughts with Prince and Pet. He wondered if they could understand Swedish. Probably, since they had belonged to Oleson. Maybe not Prince. He may have been abused by that Irishman who had him for awhile. Made him scared and stubborn. "I couldn't do that to a horse," considered Lars carefully.

"Hey, Prince, I'm good to you, eh? Can you believe Anna wants me to go to church? I once knew a man who went to church every week, not just on Easter and *Julotta*. Oh ja, he was the one who beat his wife, and lied to her too. Well, we won't have that problem...no church here." Lars chuckled softly as he contemplated the humor of seeing a church spire rise above the pines, bells pealing. "A man takes care of his family," he went on, "does his best, and works hard with his hands. What kind of God would demand more than that? If there is a God. Tell you what, Pet. I'll walk down the street today, right past that saloon, and not even go in. Not because I believe in God, but because I love my family and want to do right by them. I ask you, isn't that enough? But what do you know about churches and religion?"

It was dark when Lars returned to his rented log house in the woods. He sighed deeply as he unloaded the 100-pound sack of flour, the sugar, the coffee, and the oat and rye meal he had purchased with the money he got from selling his railroad ties. He thought he had been paid very skimpily for all his work, but he was at the mercy of the big company. After he had paid Oleson the rent money, it had been just enough. Not one penny left to buy the gumdrops and peppermint sticks he had promised his children. How could he bear to see the looks of disappointment on their small, eager faces peering down at him from the loft?

Tears filled his eyes. "I'm very, very sorry, my precious ones. There was no money to buy the candy. Can you forgive your Papa?"

"That's alright Papa," whispered Betsy, her nightgown clad form draped across his back, "Just so you are here."

"Ja," Hilda agreed, "That is the main thing."

But somehow little Charley didn't understand. "Candy! Candy!" he cried, putting out his wee hand.

"I'm sorry, Lars," explained Anna, "I shouldn't have let them talk so much about candy." She looked at Lars tenderly, noticing the sadness in his blue eyes, and the droop of discouragement in his broad shoulders. Then she caressed his hair and beard with her hands and kissed him gently. There was nothing more to say.

Thirty Seven

One morning, just before the first snowfall, Lars, Dahlberg, and several other men paused on their way to the woods by the bridge across the Leaf River. They had begun a ritual of meeting here in the sun, exchanging news, and passing around a bottle of whiskey against the cold and darkness of the forest. Suddenly they heard the sharp staccato of a hammer echoing from a nearby farm.

"Vel, I see August Peterson is working on his barn, just started and winter coming on too," Dahlberg began.

"We must help him then," suggested Lars simply.

"Ja, it is the right thing to do," the others agreed, "even if it IS August."

Lars puzzled over this last remark, wondering why he had not met this August Peterson.

"Why doesn't August come to the corner? I would like to meet him...maybe invite him and his family over to Sunday dinner sometime," Lars remarked cordially.

The men laughed a little mysteriously.

"Why? Isn't he sociable?"

"Ja, that he is. But different." Dahlberg explained, "And he's got no missus or kids, not yet. Though I heard he's married and she's coming up here before Christmas. She is sick. I think it's TB."

"Poor fellow. We sure must help him build his barn. Maybe when we're done we could have a dance there on the second day of Christmas," Lars ventured, remembering with tender nostalgia the dances in Solvesberg square. For a moment he could feel the softness of his Anna as he held her close, as they laughed and sang with old Sven the fiddler.

"Well, August, we see you are at work on your barn," Ole observed in a friendly tone of voice. "With the snow coming soon, of course."

"We came to offer help," Lars began, introducing himself. "Why, we could finish it up in three weeks, maybe less. I'm a carpenter by trade and my land is next to yours. Sorry I didn't stop by before."

Lars felt he was doing all the talking and he wondered why. August seemed such a friendly young fellow. But the other men were sort of smirkish and standoffish. Funny thing.

"I can't thank you enough," responded August with warm gratitude. "I just can't get over that you would stop your own work to help me. May God bless all of you!"

Lars was impressed with young August, who had come from Bleking, the same province as he. He saw a friendly, caring type of guy. A man who could joke and laugh too. Except he'd probably not laugh at those coarse jokes Nils Nilson tells, or use profanity either.

"August is decent," was Lars' evaluation, "I like him."

When at last the barn was finished, smelling new and clean, Lars thought it might be appropriate to ask the question Dahlberg had been laughing about.

"Say, Peterson," he asked with a kindly smile, "before you put animals in your barn, how about if we have a dance for the whole Thomastown Township?"

It was a tense moment. Lars wondered why August looked so serious, without being angry. He steadily met the averted eyes of the men with smirks on their faces. "We will have something better than a dance. We will have gospel meetings in the barn."

"What sort of meeting is that?" Lars did not comprehend.

"A lay preacher named Sandell is coming up from the cities pretty soon," August smiled, "and you will all be invited to the barn to hear him."

None of the men promised to come, but they parted with handshakes. August thanked them warmly for all their help, apologizing profusely that he had nothing else to give.

"You see now, Kristoferson, what I meant," Dahlberg remarked as they walked away.

"Ja. I see. He is a Pietist. We had many back home, too. Well, I always say, 'Live and let live!' And I like August too."

"So, will you go to the meetings then?"

"No, I will not be going. Anna can go if she likes. But she knows I never go to church, even if it is in a barn." Lars chuckled a bit at the incongruity of a church being in a barn.

"Oh," said Dahlberg, "We will go. Not that we are Pietists, but there is so little to entertain us up here in the north woods. We settlers are glad just to have somewhere to go, something new to see, someone new to hear, and mostly just to see all the other Swedes and hear their news. You come, Lars. It might be fun. We will bring eats, too."

"Ja, maybe," Lars conceded, "It might not be so bad. It might not hurt to hear what this Sandell has to say."

They forgot about it then, for nothing more was said about 'meetings in the barn' all winter. Lars concluded this lay preacher didn't want to preach in August's barn after all. Good thing he hadn't said anything to Anna.

Somehow the Kristofersons made it through those long, cold winter days. The woodpile lasted long enough to feed daily that hungry monster of a stove, and the fireplace too. The flour barrel lasted through a hundred baking days. There was coffee, and sugar. There were the gifts from Mrs. Dahlberg, eggs and milk. There was the tart cranberry jam and the wild hazelnuts. There was fish that came from a hole in the icy river. There were partridges Lars shot in the woods and venison hanging frozen on the porch.

"Ah ja," Anna exclaimed with a thankful heart to Lena Dahlberg, "God is so good! Just think, He has kept us from getting sick all winter, provided food for our table, and above all gave us a friend like you!"

"Ja, we two have been through a lot together this winter," Lena reflected, "I never would have lived, maybe, if you hadn't been with me when my baby was born."

"That was a new experience for me, but God was with us both. I'm glad I learned so much from Mrs. Stafford."

Anna realized how much she missed potatoes and onions when their meager supply was gone. And how the children missed being able to play in the snow because they had no overshoes!

One day as Anna and Lena sat rocking by the fire, they could barely hear themselves talk for all the racket of happy sounds in the loft - running, feet pounding, squeals and laughter.

"How will you stand all this noise Anna, until it gets warm enough for them to play outside?"

"Let them play. They need to move quickly to keep warm. Me? I enjoy their fun. Sometimes I go up there and join them. Don't worry Lena. They'll quiet down when their Papa comes home."

"Ja, Kristoferson, he is a good disciplinarian. But you, Anna! Well, I can't wait for mine to go outside. And soon we're going to have a school! Ja, in Bullard - two miles away."

Anna's eyes brightened. "A school? God be praised! Two miles will not be too far to walk. My children will go to school!"

A faint chill of sadness enveloped Anna just then. "If only we could have a church, too," she murmured.

Mrs. Dahlberg smiled knowingly. "Well, we have August Peterson," she thought, "but I better not say anything."

Thirty Eight

By late April ice had broken in the Leaf River, pussy willows had emerged, and the air had just a hint of the warmth to come. Robins came, singing of nest building with joy. Soft purple hypaticas came, lifting their pungent sweetness out of the dank green moss. Green buds appeared everywhere.

One sparkling spring morning a man came to Thomastown. Anna watched him come, and heard him singing, down the sandy lane to her log house. The children saw him too.

"Look Mama! He's barefoot, carrying his shoes and a big black book! And he's singing!"

> *"Tryggare kan ingen vara,*
> *An Gud's lilla barnaskkara,*
> *Stjarnan ej pa himlafastet,*
> *Fageln ej i kandanastet"*
> (Children of the Heavenly Father
> Safely in His bosom gather
> Nesting bird not star in heaven
> Such a refuge ever was given)

His rich baritone reverberated through the white pines.

"Mama! He's singing the song you taught us!" shouted Alice as she stood in the open door. Mama was in the yard planting seeds.

"*God dag*, Madam," the man spoke in Swedish, reaching out his hand as he placed his shoes on the grass. "My name is Sandell. I am a preacher of the Gospel."

"What?" thought Anna, hesitant to extend her hand to this stranger. "A preacher in blue overalls and barefoot?" But then she looked into his face. He had a singular aura surrounding him, something indescribably gentle, happy, and holy. She saw his Swedish Bible under his arm, thinking now, "Ah, yes, he is a man of God!"

Their handshake was cordial and firm. Anna noticed that his hand was hard and rough, not like the soft hand of Pastor Svendson in Willmar.

"I have come to invite you and your family to a Gospel meeting on Sunday, over at August Peterson's barn," he said with a broad smile, bowing graciously. "Will you come?"

"Oh, yes, thank you. I want to come, if my husband permits it."

"Will he not come himself?"

"I think not. Lars is a good man but he does not like church."

"I will pray for him, and that he will come. August told me Mr. Kristoferson did most of the work on his barn. He has only praise for him."

Anna beamed. She loved to hear Lars praised. And she was so grateful for Sandell's prayer. Hope began to grow in her heart, a hope that now everything would be different.

"With God all things are possible," Sandell assured her as he took his leave. "By the way," he called back gaily, "Excuse my bare feet! I need to save my shoes for Sunday. *God dag, Fru* Kristoferson!"

All week Anna had but one thought, one plan, and one prayer - that they would ALL go to the service in August's barn. While she prayed, she worked hard to prepare for the coming special day. She washed and mended their best clothes, then ironed them with the irons she had brought all the way from New York. On Saturday she baked a plain cake, sprinkled with sugar and cinnamon. Everyone would bring something to share for the dinner following the meeting in the barn.

On Sunday morning Anna woke before dawn. She could not sleep, for she did not have Lars' promise that he would go with them. He'd not answered her when she had asked him a few days ago. That, she reasoned, might be a good sign. He had not said "no."

When the sun rose she dressed quickly and came softly into the kitchen to read her Bible while the coffee and oatmeal cooked. Then she awakened the children to tell them breakfast was ready and laid out their clothes. She looked into the bedroom. Lars was still fast asleep, and her heart sank. It was not that getting there would be a problem, for it was less than a mile to August's farm. They could walk. But Lars, "Oh, God," she prayed, "Perhaps the desire of my heart was too much to ask…but please, please cause him to want to come with us."

Sitting at the breakfast table she realized the children might have dressed too early. They might get all mussed up. Just then, as Anna was feeling anxious and a little irritated with Charley, who did not want to sit on the bench with Alma and play games, she heard the bedroom door open. Lars emerged, with his best trousers on and his clean white shirt on his arm! "Glory be to God!"

He was going to put on his best shirt after he washed in the basin by the pump. He smiled a 'good morning' to his wife and children but said nothing.

"Thank you, Lars!" Anna glowed up at his tall figure.

"*Tack*? For what, my darling?"

"For going with us to church."

"Who said I was going? Or that we are going to church? I thought we were going to a barn, one that I built with my own hands."

"Well, it's the same thing."

"No, it's not. Sandell is no *prast*. Nils Erickson told me he won't go because it is a sin for Sandell to preach. That's what made me decide to come. I like Sandell. He's a good man."

"You know him then?"

"Ja, he came to my woods, special to see me. How about that? A simple man with overalls? He helped me fell trees for a couple of hours. Didn't look a bit like a *prast* to me. So I said to myself, maybe I'll go hear that man."

"Oh, Lars, I am so happy!"

"But don't count on me to change any of my ideas," he warned.

Nearly all the Swedish settlers had arrived at August Peterson's barn, sitting erect on clean new benches. Nils Erickson and a few others had stayed away because Sandell was not properly ordained; he was a man like themselves, unfit to teach the Word of God.

Except for August, the men did not often think about God. They believed He was up in Heaven. They felt that He watched them, judged them, and punished them. So it was better not to dwell upon the idea of God. They swore and drank whiskey as they told their jokes, except when women were present. Oh, it would be nice if a real *prast* could come by once in awhile to give them forgiveness in the Sacrament of the Altar, and be present in the crossroads of life - baptizing the babies, marrying the young folks, and conducting funerals. Yes, it would be nice to hear a prayer read once or twice a year. But Sandell?

"We only came because, besides work, there's not much to do up here in the woods," a woman was explaining to Anna as she sat next to her on a bench, "but we don't think Sandell has authority to preach."

Looking around, Anna noticed that everyone was laughing and visiting. She reflected that if this were a church and Sandell were a real *prast,* there would be reverent silence. Nevertheless she expected something good to happen today.

Sandell began by singing some hymns, while accompanying himself on his small stringed instrument. Anna had never seen one like it before, nor had she ever heard a man sing with such a beautiful voice, and glowing with joy as he sang. He sang some gospel songs translated from English, and then he sang some old Swedish hymns. His final song was one of Anna's favorites: *"Jag har en venn som alskar mig."*

> *"I have a Friend who loveth me,*
> *He gave His life on Calvary,*
> *Upon the cross my sins He bore,*
> *And I am saved forevermore."*

The effect of the singing was electric. Tears began to flow. Strong men bowed their heads. Now Sandell was ready to preach.

First he prayed, simply and softly: "Father, in Jesus' name I'm asking you to touch my lips, and to touch the hearts of the dear people gathered here. Glory to the Father, and to the Son, and to the Holy Spirit. Amen."

"Amen," echoed August fervently.

Then Sandell, his face radiant, lifted the black *Bibelen.* He turned to the first chapter of John's Gospel, which he read in its entirety. Anna thought his penetrating, earnest, and sonorous tones sounded every bit like he was a real *prast.* Goosebumps of solemn awe rose up her arms and down her spine. Even the children sat still and listened.

Sandell expounded for an hour on the meaning of the text. Sandell's voice rose in deep fervor. Every eye was upon him. Many became aware for the first time of a profound inner longing they could not explain.

"My dear friends," the lay preacher was saying, "The hunger that you have is not for earthly food. It is for the Word of God. It is for

Jesus Christ. He is the Bread of Life. He is the light of God sent to shine into our hearts."

"But the darkness comprehended it not," he quoted from the Bible. "Oh, my friends! In verse 12 we find out how we CAN comprehend Him, how His light will expel our darkness, how we are forgiven and cleansed of all our sins, how we can know Him as our own Savior and Lord." In a hushed voice he read John 1: 12: "But to as many as received Him, to them gave He the power to become the sons of God, even to those who believe on His name."

Sandell paused. Then his voice rose in crescendo. "Is it enough that we have received the sacraments? No, my dear brothers and sisters in Christ. We have read that only those who receive Him can become CHILDREN OF THE HEAVENLY FATHER.

Sandell was becoming more and more fervent, his voice reverberating into the very rafters of the barn. Grandma Dahlberg sat on the edge of her seat, her black shawl wrapped around her shoulders, her wrinkled face transformed in a vision of rapture.

"Is it enough that we are good and decent folks? No my friends. For the Bible says our righteousness is like filthy rags. We are saved only by God's infinite grace, given to us freely in Jesus. Only the blood of God's Son can wash away your sins and mine."

Sandell explained, "Salvation is a gift we can receive by an act of our will." He began to weep as he pleaded with the settlers to repent of their sins. His voice broke with compassion as he gave 'the invitation'.

"My friends, how many of you will come now to receive God's Gift? Is the burden of your sin too heavy to bear? How many will say yes to Jesus?"

Many came forward to pray with Sandell that day. They came earnestly, with tears of repentance. All of the Dahlbergs came forward. Anna came, and the children with her. Lars sat alone on a bench on the men's side. "I will wait and see," he was thinking, "I must consider this carefully. It may be only an emotional thing. But does it have foundation and substance? Is God real? I must find out for sure."

After the service, there was much rejoicing as the settlers shared the food that they had brought. They ate outside on the fresh green grass, sitting around the long tables improvised with boards and saw horses. It was a day of new beginning, a day long to be remembered.

August had finished their house and winter was over. His wife had come up from Minneapolis on the train. As she was a tuberculosis patient, August had worried that living in a cold, unfinished house might be too much for her.

"She looks so pretty and sweet, doesn't she, Anna?" Lena whispered.

"And she has such a lovely hat," Anna added, noting the Milan straw bonnet with its bright pink flowers.

"She's thin but doesn't look sick," another woman observed, "such pink cheeks too."

Suddenly Anna was overwhelmed with sadness. She remembered her beautiful young mother, that her pink cheeks were a symptom of tuberculosis.

August looked at his wife with tender concern for her well being. He put his arm gently around her shoulders. "Dearest, I'm sure people will understand if you go in to rest now."

"I'm having too much fun. But yes, I am tired and need to be careful for your sake, my darling," she agreed, and went in the back door of their house.

"Why does Mr. Peterson look so worried?" Alma, who had become a sensitive teenager, wanted to know.

A direct answer is best, thought Anna. "Because she has tuberculosis, a disease from which only a few people recover."

It was nearly milking time. Saying goodbye always took awhile - the lingering handshakes, the compliments, and the refusal to accept compliments by saying, "It is nothing," all the familiar Swedish rituals that must be observed.

Thirty Nine

August assured everyone that there would be another sermon the following Sunday. On Wednesday evening a Bible study and prayer meeting would be held at his home for all who had received Christ.

Anna was eager to go. She and the children walked to August's that day, carrying a lantern. While Sandell taught the adults in the parlor, August's wife, Elise, taught the children, sitting around the kitchen table.

It was late spring before Sandell was to have his last meeting. After that, August's new barn would be used as a home for the cows he had recently purchased.

Nearly all of the settlers had responded to God's call, repenting of their sins and receiving Jesus Christ as Savior and Lord. For many, the change was dramatic. No more whiskey. No more tobacco. No more profanity. No more ribald stories. Instead, the Swedish immigrants were starting to read the Bible themselves and learning to pray in their own simple words. The men were learning to lead their families in daily worship. Sandell had taught them that each husband and father was a priest in his own home. It was his responsibility to teach his children the Word of God, a task not to be left only to the women, or even to the clergy.

Still, Lars had not yet responded. One day, Nils Erickson came over to visit him.

"Oh, my, Mr. Erickson looks angry," sighed Anna, shooing the children out to play. Lars was relaxing in his rocker with his shoes off. It had been a long day in the woods

"I'm tired, Nils," he warned his contentious neighbor, "and I don't care anything about discussing your religion."

"Vel, I see you are direct, Lars. I didn't come to fight with you. Actually, I'd hoped you and I might agree."

"How so?"

"You see, I'm the only one not going to Sandell's meetings, and you are the only one going but not getting converted."

"Why don't you go, Nils? You have nothing better to do."

"Why do you go, Lars? You told me before you never go to church doings."

"I like Sandell. So I say, why not give the man a fair hearing?"

Nils' face was red and his thin lips trembled. "Now I'll tell you something. I don't know if I like Sandell or not, but the fact is I won't go anywhere to listen to a heretic, and I won't let my wife go either."

"Tell me, Nils, are you a Christian?"

Lars' sudden question made Nils bristle. Bolting upright, his face livid, he shook his workworn fist in Lars Kristoferson's face. "Nobody better say I'm not a Christian! I'm as good as my word. And I provide for my family too. And haven't I been baptized and confirmed by the State Church of Sweden?" Lars smiled while Nils took a breath.

"And furthermore," Erickson continued, "I take my religion seriously. I'll have you know I'm trying to see if we can get a real *prast* to come up here once in awhile to baptize the babies and give us the sacrament…one who wears a black robe and a white ruffle…one who has white hands because he spends all his time studying those big church books! We need the prayers of such a one when we are about to die!"

Nils finally stopped, for he was quite out of breath. Lars tried to keep from chuckling. The contrast between Sandell and this man was so obvious to him.

Well, Nils, I'm not a religious man, as I already told you. But thanks for coming over."

"Would you like some coffee?" Anna asked this question of every guest.

Nils declined. His face still florid, he bowed respectfully to Anna, and stomped out the door.

"I wonder what is the matter with him," Lars mulled over as he rocked. "Do you understand his concern with Sandell, dear?"

"Yes, I do. But he is wrong."

Erickson's remarks made Lars more interested in that last Sunday meeting than he had ever been before. Several times Anna had caught him reading from the big family Bible, looking up all the passages Sandell had preached on.

She said nothing, but rejoiced in her heart. "It is true, just as Sandell said, Lars is an honest seeker." She prayed that God would save him, soon, perhaps this Sunday.

That last Sunday turned out to be a rainy day. Even so, the barn was so crowded it would have been impossible for anyone to come to the front when Sandell gave the invitation.

Lars sat at the very back of the barn on the men's side. "Maybe he is sitting there just so he can lean against the wall," Anna whispered to Alma. She secretly feared he might be avoiding the preacher's piercing blue eyes. After all, he was the only one who had not yet responded.

Sandell began by praising God for the revival, and for the presence of the Holy Spirit in their midst, a presence that could be sensed by everyone as a hush fell over the congregation. The soft sound of weeping could be heard amongst them. There were many cries of "Glory to God!" "Jesus be praised" and "Amen!" as Sandell raised his voice in fervent praise and intercession.

Many stood to testify about works of God they had experienced. "Are there any others?" Sandell invited.

To Anna's wonder she glanced back to see Lars slowly rising from the bench on which he had been sitting, all hunched over. Every eye was upon him, and the silence was broken only by the soft patter of rain. Dahlberg and a few other close friends were apprehensive about what the forthright agnostic might have to say. Anna, however, saw the radiance in his face and knew she would not be disappointed.

"Now I must tell you something not even my wife has realized," Lars began slowly. "For me this has been a week of wrestling with God. And now, like Jacob of old, I can say I have seen the Lord and my soul is saved!" Lars was overcome with emotion and his tears were contagious. Few eyes remained dry when Lars had finished the account of his spiritual pilgrimage.

"I always used to say I doubted whether we could know if there is a God. I thought we could never be sure. The rituals of the church were meaningless to me, so I avoided them. I was proud in my sin, for I saw myself as a good man who did not need a Savior.

"But God slowly opened my eyes...eyes that were blind. I saw, with horror, all the sin and evil in me. Like David I can say, my sin is ever before me. Then I saw the cross and the terrible suffering of Jesus. It was like a picture placed before me as I was felling a tree in the woods. I saw His pain...and I saw in His eyes patience and love. As I leaned upon my ax, I realized that the one on the cross was God, and it was my sin He was bearing. I just said two words to Him: JESUS! MY SAVIOR! I wanted to say more, but I was dumb. I fell on my knees in weakness. I am a changed man, my friends. I have been born again!"

Anna wept with joy as they sang a hymn.

After the meeting, she hugged Lars tightly, unable to contain her joy. "Oh, Lars, why didn't you tell me before telling all the others?"

"I had to take a public stand before I could say I am a Christian. Can you understand, my dearest? The Bible says I must "confess with my mouth the Lord Jesus." To assembled folk. Not just to you alone, for you and I are one.

"I understand. And I love you more than ever."

The next morning Lars said he would not go to the woods until the whole family had breakfast together. Just as Charley grabbed his little spoon and thrust it into the oatmeal Lars spoke - gently, and with that same quiet authority he had always had in his home. When their papa spoke the children listened and obeyed out of love for him. And so now it was not hard for them to sit still when he prayed. It was a long prayer and the oatmeal was getting cold. Perhaps Papa was trying to make up for all the years when he had said no prayers at all or read to his family from God's Book. Now it would be different.

"Will you dear ones ever be able to forgive me? For I have not been a good husband and father." Papa's voice broke.

"You have so!" little Alice protested, "You are the best Papa in the whole world!"

"I have missed the most important part of all," Lars explained, "for I have not led my dear ones in the ways of the Lord."

It was a day of new beginnings, for Jesus Christ had come to live with the Kristofersons.

Anna's eyes were glistening with gratitude to God. "You have answered all my prayers! May your Name be praised!" She prayed softly.

Following Lars' conversion, it seemed to Anna and the children that "all things were made new," that the whole family was transformed. There was a new sense of love, tranquility, and appreciation for the simple joys of life. Especially precious was the new, fulfilling intimacy for Lars and Anna. They experienced a new dimension in their love. They became one in a way they had never known, one in the Holy Spirit. Anna felt for the first time that Lars truly understood her needs and the deepest desires of her heart.

Sandell stayed around for a few days after his last meeting. Much of his time was spent helping Lars fell trees in the woods. A special bond had grown between the two men.

"Lars, the Lord has laid His hand upon you," Sandell prophesied, you will teach the Word of God to others. You will be 'strong in the Lord and in the power of His might'. Oh, yes, my dear brother, if you will be faithful to the vision He has given you, He will bless the work of your hands and everything you do."

As Sandell spoke these words Lars felt an overpowering realization of God's presence. He was filled with the 'new wine' of the Spirit...joy, peace, and an overflowing love for the Lord that was spilling out in an amazing concern for others. For some reason he was thinking about Nils Erickson.

"Sandell, we need to call on Nils Erickson. He is mixed up and hurting."

"Have I met him?"

"He wouldn't come near you. Said you had no right to preach. Would you be willing to call on this man?"

"Of course. Let's go this evening."

Nils and his wife, Inga, were sitting on their front porch in the long June twilight. "*Valkommen*, Lars. Who have you brought along?"

"This is Sandell, the lay preacher."

"What? When you know how I feel?"

"I come as a friend," Sandell said with disarming graciousness.

"I suppose you want to know why we didn't go to August's barn." Nils peered at Sandell through half-closed lids.

"I'm sure you have your reasons. I am not offended, my friend."

"Well," Nils sighed, somewhat relieved that Sandell was not going to scold him. "Sit down."

"I'll make the coffee," Inga offered, disappearing into the house.

They talked pleasantly for awhile about the weather, the price of seed and flour, common and mundane concerns. Inga brought the coffee and inquired politely about Anna and the children.

"Enough of this," thought Sandell, remembering why they had come.

"Lars," he began, "why don't you tell about the wonderful thing that happened to you this week?"

"What happened, Lars? Did you get a new cow?"

"Well, that too as a matter of fact. The Dahlbergs gave us a cow. But something else happened far better than that."

"Well, go on." Erickson was curious.

"I found Jesus. I mean, He found me."

"Lars, are you crazy?"

Lars went on to explain that he was in his right mind and quite serious. He told the whole story, just as he had in August's barn that Sunday.

Nils was speechless with rage, his fists clenching in his lap, his mouth working nervously. "Why did Lars' good news make you angry?" Sandell asked.

"Because it is all wrong!" Nils shouted. "He is crazy to listen to you, How dare you pretend to be a priest? By what right? Who sent you?"

"God sent me, my friend. And I don't pretend to be a priest. No, indeed. I'm a farmer, just a simple lay preacher, telling the good news of salvation through Christ."

"That's what bothers me."

"I don't understand. What is it that troubles you, my friend?"

Erickson then went on to tell him that he needed a priest, but that only a true priest of the Church of Sweden would do.

"My dear friend, is it your sin that troubles you?" Sandell came right to the point, but there was such an aura of concern and kindness in his voice that Nils did not feel threatened.

"I went to the doctor in Staples because I had chest pains and spells of gasping for air. He told me my heart is failing and I might not have long." Nils began to weep. "Now you understand why I need the priest to come. I need the forgiveness of my sins in the Sacrament! And I'm angry because you are here - a pretender, and no good at all." Now Erickson was sobbing uncontrollably.

Sandell spoke gently, as to a troubled child. "I am going to pray for you, Nils, but first I want you to be still and listen to some things you should know."

"First of all, I am not against the Church or the sacraments. The sacraments are a 'means of grace', sort of like packages into which God puts His gifts. But what if we receive only the wrappings and never His gift, Jesus? And whoever said the only way to receive God's gift is by a priest delivering the sacraments? The Bible does not say this. And Martin Luther himself said, "MAN NEEDS ONLY JESUS CHRIST.""

Sandell placed an arm gently around his drooping shoulders, "My dear friend, Nils, Jesus is the only one who can wash away our sins. Come to Him for forgiveness. Will you pray with me now?"

"Ja," was his barely audible answer.

As they knelt on the floor of the porch, the angels rejoiced, for Nils Erickson was born into the Kingdom of God.

Forty

After the evening meal Papa told everyone to sit still. He took the Swedish Bible down from its shelf beside the clock and began to read. He read Isaiah 55, Psalm 1, and chapter 2 of John. Then he said a few words about what he had read, adding "I feel like a child just learning to walk...for I have so much to learn from God's Word, having neglected it for so many years."

He asked if Mama or one of the children had something to say.

Anna almost whispered, out of a heart touched with wonder. "I thank God for all of you dear ones, and especially, that He has offered us all salvation."

Alice exclaimed, "I love Jesus!"

"We do too!" Betsy and Hilda chimed in.

After Lars' heartfelt prayer Anna took her hymnal and led the family in a hymn sing, a custom that would continue throughout all the years ahead. They sang the dear old Swedish hymns; Anna still had her clear soprano voice. She was surprised to hear that Lars had a good singing voice too.

"Lars! I've never heard you sing before!" she exclaimed in amazement.

"I never had a song before. But now, God has put His song in my heart!

Anna was proud of her small garden. She spaded a patch of rich mulched earth on the side of the log house, and then planted her potatoes, carrots, onions, beans, and peas.

The older girls, Alma and Annie, helped their mother with everything. And Emma did too, when she returned from Willmar after the school year ended.

It was a monumental day when Emma, who had been missed so indescribably, arrived in Staples by train. The whole family had squeezed into the lumber wagon behind Prince and Pet on that special day.

"Emma must see us all the minute she looks out the train window!" shouted Hilda resolutely.

"What if Prince won't go fast enough? And what if Pet can't?" Annie wondered as they jogged and jostled slowly through the mud and jagged stumps.

After what seemed like an eternity, the horses and wagon made it to the depot.

The train from Willmar had already arrived and the Conductor was helping a stylish young lady to the platform.

"My, but Emma looks so grown-up!" Annie cried with deep emotion.

"Such a grand lady!" echoed her Papa, noting the fine clothing. She wore clothes he could not afford to buy.

Squeals, tears, hugs and kisses descended upon Emma. For an ecstatic moment nothing else mattered except that Emma had come home and the family was once more complete.

After the initial excitement, a strained silence pressed itself into the crowded lumber wagon. In some way, Emma seemed almost like a stranger.

"So Annie began, a bit primly, "Aren't you going to miss all that refinement and culture?"

"Silly sister!" Emma laughed, "I love Mrs. Stafford but all the nice things she gave me can't even compare with being with my family again. I missed you!"

It wasn't long before she seemed like the same Emma they had always loved. Before they arrived back at the log house they almost forgot she had ever been gone. The ride home seemed short because they had so much to talk over.

Emma felt at home in the humble log house right away. And the change in her Papa, since his conversion, was immediately apparent to her. She herself had made a commitment to the Lord Jesus, and was studying the Bible with Mrs. Stafford every day. Lars was amazed at the scriptural knowledge Emma had acquired. "Now we can learn together," he told her, "and you can help me."

The three older girls stuck together, and sometimes kept secrets from the younger ones. Alma, Annie, and Emma were now young ladies, with the interests of young ladies - sitting with needlework or a book, wearing their long hair upswept with pretty combs, pondering the changes in their adolescent bodies. Anna watched them one afternoon as they sat engrossed in quiet conversation, thinking wistfully that in a few more years they might be married, with children of their own, living in their own homes. A sadness enveloped her, for she wondered how they were to find suitable Christian husbands in this wilderness.

Betsy was only two years younger than Emma but she was small for her age. She was ten years old and stuck close to Hilda, the family 'tomboy'. Little Alice tagged along with them, a five year old trying to appear older than she was. Of course all the girls competed for a chance to take care of their only brother Charley, a two-year-old who was enormously loved. He toddled curiously around the yard in delighted indifference, oblivious that someone was always watching that he should not fall into the creek or get lost in the woods.

It was a busy summer. The girls worked faithfully with their mama to harvest and 'put up' food for the winter. They dried peas and beans in the sun. They picked baskets of wild berries...pincherries, raspberries, chokecherries, and blueberries. Anna made all the jam she could with her limited supply of sugar. Many of the sweet berries were made into 'sauce', sealed in the Mason jars she had brought from Willmar, using the new rubber rings she had bought in town the day they went to get Emma.

In the fall potatoes would be dug up and put in the cellar, and turnips and carrots preserved in sand filled crocks. This must all be done before the first heavy frost. Summer squash was eaten almost daily, but the Hubbard squash would go into the cellar for winter eating.

There were a few eggs to gather. Just as she had promised, Mrs. Dahlberg had given them four laying hens. One was a setting hen, with the expectation of a brood of tiny chicks. The generous Dahlbergs had also given them a milk cow. Lars promised he would build a cupboard for Mrs. Dahlberg to thank her for the cow.

The summer table was laden with good things - cheese, milk and butter, new potatoes creamed with peas, and fresh, hot blueberry pie with their coffee. Mrs. Stafford had taught Anna how to bake a pie, that peculiarly American culinary art. "Why didn't they ever think of that in Sweden?" Anna wondered.

Many times a day Anna thanked the Heavenly Father for the abundance of good things they enjoyed. She was especially thankful for the good health with which all her family had been blest. "Ah, yes," Anna said to God, "I will not forget your benefits. I will try to remember them all!"

"Are we rich folks?" Alice queried out of the blue one day as the girls walked down the lane looking for pincherries.

"I don't know," Hilda answered quickly, "I'll ask Papa,"

"Course we're not rich folks," Betsy interjected, wondering where Alice had heard such an expression. "Whatever does that mean, anyway?"

"Silly," Hilda declared confidently, "it means folks who have everything they want."

"We have everything we want." Alice answered her own question. Then the three played a game of naming all the things their family had.

"We've berries and jam."

"Butter and cream."

"Our log house looks pretty."

"Plenty of rain for Mama's garden."

"Pet and Prince and the wagon."

"And the brook to take baths in."

"With willow curtains so nobody can see."

When they returned home with baskets of pincherries, Alice asked the question again. "Mama, are we rich folks?"

Anna explained that real riches come from God, who gives us all we need, and that the most important riches God gives are not 'things' at all. Instead, they are the gifts of His love and salvation. She glowed as she reminded them of the revival meetings. God had sent Sandell to their settlement and now they all had Jesus in their hearts, even Papa.

"Yes, I would say we are rich folks, little Alice," her mama smiled.

After Sandell had left, Sunday school and services were held in the homes of the Swedish settlers and in the new log schoolhouse on the Klodt farm. Lars was teaching the scriptures. God had given him choice gifts, to learn quickly, to speak with clarity, and to recall everything he had learned from the Word of God. He was surprised to discover he could remember even hidden and unused treasures stored in his mind since childhood. He had been taught by a Godly mother.

There were many prayer meetings, which included a brief Bible study. They knelt beside their chairs or benches, each praying aloud in Swedish. They would pray about all the concerns of their difficult lives in the northern wilderness...the sickness of a child...a family in need of food...someone discouraged. Often they would confess their sins to

God, and also to one another…"Forgive me, my sister, I spoke harshly to you."

"Forgive me my brother, I acted in haste."

One day August received a letter telling the new Christians in Thomastown that a Pastor Sjodahl was coming to see them about organizing a church.

Pastor Sjodahl was a gentle man. He disliked controversy. He explained that he was affiliated with a movement known as "The Covenant," or "The Mission Friends."

"What do you hold on baptism?" Erickson wanted to know.

"I hold my tongue," Sjodahl asserted simply. "Our creed is Christ and our foundation is the Word of God. I can say with Paul that I am determined not to know anything among you but Christ and He crucified."

Soon the new church building was raised on a site beside the Leaf River. Lars was in charge of the construction, and he did most of the work himself. Others dedicated a few hours of their time each day and the work progressed rapidly.

"Just as our faith has a firm foundation, so must this building," Lars insisted. Stones were laboriously carried from the riverbed and cemented carefully together. Upon this solid foundation the simple edifice was erected.

At last the little church was formally dedicated to the glory of God. Dawn rose in the east with a dress of splendor and sparkled gold upon the river. Excitement filled the air as the settlers assembled in their new churchyard. Some came in horse-drawn wagons and some came on foot. Handshakes were cordial, and soft laughter rippled over the gathering congregation.

It was a day of hope. It was a day in which to give thanks to God for His gift of eternal life. It was a day to savor the bonds of love into which God had united them. Their individual lives were inexorably intertwined in worship, in toil, in rejoicing, and in suffering.

Forty One

Christmas Eve had come to the frozen northland and to the cozy log house beside Willow Brook. Betsy and Hilda snuggled deep into the featherbed, in a space between the fireplace and the big cupboard Papa had made years before. Mama had tucked them in there because they had colds and it was chilly in the loft. With excited whispers they recalled the wonders of this night. They relived Papa's reading of the Christmas story from the old Swedish Bible and his earnest praise for the Gift that had come to us in the manger. They could see the tree in the center of the room, fragrant and resplendent in the moonlight. They remembered the taste of melted butter on transparent lutfisk, and of exquisitely sweet *julakaka* and brown beans.

"Wasn't it good?" Hilda smacked deliciously.

"And the new red mittens were nice too," ventured Betsey wistfully, "even though I did long for a doll."

"Betsy! You feel hot!" Hilda touched her sister's face.

"And I don't feel so good either," Betsy whined softly.

Soon Mama was up and stirring the fire. She held a candle to Betsy's flushed face, caressing it tenderly with her hand. Betsy was indeed sick.

Bright candlelight illuminated the silhouette of the horse they visualized in the wooden grain of Papa's pine cupboard. This amazing *hasten* had been the subject of many stories and dreams as the children lay in this special bed. Hilda had imagined that a horse magically arose out of the grain of the wood on special occasions. He was gentle, with enormous blue eyes and a soft, tawny mane. An aura of subdued light surrounded him like the warm glow of fire on a winter night. Hilda told Betsy that he sometimes let her sit on his sloping back and hold his long silky mane. Then he would rise mysteriously into the night, taking her for a ride over the whole earth. The younger children loved to hear these stories.

"Tell me a *hasten* story - now, please," Betsy begged in her small, parched voice.

"Well, he's *Julehasten* now," Hilda explained. "Maybe he will be in your dreams if you go to sleep right now."

As Betsy slept her fever climbed. Mama was very worried. She woke Papa and sent Hilda upstairs. Through the long hours they sat with Betsey, applying cold cloths and bitter poultices, as they continually prayed.

At four o'clock the fever broke. Betsy opened her eyes and smiled.

"I'm not sick anymore," she announced brightly. "*Julehasten* let me sit on his back. Then we flew through the stars, right up to Heaven."

Her mama and papa exchanged worried glances. Was their precious child delirious? Could this be a preparation for her death? God, have mercy!

"Don't worry, Mama and Papa," she reassured, "Jesus made me well. He touched my hand. This is the best Christmas I ever had!"

Anna felt Betsy's forehead again and put her ear to her heart.

"Oh…" her child murmured.

Startled, Mama cried, "What is wrong, my pet?"

"Nothing…only I forgot to ask Jesus for my doll,"

Papa sighed. There were so many things he could not provide for his little ones.

Then Betsy laughed. Papa and Mama laughed too - a soft, thankful, joyous kind of laugh. Papa folded his hands and thanked God for making Betsy well in answer to their prayers. He also gave thanks that they would now be able to attend *juotta* in the little country church.

The clear, magnificent, star-filled sky held a special meaning for Betsy, as she lay snuggled down under the fur robe in the sleigh. The bells on the horses were rippling chimes of joy and praise. As they neared the church they could see candles burning brightly in every window, reflecting gold upon the new-fallen snow.

The Kristofersons arrived just in time to sing ALL HAIL TO THEE OH BLESSED MORN and to see freshly cut balsam tree with its myriad of twinkling candles.

The Pastor spoke in a gentle voice. He told of how the candlelight represents Jesus Christ, who is the worlds only true light. He read the beloved and ever wondrous story of Christ's birth from the Gospel of Luke. Then he preached on the theme, "God gave His Son for us all. Shall He not, with Him, give us freely everything we need?"

After singing "*Stille natt, Hellige natt,*" (Silent Night) the handshaking began. There were warm wishes of 'God Jul' for everyone - friends, neighbors, and one stranger whom nobody seemed to know. He was a kindly man, with a package under one arm. When Mama cordially shook his hand, he placed the box in her arms.

"This is for Betsy," the stranger explained in Swedish, "Someone asked me to give it to her." Mama was so surprised she forgot to ask his name, and he was gone before she could say "*Tack sa mycket*".

"Now I wonder who did that," she puzzled as they jingled homeward in the sleigh. "Betsy, did you say anything when we were in the store last week?"

"No," smiled Betsy, who knew she wasn't supposed to ask for things. "But I think I know who sent it."

It was a beautiful baby doll.

Forty Two

One morning in early summer as Anna was punching down her batch of bubbly yeast bread, she observed that her Alma, her mischievous, sprightly little Alma, had grown into a beautiful and dignified young woman. She was only sixteen, but was already earnest, diligent, sensitive and caring.

Alma cared that her large family did not have suitable clothes, and that the younger children could not play outside in the winter because they had no overshoes. She worried about many things. Although Papa worked hard, there was never enough money to go around.

"Mama," Alma began, as they waited for the teakettle to boil, I heard about a family who needs a hired girl - two older sisters who live in Bullard."

"You are so young, Alma. We must talk to Papa about this."

"Oh, Mama, I want so much to help our family!"

"They would perhaps not be able to pay you much, dear child."

"I saw them in the store when I went with Papa. I asked them and they said that if I worked for them they would give you a cow."

"A cow! So you have it all arranged then?"

"Yes, Mama...if you and Papa consent. Their name is Gunn."

"I will talk to Papa tonight. But Alma! Wouldn't you be lonesome living with two old women?

"They are nice, Mama."

"My, my, our little Alma bringing us a cow?" Lars chuckled when Anna brought him the news. "And why not? Working outside the home builds character."

Anna worked for the kind but fussy old sisters faithfully for several weeks, and true to their promise, they presented the Kristoferson family with a cow. Now they had two cows!

While Alma worked for the Gunns, she was asked to sew some dresses for them. They were amazed to discover that Alma was such an accomplished seamstress. Word got around. Alma was asked by many to come to their homes to sew.

The first place she went was to the Klopfer family, German settlers across the Leaf River. Mr. Klopfer was a hard man, who spoke a little English - mostly brusque words. He was the lord of his small domain - wife, children, and farm animals. Alma was terrified of him, but she adored his shy, easy-to-please wife, who spoke only German except for a few English nouns and verbs. Along with her limited English, she communicated with smiles and body language. A loving rapport grew between the little seamstress and the mistress of the house.

Alma grew to love one of her sons as well, secretly at first. His name was William. He came in from the fields early one afternoon just so he could talk to Alma. They had fun telling amusing stories and innocent jokes. When William was around Alma almost forgot about how much she missed her lively, joyous family. However, the moment his father's strident feet could be heard stomping off mud and manure before entering the door, an uncomfortable aura descended upon the entire family.

They ate in silence, fearing that if one were to reveal his thoughts spontaneously, it would displease Father. He might even explode in rage. It was not worth taking the risk. Nevertheless, Alma's and William's romance blossomed.

All the sewing was finally finished. Lars was coming for Alma in the lumber wagon that very day. William realized that he must do something quickly - that he must say something that had been weighing on his mind since the day she arrived.

"Come, son," his father snapped laconically when breakfast was finished.

"I'll be with you in a few minutes, Father. Mother has asked me to help her move some furniture," William lied. But it could not be helped.

"Mother, I'm sorry," William apologized when his father had closed the door. "It was the only thing I could think of to say. I need to speak to Alma." His voice sounded desperate.

Frau Klopfer gave the two an understanding smile and went outside to feed the chickens.

Alma guessed what he was going to say but she looked strangely displeased.

"William, how could you lie like that to your father?" Alma stormed.

"You don't know my father!" He was defensive and hurt. He'd thought she would understand.

"And how can I marry a man who lies - even if I do love him?" she blurted, tears running down her cheeks.

"How did you know I was going to ask you to marry me?"

"Well, were you?"

"Yes. Will you?"

"Yes, oh yes William!"

They were in each other's arms, clinging hungrily to one another when the bells of Lars' horses sounded in the lane.

Mr. Klopfer hurried from the barn and helped Lars tether them.

"Come in, Kristoferson," he offered somewhat courteously, "and I will settle up what I owe you for the sewing."

"That is between your wife and Alma." Lars' direct blue eyes scanned Klopfer's stern face.

"The way I see it, it's between you and me."

Lars shrugged. No use to rock the boat of a man like that.

Alma hugged her papa warmly. "Oh, Papa, I've missed you so! Is everything alright at home?"

"Ja, daughter. God is good. We are all fat and happy as usual."

Mr. Klopfer scowled behind his pointy dark mustache. "These Swedes are unbelievable," he muttered to himself in German.

William's face was red and he looked as though he were about to explode. Love for Alma gave him the courage to speak.

"Mr. Kristoferson...sir," he began slowly, not daring to meet his father's gaze. Should he go on? In his father's presence? Should he wait for a better time? Or should he now, in this very moment, get everything out into the open?

"What do you want to say, William?" Lars' eyes were kind. William saw an accepting gentleness in them that gave him the strength to plunge right in.

"I want to ask you for Alma's hand in marriage." William had said it! His words had become audible to both their fathers and he could not withdraw them now.

Lars noticed the shock and rage reflected in Klopfer's face. His big hands gripped his hayfork with an intensity that made his knuckles turn stark white. Emil Klopfer's mouth dropped open but he could not speak.

"Well, well, William," Lars answered gently, "suppose we accept your father's invitation and go inside and talk about this."

Klopfer's rage finally erupted in cold, measured words, spurting out with the short gaspings of his breath.

"How dare you, Kristoferson! I withdraw my invitation. You are not welcome in my home - you, or your daughter. You are never welcome! My son William will never marry a Swede. Go!" the angry father hissed, thrusting a five-dollar bill into Lars' hand.

Lars looked steadily into the steel gray eyes of his raging neighbor. "What will you do if he does not obey you, Klopfer?"

"I will beat him until he bleeds."

"If you do that you will answer to me...and to William." Lars spoke softly. Then he reached out his hand to the young man, whispering "Come to our house, William. We talk then."

Alma was trembling under the warm wool robe as the horses pranced down the lane. "Oh poor William," she said over and over, sobbing bitterly.

Her father put one arm around her shoulders, guiding the horses with the other one. "I can see that you love him," he said.

"Oh, yes, Papa. I really do love him...even though we have only had a chance to say only a few things to each other - on account of his father."

"Ja, I can see that his father is a very frightened man."

"Frightened? Him? It's more like everyone is frightened of him! Scared to death, I would say. And Papa, he just hates Swedes!"

"*Nei, da*, He's kind of like an animal defending his territory...like a little dog barking real loud so no one finds out he is a little dog."

"Well," said Alma, shuddering, "I still see him as a very dangerous dog!"

"I see him as a man who needs the Lord Jesus," Lars added, softly.

The very next evening, William came to call. Alma was overjoyed to see that he was still alive and able to walk. She wondered if there were wounds on his bare back, under his shirt, but she was too shy to ask. Finally she got up the courage to ask, "What did your father do, William?"

"Nothing. He hasn't spoken to me since. To him the subject is closed. Final. Never to be brought up again."

"Are you going to tell him you came over here?"

"Of course not."

"Are you going to lie then?"

"It would be easier."

"No, William, no."

"Don't worry. I always go for walks on nice evenings. Sometimes I swim in the river - or take my horse and ride. He won't ask. He doesn't want to know."

"How old are you, William?" Lars asked.

"Twenty three."

"You are a man, William. Your father knows he cannot force you to obey him," Lars counseled, "but he is afraid of losing you. He needs you. And he knows you are free to leave. Just as I was free to leave my father in Sweden. Just as your father left his father in Germany."

"I respect your wisdom, sir. Tell me, do you think I should leave my father's house?"

Lars paused to reflect. "Perhaps," he began slowly, "Perhaps you should think of your plans and goals. I can't tell you what to do, William. Only God can guide you."

The time had come for Lars to ask the most important question of all. "William, have you ever received Jesus Christ as your Savior?"

William looked puzzled. He wasn't sure what Lars meant by that question. He had never heard that expression before. Lars felt uncomfortable trying to explain the Bible in English to William. And it was no good to invite him to the little white church by the river, since the sermons were all in Swedish.

"Maybe the Methodist pastor in Staples can explain the gospel to you, William. He would have the Bible in English.

Lars and Anna felt sad they could not share with William the language of faith. They liked William very much, but neither of them was ready to give their blessing to a marriage. There was no hurry. After all, Alma was only sixteen.

William did not give up. All summer he came courting Alma without ever telling his father what he was up to. William loved Alma, and he loved her family. When he crossed the river and started up the dirt road to the log house he left a dark world of oppression and entered a world of light and joy...a world in which laughter bubbled up like a spring, and in which a harsh word was never permitted. Except for that one restriction, free speech was the abundantly exercised right of all. It didn't matter that most of the talk was in Swedish. William was even beginning to learn a little Swedish himself.

By fall everyone seemed to accept the fact that Alma and Will were to become engaged, everyone except the immovable Mr. Klopfer. Their love had overcome many obstacles - her youth, their language differences, and his lack of understanding of their faith in Christ.

Finally, after harvest, William summoned his innate bravery and told his father point blank that he intended to marry Alma. This time Mr. Klopfer was calm. He didn't even change his expression when he announced with finality, "Vilhelm, if you marry that Swede, you will no longer be part of my family. I will no longer have a son."

"Well, then," William asserted firmly, "I will make my own way." That was all that was said. William went into his father's house, packed his few belongings, and kissed his weeping mother.

"Where will you go, my son?" she sobbed.

"I think Mr. Kristoferson will let me move into his barn."

When William told Lars and Anna what happened they could not refuse to give their consent to a young man who was willing to give up everything for his love of Alma. Besides, they had grown to love William.

"He will be a good husband for our little Alma," Lars reasoned.

"But she is so young," worried Anna.

"No matter," Lars reasoned, "Alma is far older than her years. She will be a good wife."

"I couldn't love William more, even if he were a Swede," Anna considered, "but one thing troubles me. Do we know if he is *frelst* (saved)?"

"It troubles me too," admitted Lars, "and it troubles me that I have no English Bible to explain the way of salvation to William. I'll take William to Staples to visit Rev. Phillips, the Methodist pastor.

Rev. Phillips received Lars and William graciously. He was a true man of God, having been converted under the preaching of D.L. Moody. The Lord had prepared William's heart, for he listened attentively as the kindly pastor explained God's plan of salvation in Jesus Christ. He lovingly read the life-giving verses from his King James Bible.

Then the three of them knelt beside their chairs in the pastor's cheery study. William told God he realized he was sinner, and asked forgiveness in the name of Jesus Christ, who paid for all our sins on the cross. William wept as he cried out, "Jesus, please forgive me and take away the bitterness I have for my father!"

William arose with peace in his soul.

The marriage of William and Alma was celebrated on a sunny afternoon in December. Anna and her girls took great pleasure in decorating their sparkling clean log house with spruce and pine branches.

The bridal couple stood facing each other in their best clothing on Anna's prettiest rag rug. The fire burned brightly. Reverend Phillips faced them as he read solemnly the English vows from his little black book. William's brother, Emil junior, had come secretly to be his Best Man, while Alma was attended by Annie. The Dahlbergs and the Petersons were invited guests. After the ceremony Lars asked the pastor if he would mind listening to some Swedish hymns. "I'd be delighted," Pastor Phillips said with a wide smile.

Afterwards Anna served cake and open-face sandwiches with coffee. Everyone glowed with joy as they watched Alma and William.

The newlyweds were invited to live in the log house as they had no other place to go. "At least until spring," Lars promised, "then I will help you build a little house." William had saved enough to make a small down payment on forty acres north of the farm on which Lars was working so hard to develop.

"Let them have our bedroom, Lars," Anna pleaded, "and we will go upstairs with the children. It will only be a short time. Remember, they are 'honeymooners', as the Americans say. Remember how we were long ago?"

"Oh, was it long ago?" Lars teased, "My love, it seems like only yesterday!"

"You flatter me, Lars," she crooned gently, brushing his graying hair tenderly with her lips as he sat rocking.

"Lars, are you asleep?"

"Ja."

"I feel so sorry for William's mother. She wanted so much to come to the wedding. Sometime I will go over there and visit her when Mr. Klopfer is not there. I'll find out what day he takes the cream to town."

Lars and his new son-in-law spent the winter cutting trees in the forest and hauling them to the Staples mill to be cut into lumber. Two new homes must be built...Lars' large new home on his farm and a small home for Alma and William on the forty acres farther north.

Lars' first priority was to finish William's home.

"Anna, I'm so sorry. It seems that to finish your house always comes last - after August's barn, after the Church, and now a house for Alma and William."

"Lars, don't feel bad that I have to wait. I'll never forget how hard it was to share a house with another family. I don't want that for Alma and Will."

"Of course it is not the same as it was for us," commented her husband.

"Why not, Lars?"

"Because you are not like Svenborg," he laughed.

A spring thaw came early that year. Snow melted, flowing in rivulets through the ruts in the trail. Pussy willows lined the branches beside Willow Brook. White crocuses bloomed in receding patches of snow.

Lars and Will worked long days, and by the end of April they had finished a sturdy frame home for Alma. It had an airy living room across the front, and two rooms in the rear - one a kitchen, and the other, a bedroom. Upstairs there was a loft. Lars promised to finish that and to put a dormer window in when their first child was big enough to climb the ladder. Still to be finished was the outhouse, a shallow well, and a small barn for the animals Will would acquire.

Alma had not yet seen the house. Lars and William wanted to surprise her. They told her it was just a shanty made of sticks.

"Stop teasing her!" Anna ordered at last. "Otherwise, how is she going to get the curtains ready?"

"Well, there are five windows," Lars admitted.

"Five windows! Real windows?" gasped Alma in disbelief

"So?" her mother shrugged, "That means five curtains. You have to get busy, daughter."

The trouble was they had so little money. Lars had not sold many logs over the winter, since he was so busy helping William. Alma had a little money she had saved from her sewing, but she would need so many other things.

Her mother had an idea. She dug into her old Swedish trunk and found some lace she had made long ago, and she had saved several muslin flour sacks.

"Alma," she suggested, "why don't we make tops for the windows with this lace and muslin, and you can put pretty geraniums on the sills? That way you can see out better."

Alma thought that was a good idea. By moving day the curtains were ready, and they had also made some quilts and rag rugs for the floor.

The little house was more beautiful than Alma could ever have imagined. Will had plastered the walls a glowing white. Lars had planed the pine floorboards smooth and fine. There was a stone fireplace, and some neighbors had given them a small iron range for the kitchen. And the sink - with a pump right beside it! He had also built a table, with two benches. In the bedroom they had made a bedstead and filled a tick with straw.

"I love you both, and I thank you so much!" Alma said, weeping and hugging all at once. Never mind they had no furniture for the parlor. That would come later. The great wonder was the kitchen pump.

"How did you do it? A pump in the kitchen!" Alma was breathless.

"Will's land has water close to the surface," her father explained, "We just drove down a shaft and there it was."

After Alma and Will had gone to live in their own house, Anna often found herself crying with a loneliness she could not explain. Strong emotions and longings began to fill her heart. At the same time she was often taken with weariness after performing the simplest tasks. This was not like Anna. Lars began to worry.

"What is wrong, my love?" He inquired anxiously, "Where has my songbird been hiding?"

"I don't know, Lars. I tell myself it's because I miss Alma so much. But I think it may be something else."

"What is that?"

"That I am an old woman."

"Nonsense."

"Alma is a married woman. Grandchildren may be coming. I have begun the 'change of life'."

Lars gave her a hug of reassurance, "Don't forget, old woman, that I love you more than ever...and how come getting old makes you so beautiful?"

That brought a smile to Anna's face.

Forty Three

As the summer went by it became apparent to Anna that her problem was something far different than what she had thought. To her great surprise, a new life was again growing within her. When she felt the baby wiggle and squirm within her swelling form she felt young and happy again. She thought of a verse from the 103'rd Psalm: "He will renew thy youth like the eagles" - and she burst into song.

Lars heard her. "May God be praised! My songbird has returned!"

Lars worked on Anna's big new house all summer. He wanted so much to have it finished before the baby came, but this was not possible. When the last red maple leaf had fallen, ice formed a thin layer on top of the river.

One morning Anna peered through her tiny window at a world of shimmering white. Each twig wore a resplendent halo as the dawn crescended red in the east.

"Good thing Lars brought lots of wood into the lean-to last night. He is a good man."

Just then she felt a tiny relentless squeeze in the small of her back. She smiled knowingly.

"Ja, we shall see…could be a false alarm." Anna filled the coffeepot with water from the pail. Then she stirred up the coals and put kindling on top.

"Uff! Another one. When it comes to baby number eight, I should know. Shouldn't I?" She dropped the coffee scoop.

"Lars!" Her cry was loud and insistent.

Her husband leaped from the bed where he sat with his underwear on. Something in her tone made words unnecessary.

"Ja, Anna. I go for Mrs. Dahlberg." He dressed quickly, and giving his wife an encouraging hug, hurried to the door.

"No hurry, Lars. We have coffee first."

"I'd better go first. Then we have coffee."

She was starting to protest, but another squeezing pain stopped her. "Ja, go, Lars!"

174

Anna built up the fire, but she still shivered with cold. "December it is. No wonder I am cold." Then she remembered that same feeling before her summer babies were born.

The older girls were now up and helping Charley dress. Annie made the gruel and set the coffeepot back on the stove.

"Mama, please sit down," Emma pleaded. She had seen this before, and suddenly became frightened. "Mama, you will need all your strength!"

"It's all right Mama reassured, "The pain is not so bad, not yet. Best I should keep busy." She bit her lips as she fed the stove again. Then she sat down wearily.

"Maybe I'll have a little coffee now. Annie, I want you to take charge, and put the warmest wraps on everybody, especially Charley. Then I want all of you to walk over to Peterson's for the day. All but Emma. I need you with me, Emma."

Just as the children had started down the lane, Lars returned in the wagon with Mrs. Dahlberg.

Mrs. Dahlberg was herself again great with child and moved slowly but resolutely about the kitchen. She boiled water and made some chamomile tea for Anna. Then she dropped the scissors in a pan of hot water.

She snatched Anna's coffee away. "Not now, Anna. This tea is special for times like this. My sister learned it from an Indian woman."

"Mmm, I do think it helps," Anna agreed after a few sips. "Makes me warmer and more relaxed."

Between the pains they talked of many things, while Lars went out to do the chores.

"Soon you'll be helping me again, Anna. I'll be going through the same thing."

Anna managed a little laugh. "Well, Lena, it's not like we haven't been here before."

"Anna?"

"Ja?"

"You know I've been praying. God is the one we need to get us through this."

The possibility of childbed death lingered like an apparition in the dark room. Every woman knew of someone to whom this had happened. Many babies did not survive.

"Lord, let it go well," Lena whispered as she helped Anna into bed. She noticed that Lars had finished his chores and was kneeling beside

175

the big rocker in the corner. Emma knelt beside him as he cradled her small hand in his. They continued to pray with fervent faith, and then to sing the dear Swedish hymns until Mrs. Dahlberg emerged from the bedroom.

Lars studied her face. She was grave and pallid.

"Ja?"

"It's another girl, Lars. Anna is fine. The little one is blue and cold - but alive."

Lars bolted to Anna's side.

"Sh...don't wake her. She must rest."

Lars turned to the baby girl. "Oh, my, so small and blue. Yet, she is breathing. Praise God! He has given me faith she will live."

"Lars, I know what to do," Lena asserted capably, "Can you fix up a box for the baby with room for warm bricks? I will line it with flannel."

"I have such a box!" he answered. Quickly, they improvised a little incubator for little Ruth, as they decided to call her. And in a few days, she began to thrive.

Lars Kristoferson's dream was to build a fine house for his family, the finest house a poor man could build as he carved a place for himself in this wilderness of trees. For several years he had been clearing his land by the Leaf River - cutting down the pines with bare, scarred hands and hauling the logs to the sawmill in his old rusty wagon. Each time, he sold some and took the rest home transformed into lumber. Finally, he had gathered enough lumber to build his house.

Anna and the children helped him draw up the plans. He wanted this to be the 'family home', a center for the gathering of their loving circle - a circle in which Christ would always be the head.

After Lars had given his life to the Lord, it seemed that the work of his hands prospered as never before. The work on the new home progressed rapidly. There was always just enough money to buy the nails, plaster, and other things Lars needed.

In May another life had been added to the family. Alma and Will had a sweet little girl they named Clara. She was only a few months younger than little Ruth.

Carefully selecting and carrying the stones from the river had been hard and took Lars a long time. "Ja, the foundation is everything," he would say. Then he would give this thought a spiritual application.

"Children, build your lives on the Rock, Jesus Christ - or everything you do will crumble and fall like a poor foundation."

The new house rose grandly from the middle of the clearing. Lars worked on his house from sun-up until there was barely enough light to see. A sturdy roof must be in place before the heavy winter snow.

Windowpanes were bought a few at a time, wrapped carefully in rags so they would survive the bumpy wagon ride. There was a larger, more beautiful window for the parlor, a grand, special window with stained glass across the top.

"Oh, Lars, I will feel like a queen standing in the sunlight of my splendid window," Anna exclaimed, tears wetting her face.

Lars' long arms enfolded her. "Ja, just like the queen you have always been!" he chuckled. "You'll be standing in your window watching the chickens pecking in the grass."

"And then going out to gather the eggs," Anna added. They giggled for a moment like two silly children.

The thought of such a house did make Anna a little giddy - giddy with pride in her man, and with the joy that now she and the children would have a beautiful and proper home. She visualized lovely weddings in the parlor. And the Church Ladies Aid might meet there for quilting and coffee. There would be prayer meetings too, with a nice rug upon which to kneel.

"What an imagination I have!" Anna thought as she looked around her.

It was nearly Christmas, and they had just moved into their new house. Anna looked up at open beams and unfinished walls. She shivered in the early morning cold.

"Uff-da! Ice covers the wash basin!" she cried, "Where is the kindling? Oh well, it is better we should be here where Lars can work inside all winter...but I wouldn't be so cold in the log house."

Lars heard her mumbling as he came into the kitchen to build the fire. "Ja, but the log house was small with a low ceiling. This is a big house without insulation yet."

"Lars, you don't have to explain that to me," she exclaimed between chattering teeth, "I dreamed of this house, and when it is finished it will look just like my dream!"

"So much left to do," Lars sighed.

The fire in the kitchen range popped cheerfully as the coffee boiled and the ice in the basin began to melt. Anna and Lars now enjoyed their special, private closeness, coffee cups in hand and feet pressed against the oven door.

"Anna, did I ever tell you I wasn't sorry we got married?"

"Never, Lars," she teased.

"Well, I want you to know that all these years you have been everything to me."

"Next to Jesus?"

"Ja, next to Jesus…now He comes first." Lars reached for her hand. He could never know the depth of thankfulness her smile expressed, nor the depth of love for her husband. At last, the two had truly become one.

Soon the children awoke, shivering in their beds upstairs. Wrapped in woolen shawls, they raced downstairs, heading for the warmth of the radiant black stove.

Papa discreetly turned his head while the girls put on their long woolen underwear and struggled to pull their long black stockings smoothly over the underwear. "This is not easy," Alice observed, "especially when my fingers are all numb."

"And with my teeth ch…ch…chattering," Betsy complained, "I'm shaking so hard I can't dress, Mama. May I come to the table in my shawl?"

Mama laughed, and replied with an old Swedish proverb. "Things don't get better until the worst has passed." She added a little speech about patience and persistence, and not grumbling. By then everyone had warmed up a bit.

The oatmeal was cooked and the coffee was deliciously aromatic. As the family sat around their long table, covered with blue oilcloth, they reverently bowed their heads while Papa prayed. Bright sunshine filtered through the east window. On this day he prayed for "children's children yet unborn." Then he took the Swedish Bible carefully from its shelf and began to read Psalm 103. By the time Papa had finished his journey to the Throne of Grace they were amazed at how warm and cozy the kitchen had become.

After breakfast, each Kristoferson was imbued with enthusiasm for the day: Mama, for setting her bread; Papa, for his plastering; and the children, for their trek across the river to the Bullard school on the Klodt farm…that is, the four who went to school. Annie and Emma had finished their elementary education but it was out of the question for them to go to Staples to High School, ten miles away on a dirt trail. So Mama had lots of help in caring for Baby Ruth.

By Christmas the whole downstairs was nearly finished. Anna thought it looked very pretty. It was a fitting place into which Lars would bring the fresh green spruce from their woods on Christmas Eve.

Lars had taken great care with the polished oak floors, made of boards from sturdy oaks by the river. The shiny floors made Anna's parlor as splendid as Queen Victoria's, even with the old rag rugs. "Someday," Anna dreamed, "I will have a nice wool Oriental rug on the parlor floor, and a red velvet chair and settee."

Anna covered the table with a lace cloth. She opened the curtains so that the afternoon sun could stream through the stained glass window panel. The plastered walls sparkled white with newness. Some day they would be covered with paint or wallpaper. But for now she relished the clean, delicious fragrance of her brand new house, with the luxurious fir standing in the parlor.

Anna and Lars shared the fun of trimming the tree with the older girls. They would light the candles just before the little ones came downstairs to behold the awesome, resplendent sight.

"God is good!" Anna breathed as she glanced around her homey parlor. She looked at the photographs of her dear ones in Sweden that adorned the white walls, peering lovingly out of their beveled frames. Then she saw the motto by the door: *Gud valsigna vart hem*, (God bless our home). "Oh, yes, Lord Jesus," she prayed, "Be the heart and center of this home - always!"

Something else must be put up on the parlor's west wall. On the eighth of December, Lars had gone to the county court house in Wadena to receive his citizen paper. "Now I am an American at last!" he exclaimed triumphantly as Anna ran out in the yard to meet his jingling sleigh, "And you too, as my wife, are an American citizen."

Lars gave his home a name - *Homecroft*. He had come home at last. *Hembignen* had found its fulfillment. And their Christmas was the merriest ever!

Forty Four

The languid days of summer had come again. After all the work that must be done, there were occasional afternoons for fishing in the river, and for dreaming, while inhaling the pungent fragrance of moss and the aromatic pine and balm of Gilead trees.

There was a special place made for the dreams of childhood, a meadow behind Papa's unfinished barn. It was a piece of low land that needed no clearing because its frequent flooding discouraged the growth of trees. It was a home for strong green frogs, leaping bravely from small hands that tried to hold them captive. It was a place where lacey grasses and delicate wild flowers nodded gracefully in the warm breeze. White daisies, yellow buttercups, and tiny purple periwinkle were chosen carefully and taken into the house to be arranged in bouquets. The Kristoferson children were continually amazed by the intricacies of God's creation. The flowers and the colorful butterflies resting briefly upon them, offered Anna the opportunity to point out evidence of God's existence.

"Down in a green and shady bed a modest violet grew," she would sing, teaching at the same time an unforgettable lesson in humility.

One glowing June morning, when the golden leaves of the balm of Gilead were resplendent with dew, Anna did an unexpected thing. After she fed the pig, she looked across the summer field behind the barn, seeing the expanse of nodding white daisies. Suddenly Anna became a young girl again. She recalled a German song she had learned long ago:

> In summer fields
> I lie in deep green grass,
> I lie and watch the boundless blue above me,
> The whirr of tiny wings is never still,
> To wondrous visions, Heavenly glories move me.

"Why not?" she said to a little brown hen, "No one will see me." And with that, she rolled impulsively down the hill and lay down on the meadow grass. It was a delicious reverie of seeing, as if for the first time, the wonder of intense blue sky, brushed lightly with white goosedown, and the miracle of detail in each cloud. It was a time in which the Spirit of the living God bathed her gently with His tenderness and great love, giving her a small glimpse of His glory. She felt detached, and at the same time connected to the earth upon which she lay.

"What was that?" Anna rapidly got to her feet, feeling a little foolish. "Uff--da! And me a grown woman!"

"Anna, where are you?" Lars called in English.

"I'm coming, Lars. I was just feeding the pig."

"And gone so long? I was worried. Anna, your dress!"

"So?"

"It's wet and moss is clinging. Sweetheart, did you fall down?" He put his strong arm tenderly about her no longer tiny waist.

"Lars, only to you could I tell this secret."

"Is something wrong, my love?"

Anna burst out laughing at his serious, anxious expression.

"Forgive me for being so silly. The truth is, I was just laying down in the daisy patch and looking at the sky. I was a *flicka* again! "

"Oh, my," Lars sighed. His serious expression did not change. This was something he must ponder very carefully.

Forty Five

One summer evening August Peterson and his fragile young wife were walking together in their grove. He held her close. Despite his tender care, she had continued to grow weaker. She had tuberculosis, a disease for which there was no known cure.

"But some people do get better," a doctor had told August. So August Peterson, a young man of great faith, did not give up hope, or stop praying for her recovery.

At the same time, he had noticed a growing pallor and fragility that could not be ignored. He was frightened by the fire of other worldly joy that glowed in her deep blue eyes, and her constant talk about Heaven. Perhaps she was preparing him. He knew he must accept God's will. However bitter for him, it was for her good.

"What is that?" She had that scary, rapturous look again.

"I don't hear anything."

"It sounds like angels singing."

"Oh, no ... dear Lord, no. Not now," August whispered.

Then he heard it too. He heard the singing, with Swedish words, wafting gently on the wind from the other side of the grove.

"Han skal opne parleporten" (He the pearly gates will open.)

August laughed with relief, it was not the angels coming for her. It was simply the Kristoferson family singing on their front porch as they did almost every evening.

"Let's go over and visit them, August."

"Now? Do you think you can walk that far?"

"Of course. We have our shortcut, don't we?" Lars' and August's farms adjoined each other and their homes were not far apart. They had become very close friends, united by a common faith in Jesus Christ.

"August! They're still singing!" she exclaimed as they neared their neighbor's house. "We could hear them all the way. What fun! It's almost like Heaven!"

"Don't, my darling." August squeezed her hand.

182

"Don't what?"

"Oh, nothing."

She was too enthralled with the music to care what August was getting at.

As the Petersons approached, the Kristoferson's heard two voices joining theirs "*Trygare kan ingen vara…*"

"Hurrah! We have company!" shouted Alice.

"*Valkommen*, dear friends, come in," Lars invited, reaching out his hands to touch them.

"I'll put the coffee on," exclaimed Anna with obvious delight. What excitement to have company on this perfect summer evening!"

The good friends talked of many things as they sat in the screened-in porch, watching the rosy hue of the setting sun, and listening to the frogs singing their sweet cacophony from the meadow.

"The coffee is very good, Mrs. Kristoferson. How do you make it so flavorful?"

"Well, you see Elise, I put an egg in now that our hens lay so many." Anna beamed.

"Really? I have so much to learn."

"Your family singing warmed our hearts so we just had to come over," August explained.

"What?" Lars responded in amazement. "How could the sound travel all the way over to your place?"

"It's hard to believe, but I have heard others speak of it. One man said it went all the way over to Bullard Township."

"Oh, yes," added Elise, "when there is no wind your singing goes far, bringing the blessing of the Lord to all who hear."

"My, oh my," marveled Anna.

"Praise God! Now will you and Elise please join with us in singing? You will add much to this blessing going over the air waves."

"What will it be?"

Mrs. Peterson suggested a song about Heaven.

> *"I have a future all sublime,*
> *Beyond the realm of space and time,*
> *Where my Redeemer I shall see,*
> *And sorrow never more shall be."*

When they had finished, August wiped away a tear, and Lars closed the evening with a prayer so anointed, that even the children knew Jesus was in their midst.

One morning soon after August came running frantically down the path and pounded on Lars and Anna's door.

"Elise is very sick. She's breathing, but I can't wake her up! Oh, Anna, I fear she is dying!"

"Get in the wagon, August. Anna and I will both go," instructed Lars.

"Annie, take charge. All of you stay in the house," Anna said.

After they left, Emma began to cry softly. But the younger children chased each other around the table, feeling free because their parents were gone.

"How can you do that?" Emma shouted, "When our Sunday school teacher is dying?"

There was silence. Shock. "What? How do you know?"

"I just know. Besides, Mama has been going over there with soup and things all week."

"August, how long has she been this way?" Anna inquired gently. "Yesterday she seemed better - and so happy."

"Yes," August told, his voice breaking, "She talked and even sang. Jesus was so near to her - to both of us. And this morning…she just lies there."

"We must hurry," Lars said, whipping Prince with unusual sharpness. In five minutes they were at August's house.

Elise was lying on the big double bed, her head elevated by two pillows. Her face was white, except for two rosy spots on her cheeks. Anna had seen many with tuberculosis, and knew this false bloom on the cheeks was typical. Elise breathed shallowly, with great difficulty. She coughed weakly, and each time a small trickle of blood ran down the corner of her mouth. There was no doubt the sweet and beloved young wife of August Peterson was dying.

August sat beside her, head bowed in grief. "Why so soon, Lord?" he cried, "I didn't even send for her mother."

"We must send a message to her mother by telegram at once," instructed Anna.

"Ja, I will ride Prince to Staples. That will be quicker than the wagon," Lars decided.

"It will be too late," August sobbed, "Oh, why didn't I know before? I didn't want to know. I kept writing her mother and sister that Elise was no worse, maybe even a little bit better. Why was it so hard for me to face the truth? Oh what a shock this will be for her dear Mother and sister Tillie." August trembled in his pain. He kept rambling on. The strong spiritual leader, whose prayers had brought about the Thomastown revival, had become a helpless, babbling child in his grief.

But then he took his Bible, and began to read aloud the familiar, comforting words, "Let not your hearts be troubled...My peace I leave with you...I shall abide under the shadow of the Almighty." It seemed to August that every place in the Bible to which he turned was a source of peace and comfort.

While Anna tended to Elise, August continued to read. The more he read, the calmer he felt. The peace of God seemed to permeate the room. There was no more coughing and it seemed that Elise was breathing more easily. Her eyes opened, and a faint, serene smile played upon her lips. Her pulse steadied, and it seemed her pain had ceased. Elise appeared to be conscious now, even though she was too weak to talk. Anna wondered if she could comprehend the words August was reading.

"August," Anna whispered, gently touching his arm. He did not seem to hear. He continued to read. Finally he closed the Book and reached for Elise's hand. He gave a prayer of praise and thanksgiving for the love they had shared - a prayer of relinquishment too. "Not my will, but your will be done. Do what is best. Bring glory to your name, by life or by death."

When Lars returned several hours later, August was at peace, and Elise was conscious and resting comfortably.

"I have a surprise." Lars put an arm around August's shoulder. "When I got to the depot to send the telegram a train was just pulling in, and look who got off. Mr. Olson loaned me a buggy to bring her in."

"Praise God!" August exclaimed, rising to embrace her. "Mother, how did you know?"

"Your Pastor wrote me about a month ago, saying I should come. He said, "Elise never complains but I can see that she is failing." So as soon as I could arrange it, I came."

"God arranged it," August said matter-of-factly.

"Elise?"

She lifted her thin arms and smiled. "Mother, you have come!"

Elise improved a little and lived for several more months. There was time for talk, for prayer, time to prepare them for her 'home-going', time to say the really important things to each other. August and his mother-in-law nursed Elise with great tenderness. Although very weak, Elise remained aware and free of pain. There were days when she was able to sit in a rocker by the window, watching the leaves of the sugar maples turn red, and the robins beginning their flight to the Southland. Nearly everyone in the settlement came to say good-by, and Elise had a kind word of blessing for each one.

Then one day as the red leaves began to fall, she quietly slipped away to be with the One she loved the best, the One who loved her most - Jesus.

Lars had built a coffin for her from his best pine boards, and they laid her to rest beside the little white church.

After the funeral, Elise's mother stayed on to help August get through the winter. Her other daughter, Tillie, had been with them the last week of Elise's life. She came just before Christmas to stay with them. The three nourished one another in the healing of their common grief. They sought comfort and peace, not so much in one another, but in God who continued to encourage them in His Word. Sometimes August would take down his Bible after breakfast and read for hours. Then they would sing the dear Swedish hymns - over and over.

Also, there was the healing power of work. For August, there was wood to cut and pile, cows to milk, and chickens and pigs to feed. There was snow to shovel, and fires to build. For the women, there was always the cooking, bread baking, and the difficult task of washing clothes in the winter. Winter was a time for knitting stockings and piecing quilts. The hands of an immigrant woman were never idle.

Years went by. August and Tillie had been blessed together by the comfort of Heaven. Their hearts were blended together by common interests, and the common desire to serve God. In time, their hearts became blended with love. August and Tillie were married, and faithfully served the Lord in the Thomastown congregation for many years.

Forty Six

The warmth of summer came finally after a long hard winter. The Swedish settlers of Thomastown were enjoying the busy days of summer.

"Seems times we are busiest we have the most fun," Anna confided to Lars one evening as they shared an intimate moment on the porch.

Every muscle ached from his long day in the cornfield; every bone creaked with weariness as he savored the luxury of the hammock. Nevertheless, he beckoned Anna to come lie beside him.

"You silly man! The hook will break and then we will both look foolish! And besides, the children will come in at any moment." She protested in vain.

He cuddled her. "How precious you are to me, my tiny Anna," he whispered.

"Haven't you noticed lately how fat I have become?" she pointed out.

"No, I haven't noticed. You are the same girl I married."

A spontaneous idea came to Anna. "Lars, how long has it been since we've had a picnic down by the river?"

"I don't know. A month?"

"Way longer than that. Let's do it on Sunday."

"Good. I'll get the boards and saw horses set up ahead of time."

Very early on Sunday morning lightning blazed and thunder shook the silence of the sleeping household. The sky opened and abundant rain cascaded down.

"Uff-da, why should it rain on the day we planned a picnic?"

"Now, Anna," Lars said pulling on his overalls (for cows needed to be milked even on the Lord's Day) "Don't you remember? We prayed for rain, and God in His mercy has heard our prayer. He is mindful of our need."

Hilda got up to help close the windows. "Cheer up, Mama," she said, "Remember the old saying, RAIN BEFORE SEVEN, QUIT BEFORE ELEVEN."

Sure enough, before church time the rain had stopped and the sun sparkled on the Balm of Gilead's wet leaves. The air was moist with the fragrance of fresh pine. Alice inhaled deeply as she sat beside Papa in the wagon. The horses whinnied with excitement.

"On such a morning we must sing all the way to church, "Lars announced, "songs of praise and joy, and thankfulness for the rain."

"I'll start!" Anna's voice was clear and beautiful as ever. "Let's sing *TACK FOR ALT.*"

Thanks to God for my Redeemer,
Thanks for all He doth supply...

As they neared the church, the congregation could hear them singing. They stopped their friendly visiting on the church lawn to listen to the familiar strains.

"I felt real good in church today," little Ruth remarked on the way home. Then she made up a little song of her own…"Thank you for the sunshine. Thank you for the picnic we're going to have today!"

It was a memorable picnic. Alma and Will had come in their new buggy and were waiting at the house for the family to return from church.

"Clara!" Ruth exclaimed. This is going to be some day!

"Ruth!" Clara cried, happily hugging her aunt.

The little girls had so much to talk about and show each other they were in no hurry to go to the woods. The upstairs was now finished, with a little room of Ruth's own, which she could hardly wait to show Clara.

Alma had brought a pot of her own special rice pudding, along with some homemade rolls, fresh from the oven. And there was a big pot of Swedish brown beans Mama had simmering in the oven. There was also the chicken Betsy had fried on the top of the stove and put into the warming oven. There was the last minute cooking of tiny new potatoes and tender green peas. Annie smothered them with rich cream. Annie had baked a chocolate cake, and Hilda had made her favorite - sunshine pudding, which was red and elegant, swirled with cream. She made it with the wild currants she had picked herself in the very spot they were going to have the picnic.

Papa and Mama went on ahead in the wagon with all the food, the red-checked tablecloth, some blankets, and some boards for the improvised table.

The children walked, ran and skipped, avoiding the cow piles and stumps along the way. They were too hungry to pick daisies and buttercups or look for squirrels. That could wait for later, when with full stomachs they could explore the woodland paths.

I wonder if Mama will let us go swimming. I brought my bloomers just in case," Alice wondered.

"At least we can go wading and play in the sand," Ruth added.

Papa arranged the boards on the sawhorses he had brought the evening before, making a long table with benches. Mama stretched two bright checked tablecloths over the rough boards and an elegant table emerged. After Papa had taken all the food from the wagon, they sat on the benches around the table and bowed their heads.

> *I Jesu nam-n till bords vi ga,*
> *Valsigna Gud den mat vi fa,*
> *Honom till ara - oss till gagn,*
> *Vi ga till bords i Jesu namn. Amen.*

"Clara, I didn't hear you pray," Ruth gently scolded her niece and best friend.

"That's cuz my Papa and me don't know it." William squirmed uncomfortably.

Lars felt sorry for him. Perhaps his affable son-in-law felt left out when all their prayers were in Swedish. Next time, Lars resolved, he would ask William to pray, in English. And today he would make sure most of the mealtime chatter was in English. Why not? By now, even Anna had learned to talk 'American' - even though she preferred not to. Lars whispered that they must consider William and their little granddaughters.

"Funny how everything tastes so good outdoors," William remarked.

"That it does," Anna said kindly in English, "and especially your wife's good rolls."

"I think it's the air - the clean, washed, blossom-scented air," Hilda offered.

"Well," Betsy teased, "We have a poet and didn't know it!"

"I think it's the birds singing to us while we eat," contributed Alice.

"Maybe it's the sound of water running over the stones," added Alma.

"I just love picnics, don't you Clara?" Ruth concluded.

Mama and Alma decided that Ruth and Clara must wait at least a half-hour after eating to go near the water to prevent 'cramps'.

"Time for our walk!" Annie proclaimed. "I'll be the leader."

"I'll stay and rinse the plates in the river," Emma volunteered.

I'll play with Ruth and Clara so Alma can get some rest," Betsy offered.

"She seems so much older since she got married," she whispered to Hilda, I think perhaps I won't ever marry."

"I will," Hilda said, "but I will marry a Swede!"

"Can't we go walking too?" Clara pleaded.

"Can you keep up? Sure you can. Come, let's follow Annie. Let's see how many kinds of flowers we can find," Betsy suggested.

"Does weeds count?" Ruth wanted to know.

"If it's pretty, 'tis not a weed. Right?"

"A weed is a plant out of place."

"None of these are out of place in the woods."

"How about thistles?"

"Who knows? Didn't God make them too?"

They found shiny yellow buttercups and prim white daisies, solemn and straight. Wild roses were still in bloom but they were hard to pick. There were trilliums and jack-in-the-pulpits. And they found the state flower of Minnesota, pink lady slippers, growing in abundance.

After exploring all the paths, it was 'coffee time'. While Mama cooked the coffee over the open fire, the little ones donned their bathing bloomers and played in the shallow water, making castles in the sand, Charley and Alice went farther out in the 'swimming hole'. The coffee tasted so good in the tin cups, with sugar lumps and Annie's chocolate cake.

As the sun neared the western horizon the Kristoferson's looked wistfully at the flaming splendor while they loaded everything into the wagon.

"Time to think about chores," Lars said, "Let's go before the mosquitoes eat us alive."

"Good-by, dear little picnic place" Ruth waved.

"Be seeing you again," little Clara added.

Forty Seven

Preparations were made in advance for the expedition to Blueberry Woods. Everything must be carefully choreographed for this was no ordinary adventure. It was nothing like going to the meadow by the house to pick strawberries. This was an expedition into the forbidden and the unknown. No matter how many summers they had ventured forth, each time all was new, uncharted, and peculiarly ominous. Nothing ever looked the same. And yet everything looked the same...a jack pine here, a popple over there, blue bells in a small clearing, black eyed Susans in a peat bog, a little hill - a dejavue aura and yet reason telling one this was the first time a human being had seen this sight. There was always the fear of getting lost, of going round and round and losing one's bearings amid all this hypnotic, enchanting sameness. There was the fear too of encountering a mother bear, of picking her berries, and especially of getting between the cub and her angry, protective presence. And there were other fears... the fear of stepping on a nest of hornets, or encountering an army of furious wasps...of unexpectedly startling a skunk...or putting one's searching hand into the fur of a porcupine. There were many dangers deep in Blueberry Woods, as well as many inconveniences...like being dinner to hoards of hungry mosquitoes, or victims of the wood tick's silent attack. There was even the dire possibility of eating too many blueberries and putting too few into one's basket.

They established rules and organized the trip long before Mama and her girls ventured forth to the deep woods. Of course the smallest children must be left behind with one of the older girls to look after them. There must be a lunch prepared to take along, with a jar of coffee wrapped in woolen rags, and sandwiches with homemade bread and butter, together with some hard-boiled eggs and cheese. There would be a cake for dessert and a jug of water in case someone was thirsty. They must also remember to take their sweaters or shawls in case it got cold or rained.

Anna and her blueberry pickers walked resolutely in a line, they meant business. "Girls, the important thing is that we stay together. When we find a nice place to pick berries we will all stay there until we get them all. Then we move on. Of course we will be somewhat separated because of the bushes, but we must always be within calling distance."

"Yes, Mama. We know all that!"

"It would be hard to get lost when we can't stop talking!"

"And laughing! That will help scare away the bears!"

"And the wolves!"

"And the skunks!"

"Mama, where can we go in? Can't we find August's path?"

"That will be hard. It rained since he was there."

"Let's go in here. Here's a break in the thicket."

Annie led the parade. It seemed they had gone quite a distance and to higher ground when they heard Alice squeal, "I spy!"

Sure enough, lots of blueberries, large and sweet, on stubby bushes pushing out of the sand.

"We can pick here awhile. My, they are nice this year - so big!"

"And so sweet!"

"Remember, don't eat too many!"

And so the baskets began to fill with the tiny berries. They were large for wild blueberries and luxuriously abundant. The girls were so busy picking and talking they lost track of time. Mama had to remind them that the sun, high in a cloudless sky, was announcing that it was dinnertime.

They sat down on some soft grass beside a little brook under a basswood tree and spread out the red checked cloth that covered the picnic basket.

"Sh...look!" Emma pointed out, as everyone froze silent and quiet. A sense of joy and wonder surprised them as they watched a mother deer and her little one drink from the brook only a few feet away. Then Alice sneezed and the two gracefully leaped the brook, blending into the forest.

"How beautiful!" gasped Anna, "Did you ever see anything with such grace?"

"Alice, why did you have to sneeze and spoil everything?" Hilda complained.

"She couldn't help it. So don't be mean." Betsy was always the kind and practical member of the family. "They would have run away soon anyway."

"Course. Deer don't like to sit around with humans. Anyway, I'm sorry."

After the noon meal, the girls begged to take off their shoes and stockings and wade in the brook.

"Of course," Anna agreed, "maybe you're old mama too. Why not?"

Since it was a hot day no one minded that Hilda splashed water on everyone. "Look out!" she yelled, cupping her hand in the clean, surging water.

"Stop it, Hilda!" they cried, screaming and laughing.

"Oops! Alice just fell in and got all wet!"

"I slipped on a stone!"

"Take off your clothes and hang them on that willow bush in the sun," Mama ordered.

"Oh, goody!" Alice giggled at the prospect of swimming naked until her clothes got dry. The other girls looked at each other with shining eyes.

"Oh, no you don't - just to the knees, that's all." Mama's word was final.

Another hour passed, oh so quickly. "Well, girls, no more fooling around. The clothes are dry and we must be on our way. Maybe we can find some more blueberries over there." Mama pointed to the other side of the brook.

"But I have my shoes on," Annie said.

"No matter. We can walk on the stones,"

After they had walked a short distance on the other side of the brook, Mama announced, "Berries are scarce over here. Best we go back."

"Where is back?" Annie was starting to wish they had not come so far. The sky was clouding up, the sun half hidden.

"We just look at Papa's compass and see which way is south. Then we go that way."

Mama made it sound so simple...until she reached deep into her pocket and realized there was a hole. "Oh, my! The compass is gone!" Mama yelled so unnaturally loud that she startled the girls.

"Oh, Mama, should we go back and look?"

"That would be useless. Who knows at what point it slipped through the hole in my pocket? Oh, how careless of me to forget to mend my pocket!" Tears filled Mama's eyes. "And poor Papa. My Lars held that compass on the ship coming over from Sweden." Anna sat down in shock.

"The point is," Emma reminded them all, "How are we going to get out of the woods without it?"

"I can't see the sun," Annie noted, "Do you suppose it's going to rain?"

"I wonder how far we have walked."

"Probably miles."

"Let's sit down and plan what to do." Mama decided it was no use to mourn for a lost compass. "Let's see. The sky is darker over there - so it must be west. No, that makes no sense...only if a storm is coming our way." A feeling of helplessness and indecision enveloped Anna, she who was always so strong.

"Well, let's try to find the brook again," someone suggested.

"But how?"

"It's simple...follow our tracks."

"Don't have to do that. I hear the brook! It's right over there!"

Quickly the group followed the rippling sound. And there were stones to cross. "Now all we have to do is go in the opposite direction from the brook and pick blueberries as we go!"

The blueberries were abundant there. The baskets filled fast. Laughter and fun were now restored.

I just thought of something," Annie said, "A terrible thought!"

"Don't say it!"

"I must. What if the brook turned?"

"Then we could be heading in most any direction." Their new balloon of confidence had just had a pinprick.

"We need to pray." Mama wondered why she had not thought of this in the first place. They all held hands in a circle while Mama prayed. "Lord, forgive me for waiting so long to come to you with our problem. Thank you for all the nice blueberries. Now we need your help to get home. Please show us where to go. In Jesus name, Amen."

"Amen," the girls chimed together. "And Lord," Hilda added, "Please hold off with the rain 'til we get home."

They finished the patch they were picking silently, each wondering how God was going to direct them.

Suddenly, the sun nodded its shining head above the clouds. Mama knew then which way to go. They walked and walked, growing more and more weary as the sun settled lower in the western sky.

"Aren't we ever going to get out, Mama?"

"We might be too far east but God will help us."

Just then they heard a familiar sound - the resonant tinkling of a cowbell.

"A cow! We're in someone's pasture!"

Betsy and Hilda peeked through a hazelnut thicket at the cow. "Hoo-ray! It's Mollie - our Mollie!"

"Mollie, it's milking time. Let's go to the barn."

"Papa! What are you doing here?"

"Looking for Mollie, of course."

"Why weren't you looking for us?"

"I thought you could find your own way home."

"You didn't worry about us?"

"Why should I? The Bible says not to worry about anything, just have faith."

Anna hurried into the house. She couldn't bear to tell Lars about the lost compass.

"Mama!" Hilda screamed, "The compass is right here beside Papa's Bible!"

"How could this be?"

Ruth's little voice piped up. "I'm sorry, Mama. You told me to put Papa's compass in your pocket. But I forgot! Will you spank me?"

"Oh, no, my darling child. I'm too happy!"

April 1900

L ars and Anna are sitting in their cozy parlor.
"What, Lars?"
"I was wondering what you were thinking about."
"Oh, I was just thinking about how rich we are, Lars."
"I love you, Anna."
She smiled. No more words were necessary.
"Lars, I think I'll write a letter to my brother Jon before I go to bed."
"You'll need the lamp. It's nearly dark." He lit the Aladdin lamp, which sat in the middle of the polished table.
"I can't help thinking how elegant my Christmas gift looks when lighted - and how bright it is!"
She took some sheets of lined white paper from Lars' desk and began her letter.

Dear Brother and Sister-in-law,

God's peace! Many thanks for your letter and the pictures you sent. I will send you our family picture, which was taken before Christmas.

It would be so wonderful if we could travel across the ocean to see you once again. That would be costly. Besides I remember the hard trip of coming to America. So it cannot be.

I miss you so much. How quickly the days of childhood pass away and we are suddenly old! Lars is fifty. And I believe you are fifty-four, but my dear brother, we shall meet again in that land above, where Jesus will wipe all our tears away. I often sit in my rocker in the twilight, thinking of that Home above, and singing 'Min Framtigs Dag.'

Lars and I gave our hearts to the Savior, nearly ten years ago, when we experienced an Awakening in this Swedish settlement. We have built a little white church by the river, quite close to our home. Lars did most of the work on the church. He also built us a nice home on our own land. And Jon, I want you to know (in case you have been worrying all these years) that Lars has always been kind and good to me. I have the dearest husband in the entire world, and now that he is a Christian my joy is complete.

Our eight children are all well. How God has blessed us, that all of them should live and not often be sick. Surely it is His hand alone that has kept us from many plagues and suffering.

Our eldest, Alma, who was a mischievous little one-year-old when we left Sweden, has become a mature and capable woman. She is married to a good-natured young man and they have a little girl only a few months younger than our Ruth. The two girls are great pals.

Annie is engaged to marry a Swede from Smaland - a fine man who drives a locomotive. He is building a large, square house in Staples. Annie has a gentle, patient spirit, always ready to help. She was easier to raise than Alma. Sometimes the girls get very loud around here discussing their ideas, except for Annie, who tends to keep her thoughts and feelings to herself like a true Swede.

It gets very exciting here at times. We all have fun together; most anything is permitted but harsh words. This Lars will not tolerate. He always says, "Remember children, Jesus is the Head of this home. He likes to hear you laugh, but He weeps when you quarrel."

Emma is only seventeen, but she is already 'working out'. A neighbor lady has a terrible sickness, what it is I do not know, but her husband has hired Emma to care for her. Emma is our serious one - yet always cheerful. She has a practicality and concern for others that almost scares me. Who knows what God may have in mind for her to do in life, what burdens my little Emma might be asked to carry?

Betsy and Hilda are fifteen and thirteen. They are both jolly girls who work hard on the farm. Lars calls them his 'boys', for there is nothing they cannot do.

Alice is ten, and Charley, our precious and only son, is eight. They walk three miles to school every day. Isn't that brave of them? Every morning I bundle them up as best I can, committing them to God's care. Even though I know He sends His angels to protect them, I sometimes think about the timber wolves that roam about in the forest. Lars doubts that anyone has seen a wolf. But everybody talks about them, and often we hear them howling in the night.

I have already told you about our sweet baby, Ruth. She is four years old. What a comfort to have her in the house with me, singing to her rag doll beside the stove. She was a sickly baby and I am so thankful to God that He made her well and rosy.

If you see Lars' brother Marten please greet him from us. Perhaps Lars will write to him someday.

May God bless you and keep you in His care,
Your loving sister, Anna

"Are you coming to bed, Anna? It's very late." She was surprised to hear his voice calling from the bedroom, for she supposed he had fallen asleep.

"I'm sorry, dear," she called back. "Did I keep you awake with the lamp on and the scratching of my pen?"

He had a way of softly chuckling, as if pausing to relish some sweet and secret memory lurking in a comer of his soul. He mumbled something.

"What did you say, Lars?"

"I said it wasn't your lamp or your pen that kept me awake. It was my wanting your warm body close to mine! Besides, I was thinking about Marten."

"Marten? I told Jon to greet him from us."

"Good. I thought of a verse from Proverbs 13:22 that we had in our reading this morning.

"How does it go?"

"A good man leaves an inheritance for his children's children."

"What a precious verse!"

"Now take Marten. He will leave a BIG inheritance - money, lands, education...But I..."

"Oh, Lars, you are thinking the same thing I am, I just know it!"

"What is it then that I am thinking?" he asked with the tiniest chuckle."

"Now take Lars. He will leave a really BIG inheritance...faith in God, unfailing love and joy, gentleness, understanding, patience, and prayers that reach beyond this generation - into the lives of our grandchildren, and their children's children."

Lars smiled. "Only by God's grace," he whispered softly.

Lars and Anna

About the Author

Elisabeth Mai Johnson lives in the home she was raised, situated on 17 wooded acres outside Moose Lake, Minnesota. She was born in Brainerd, Minnesota to Peter and Bessie (Betsy) Johnson, daughter of Lars and Anna Kristofferson. A graduate of Saint Olaf College, Northfield, Minnesota, she married Jean R. Johnson and moved to Washington State where she was an elementary school teacher and raised 6 children. After retiring she moved back to Minnesota.